Diamond in the Rough

Diamond in the Rough

Jane Goodger

LYRICAL PRESS
Kensington Publishing Corp.
www.kensingtonbooks.com

LYRICAL PRESS BOOKS are published by

Kensington Publishing Corp.
119 West 40th Street
New York, NY 10018

All Kensington titles, imprints, and distributed lines are available at special quantity discounts for bulk purchases for sales promotion, premiums, fund-raising, educational, or institutional use.

Special book excerpts or customized printings can also be created to fit specific needs. For details, write or phone the office of the Kensington Sales Manager: Kensington Publishing Corp., 119 West 40th Street, New York, NY 10018. Attn. Sales Department. Phone: 1-800-221-2647.

Lyrical Press and Lyrical Press logo Reg. U.S. Pat. & TM Off.

First Electronic Edition: August 2018
eISBN-13: 978-1-5161-0166-5
eISBN-10: 1-5161-0166-9

First Print Edition: August 2018
ISBN-13: 978-1-5161-0167-2
ISBN-10: 1-5161-0167-7

Printed in the United States of America

Preface

Nathaniel Emory, soon to be Baron Alford and possessor of a moldering estate long stripped of anything of value, including the family's honor, looked through the window of his hired hack to Lion's Gate, his legacy and burden. A cold, driving snow stung his face as he gazed up at the home, at broken windows, rotted wood, stone covered in moss, and shutters hanging askew.

The hack's driver, huddled against the cold, blew on his gloved hands before calling down, "Are you certain this is the place?"

Nathaniel pushed open the door, allowing a gust of the frigid air into the hack, and turned his head against the icy wind. "I am," he called, then dug into his coat pocket to pull out the coin to pay the man. The driver took the coin, then looked back at the dark house, which appeared completely abandoned and inhospitable.

"Good day, then." He lifted the reins, then stopped. "You want me to come back tomorrow for you?"

It was a real possibility that his grandfather was already dead, and he would be stranded here without food or heat. Then again, the old man might linger for days. It was a six-mile trek back to the village, but he could hardly ask the man to travel back and forth—and Nathaniel couldn't spare the coin to pay the driver for his time. "No, thank you." Nathaniel pulled up his collar, picked up his carpet bag, and stepped forward toward the front entry. Behind him, the hack drove away, and he wondered if he should have told the driver to wait. If his grandfather was dead, he wouldn't want to spend the night here, and he didn't relish the thought of walking six miles in this cold. It was too late now, though, so he forged ahead and ascended the shallow steps to the heavy door, wondering if he should even bother knocking.

It had taken him four days to reach Lion's Gate after he'd received a note from his grandfather's valet, clearly written by a hand that shook with age. Or desperation. Mr. Barber was nearly as ancient as his grandfather, a man who had loyally stayed with him, caring for him without complaint. Or pay.

Nathaniel gripped the cold doorknob, twisted and pushed, feeling the wood give a bit. Leaning against the door, he put all his weight against it, and the door screeched open before stopping abruptly. Looking down, Nathaniel could see that the door had become uneven so that the bottom scraped against the stone floor; he had just enough space to squeeze through. After shoving the door closed, he looked around, shocked by what he saw. The last time he'd been to Lion's Gate, he'd been just twenty years old, newly out of university. Even then, he'd been taken aback by how rundown the place had become. Now, five years later, the old place was a victim of neglect and disuse.

A thin fog streamed from his mouth when he let out a long breath; it was nearly as cold inside as it was outside. Dust, thick and covering every surface, gave everything a ghostly appearance, and floating strands of cobwebs danced from the chandelier that once lit the opulent foyer. Now, with the windows coated with grime, only a muted light filtered through, and Nathaniel suspected that even on a sunny day, the room would be gloomy and dull. A noise coming from the second floor caught his attention, and he made his way toward the grand staircase, leaves crunching beneath his feet. There at the top of the landing sat a black cat, its green eyes staring down at him unblinkingly, and Nathaniel had to suppress a shiver.

"Hello, cat," he said softly. The cat immediately ran down the stairs, its tail high, and before it had even reached Nathaniel, he could hear its purring. If the cat portended doom, it was a friendly messenger, he thought, as he watched it wind around his legs, rubbing his shins in an exuberant greeting. He bent down to pet the creature, and it lifted up its forepaws to butt against his hand. The cat was well fed and obviously friendly, which heartened Nathaniel despite the ruin surrounding him.

Calling out a hello to whomever might be home, he started up the stairs, his new friend skirting by him to lead the way. At the top of the stairs, though it was even darker than down below, he sensed a small bit of warmth and continued toward his grandfather's suite of rooms. A slice of light showed beneath his grandfather's door, and Nathaniel let out a sigh of relief. The old man was still alive.

Nathaniel pressed his ear against the door, but it was ominously quiet on the other side. At his feet, the cat looked up at him expectantly. "Shall we go in, then?" he asked. As if in answer, the feline head-butted his shin affectionately.

Pushing open the door, he stepped into the room and blinked. If it was neglected and cold on one side of the door, the other side was the complete opposite. He was struck by a blast of heat and the sight of a neat, well-tended, well-lit sitting room with a cheery fire in the hearth. Sitting in a large, wing-backed chair was Mr. Barber, impeccably dressed and sound asleep, his mouth open slightly, his hands folded on his stomach. Before Nathaniel could stop it, the cat leapt up and onto Mr. Barber's lap. The old man started, then, his eyes still closed, lifted a hand to pet the creature, which immediately started kneading his chest.

"Not so rough," Mr. Barber said, his voice raspy from age.

Nathaniel stood there a moment, wondering how he should make his presence known, not wanting to startle the old gent. There was nothing to do but quietly let Mr. Barber become aware he was not alone.

"Mr. Barber," he said softly. Nothing. Nathaniel recalled that the last time he'd seen Mr. Barber in his grandfather's now-sold London townhouse, the man had been quite deaf. With a sigh, Nathaniel said much louder, "Mr. Barber."

Mr. Barber's eyes snapped open and he sat up so quickly, the cat sprang off him, no doubt leaving behind claw marks on the poor man's chest. "Mr. Emory, my apologies," he said, face alight as he hurriedly stood.

"No need, Mr. Barber. You were not aware when I was arriving." He looked toward his grandfather's door. "How is he?"

His face fell. "Not good, I'm afraid. I am so sorry, sir. He is asleep most of the time. He would not allow me to write to you until his death was imminent. His lordship never did care for sentiment, but he was adamant you see him before he passed."

Nathaniel looked to the floor, fighting the emotions that flooded him. His grandfather was the only person on this earth whom he loved, whom he had ever loved. Despite the fact his grandfather had been in a wheelchair since before he was born, the two had had a great deal of fun together when Nathaniel was a lad. They would spend long hours together working on automatons and other inventions, anything to keep Nathaniel occupied and away from his wastrel father. Whenever his father would come home drunk and wild-eyed, his grandfather would have Mr. Barber push him into their workroom, where they would remain until Nathaniel's father's shouts turned into snores.

All his life, Nathaniel was aware there were secrets surrounding his family, and now with his grandfather dying, and his father already gone, this would be his last chance to have the answers.

"I'll go in, shall I? Will he know I am here?"

Mr. Barber shook his head, his eyes filled with sorrow. "That I cannot say. When he is lucid, it is as if he were a much younger man. But those times are getting more and more scarce, I'm afraid."

His grandfather's room was dark, but neat and clean, and a fire warmed the large area. At first, Nathaniel didn't see his grandfather in the large poster bed, and it wasn't until he was standing by its side that he finally saw the pale, still form of his grandfather. Given his infirmity, Jonathan Emory, Baron Alford, had never been a robust man, but Nathaniel didn't recall his being quite so diminutive.

"Hello, Granddad," he said, and searched his face for any reaction. It was hardly like looking at the man he'd known forever. The man lying on the bed was gaunt, nearly skeletal, his mouth open, his lips dried and cracked, his eyes sunken. If not for the shallow but steady rise and fall of his chest, Nathaniel would have believed him already dead.

He took his grandfather's hand, smiling, because it still looked like part of him, the hand that had created all those lovely little machines. The hand that had lain on his shoulder, strong and comforting, as he silently gave his grandson courage.

"I came as soon as I received Mr. Barber's message."

His grandfather's eyes fluttered open, and for a moment Nathaniel's heart dropped, for his gaze seemed unfocused, as if his soul had already gone. Then, the old man turned his head and he was back, blue eyes faded just a bit, but sharp with intelligence and, most importantly, life.

"Still breathing," he said, then let out a rusty chuckle, making Nathaniel smile. "Help me sit up, will you?"

Nathaniel put his hands beneath his grandfather's arms, trying not to wince when he felt how thin the old man was beneath his palms. He easily lifted him up, then fluffed his pillows behind him until his grandfather swore at him.

Letting out a laugh, Nathaniel sat back down, then leaned on the bed with his elbows on the mattress and his hands fisted beneath his chin. "I'm sorry I haven't visited," Nathaniel said. Guilt and desolation swirled around his gut, making him nearly nauseous.

His grandfather moved his fingers slightly, flicking away his comment the way someone would flick away a fly. "Regret is a cancer on one's soul; I have enough regret for the two of us." For a terrifying moment, it appeared as if his grandfather were about to weep.

Nathaniel sat up, not prepared to hear his grandfather's confession, for that's what seemed to be coming. He wanted to savor his memories of his grandfather and didn't want them tainted by whatever it was the old man needed to get off his chest. "Everyone has regrets, Granddad."

The old man chuckled in response. "You need to hear my story, Nathaniel. I'm dying and I'll be damned if I go to the grave with this secret."

"Secrets that are no longer secrets can sometimes alter us in ways not foreseen."

"That is what I am hoping for, my boy."

Nathaniel studied his grandfather for a long moment and couldn't help thinking that he seemed rather hale and hearty at the moment for a man who'd seemed on the brink of death not moments before. "All right, then. Tell me your story."

His grandfather relaxed into his pillow and closed his eyes, and for a moment, Nathaniel thought the old man had dozed off. Until he spoke.

"I was twenty-five years old, just your age, when it all began. My friend, Zachariah Belmont, and I considered ourselves adventurers. We were a bit in our cups one evening when he suggested an adventure to Brazil. We'd just attended a lecture about the flora and fauna there, and it seemed like a paradise to us, something that would pull us away from the monotony of being wealthy aristocrats." His grandfather, eyes still closed, let out a bitter laugh. "So we went. I won't bore you with the details of our trip. It was long, tedious, and more than once I questioned my intellect for agreeing to such a journey.

"But once we were there, by God, it was all we'd thought it would be. Nothing had prepared us for the lushness of...everything. It seemed as if the very air were alive. Coming from England, we found it a paradise of riches. Women"—he smiled, and Nathaniel smiled with him—"exotic plants and animals. Insects, by God, they seemed gigantic compared to what we were used to. It was a grand time for us both, a true adventure."

His grandfather was silent for a time, and Nathaniel thought perhaps he had, indeed, fallen asleep. "We can finish later," Nathaniel said quietly.

The old man's eyes snapped open. "Am I boring you?"

"No, sir," Nathaniel said, chuckling. "Please go on."

"We met a man in Mariana who told us about the diamonds, that you could pick them off the ground, some larger than a bird's egg. Of course, we wanted to have a go at finding them. I thought it would be a nice souvenir, something to bring back home, a gift for my wife. I had always been fascinated with geology. Did you know geology was my specialty at Cambridge?"

Nathaniel shook his head, then realizing his grandfather had closed his eyes again, said aloud, "No."

"Zachariah wanted to find diamonds for an entirely different reason. He was, to put it politely, scarce of funds. He was a third son with no property and little interest in the military or clergy, and he'd used the last of his money to fund our great adventure. Looking back, I can now see his desperation. But then, I was blind to his ambition. On a lark, we went to the area where the diamonds were being found, and we did find them, though not in any great quantity. I was happy to have something to give Elizabeth, who was none too pleased about my journey. I wanted to leave, but Zachariah...something changed in him. A fever, fueled by his desperation, I suppose. It came to a head one evening when I told him I was leaving, with or without him. I wanted to go home, and he wanted to stay. I agreed to one more week. One more, and then we would return to Mariana and board the next ship to England.

"We were to leave the next day when we found it."

"Found what?" Nathaniel prompted, slightly amused that the old chap had paused for dramatic effect.

"The blue diamond. Five hundred sixty-four carats of nature's might. It was stunning."

Nathaniel let out a low whistle. "And worth a king's ransom, I'd say."

"Yes. And Zachariah wanted to cut it up into smaller diamonds, thinking we would be able to get more money for them. To me, though, to break up such a miracle would have been an abomination. Do you have any idea how rare a diamond that size is, never mind something as precious and beautiful as a blue diamond? It belonged in the hands of a master cutter, and then in a museum or on display at Buckingham. That's what I wanted. We fought bitterly, nearly came to blows."

"Who actually found the diamond?"

His grandfather narrowed his eyes, a spark of irritation showing. "I tripped on it, Zachariah picked it up. So you see, we were at odds. In the end, I did what I thought was right."

"You took it."

"I did. When I got back to England, I kept it with me at all times. I felt guilty for doing what I'd done, but I was as stubborn as Zachariah was desperate. I planned to give him half of whatever I was able to sell the diamond for, and he knew it. But he wanted it all. One day, my entire flat was ransacked, violently, and I knew he was behind it. I thought Zachariah would be more reasonable once he was back in England, but instead he became more and more unhinged. He actually confronted me on Piccadilly, demanding that I give him the diamond. I always assured him that I would compensate him fairly for his share, but that did nothing to reassure him. He'd decided that all proceeds should go to him. He'd picked the diamond up, he'd suggested the trip in the first place. That's when I decided to hide it, far from those I loved."

His grandfather closed his eyes again, taking a few shallow breaths. When he opened them, Nathaniel let out a small sound of surprise. His grandfather's eyes were filled with tears. The old man swallowed, then shook his head. "He did this to me," he said, motioning to his legs. "He sent thugs to beat the location of the diamond out of me. Broke my back, but I didn't say a word. Unless screaming is a word."

"My God."

"When they were done, Zachariah came out from his hiding place. I'll never forget the look in his eyes, that cold, blank, dead look. 'Kill him,' he said." His grandfather lifted the hair away from his forehead with a hand that shook. "You see that?" he asked, pointing to a long, deep scar on his scalp, one that Nathaniel remembered asking about when he'd been young. "One of the bastards shot me in the head and left me for dead." He smiled, giving Nathaniel a glimpse of what his grandfather had been like as a younger man. "I didn't die," he said, letting out a laugh that ended with a weak cough.

"The diamond, did you ever retrieve it?"

His grandfather shook his head. "I couldn't. It was months before I could even sit up in my bed. It's still there, buried."

"Where?" Nathaniel could feel excitement growing.

"St. Ives."

Chapter 1

Clara Anderson, chin propped on one fist, gazed out the window of her room, a smile on her face. It was a gloriously sunny morning, unusually warm for late September, and she and Harriet, her younger sister, had planned to spend the day at Porthminster Beach. Mother had finally agreed to allow Clara and Harriet to go out on their own, without the benefit of a chaperone, and Clara could hardly stop the excited smile on her face.

Clara couldn't really blame her mother for being a bit overprotective of her reputation; after all, looks and money would mean far less if her reputation wasn't pristine. Mother had grand goals for her eldest daughter and no local man could even be considered as part of those plans.

When she was sixteen, Mother had sent her off to finishing school, determined that she should, if not be a lady, then at least act like one. There, she'd learned such brain-tasking matters as How to Write a Proper Letter of Thanks, and How to Speak to a Gentleman without Exposing One's Intelligence. Because the Andersons lacked the social standing to gain entry into the more exclusive academies, both Clara and Harriet had gone to Mrs. Ellison's Seminary for Young Ladies. Clara loathed every minute she'd spent there, but knowing how important it was to her mother that she marry well, Clara did her best to comport herself as a lady should. She learned to smile and nod at whatever great scheme her mother came up with because arguing upset Hedra and never worked at any rate.

Today was one of those glorious days in which her mother had nothing planned for Clara, which meant she could do as she pleased. And on this day, it was a trip to the beach with Harriet.

Below her, their new gardener was beginning the Herculean task of putting the garden to rights. The Andersons had been living in the home for years now, and while the interior had been completely redone and modernized, the outside was sadly lacking any sophistication.

Harriet, bonnet in hand, erupted into her room without knocking, as she usually did, with an exuberance she rarely showed. No doubt she'd learned Mother planned to allow them to go to the beach without her. Harriet might be two years younger, but she was far more serious and more mature than Clara could ever hope to be. Clara had disliked finishing school, but she'd gone along, learned her lessons, smiled through the monotony of comportment lessons. Harriet had wilted and become even more serious.

"What are you looking at?" Harriet asked, rushing to her side and looking out. She frowned when she realized it was nothing of interest.

"Just at this beautiful day," Clara said. "Our gardener has begun work. I wonder what he'll do? I fear we've started far too late in the season, with winter nearly upon us. I don't know what Mother was thinking."

Harriet peered out the window. "Look at all those holes," Harriet said.

"Mother wants roses." Clara wrinkled her nose. "I do love roses, but I fancy gardens that have a variety of horticulture." She squinted down at him. From her vantage point, she could only see his broad back and the top of his cap. As she watched, he stopped digging and rested his chin atop a hand still clutching the top of the shovel. After a moment, he started up again with sure, strong movements, then bent to pick up what looked like a rock, which he flung into a growing pile of similar rocks. Perhaps he planned to build a wall?

"Let's go down and see what he's planning to put in our garden," Harriet said, shoving her bonnet onto her head.

Clara agreed, even though she had little interest at all in the garden or in plants, for that matter, other than the ones that produced food. She secretly thought it a waste of resources to hire a gardener. But Mrs. Pittsfield, her mother's dearest friend and Purveyor of Proper, as Clara secretly called the woman, had said every great home must have a garden. Mother had immediately put out an advertisement and within a week, she'd hired the gardener who was even now digging holes in preparation for planting things one could not eat.

They'd lived in their house fourteen years, since Clara was ten years old. She would never forget entering its halls and speaking in the hushed tones reserved for church on Sundays. It had seemed to Clara the largest, most opulent dwelling in all of England. Ceilings soared above her head, great chandeliers sparkled in the sun, the marble floor beneath her feet shone from vigorous polishing. For Clara and Harriet, who had not only shared a room but also a narrow bed crammed beneath the rafters, the idea they would not only have their own rooms, but rooms that one could dance and run about in without smashing into furniture every two feet, was a wonder.

It hadn't taken more than a month, though, before Clara began to long for their old cottage, for that homey smell of her mother's fine cooking and her father's pipe. Mother no longer cooked, and even if she had, the kitchen was so far from their rooms they couldn't smell it at any rate. And Hedra had forbidden any sort of smoking in the house.

"What's your favorite flower, Clara?" Harriet asked as they pushed through the back door.

"Bluebells," Clara said, just to be contrary even though the common flowers were her favorites.

Harriet laughed. "Wouldn't it be fun to ask the gardener to plant rows and rows of them? Mother would be so cross."

Clara shook her head, the wide brim of her hat flopping about. She never could understand why Harriet liked to make their mother cross. She found life was so much easier when Hedra was pleased and happy, which might explain why their mother was constantly frowning at Harriet.

As they approached their new gardener, he stopped what he was doing and straightened.

"Good morning, sir," Clara called, and gave the man her friendliest smile. He stared at them, his eyes shadowed beneath the brim of his cap, before jerking his head in greeting. He thrust a hoe into the earth then stamped on its rim, shoving it deeper into the ground, dismissing them.

Clara frowned. In her experience, few people didn't smile back when she smiled at them. Gamely, she said, "We're very pleased to have our garden. What sorts of plants do you intend to use?" Another of her trademark smiles followed. One of the lessons she'd learned was that people loved to talk about whatever interested them. Ask an equestrian about horse breeds, and the conversation would be off and running, so she reasoned a gardener might like to discuss his garden.

Instead, their taciturn gardener, after another unsettling stare, nodded toward a large group of plants, roots balled up into burlap bags.

Bored by this point, Harriet gave Clara a look, then said, "Perhaps we should ask Cook to pack a lunch for our picnic." She gave a subtle jerk of her head.

"Why don't you do that while I look over the plants," Clara said. Few people knew that Clara had a competitive nature, and having their gardener resist her friendly overtures was tantamount to throwing down the flag of challenge. She would get the man to smile or at least utter a syllable, before heading to the beach. Unless he was suffering from some malady that prevented him from smiling or speaking.

Harriet made a face but headed back into the house, calling back, "If you do not like what I choose, I cannot be blamed."

"No beet salad," Clara called.

"I adore beet salad," Harriet responded, then giggled and rushed into the house as if Clara would give chase.

The moment she was alone with the gardener, Clara regretted her decision. He was gripping the shovel in his meaty fists, his eyes still in the shadow of his brimmed hat, and Clara felt the smallest niggling of fear. He seemed quite a fearsome creature.

"Would you mind telling me what you're hoping to plant?" she asked cheerfully, looking about the garden at the neat lines of holes. "Knowing my mother, it's likely all roses."

The gardener glanced at the plants, then shook his head, but Clara swore she saw his lips turn up just the slightest bit before his expression changed to stone once again. Normally, Clara would have not counted that slight movement of his mouth as a smile, but in this case, she decided to settle. Truthfully, their gardener was a bit frightening. He was a strapping man of indeterminate age, broad and tall, with a jaw that could have been carved from the good Cornish granite.

"I'll leave you to your holes, then, shall I?"

Without a nod or even the slightest indication he'd heard her, he shoved the blade into the dirt. And winced.

That's when Clara noticed the blood on the handle.

"You've injured yourself. Let me see," Clara said, reaching for his great paws. He moved away quickly for a man so large. "Don't be such a baby. I won't hurt you, will I? Let me see what's to be done so I may tell Cook. She's our resident healer." When he continued to stare at her stonily, Clara put her hands on her hips. "I demand you show me your hands," she said kindly. "If you are injured, how will I get my garden?"

He let out a small huff of air, then held out his hands, torn and blistered from his labors.

"Oh." She darted a look to his face, but it was still in the shadows of his cap. "I'll send Cook out with a balm. And gloves."

As she was turning away, she heard a low, "Thank you."

It seemed he could speak after all.

Nathaniel prayed the chit was dimwitted enough not to wonder why a gardener would have blistered hands from digging a few holes. When he'd taken the position, it was something he hadn't given a thought to. He looked down at his hands, amazed at the damage that had been done in such a short time. Hard labor was something he was entirely unfamiliar with, but it appeared it was something he was going to have to get used to.

The bloody garden was massive, stretching more than three acres before ending at a small pond. His grandfather had been surprisingly theatrical. He'd managed to tell Nathaniel the name of the property where he'd buried the blue diamond, but gasped his last breath before he could tell him where in the garden he'd buried the blasted thing.

"I buried it the garden behind the house. It's…" Then a gasp, then nothing. At the time, Nathaniel had been far more concerned about the fact his beloved granddad had died. He didn't give a fig about a diamond nor truly believe it could be worth the extraordinary sum of a half million pounds. Since leaving Oxford, he'd quietly been making a respectable living as a solicitor. Not the thing for a man who would one day inherit a barony, but it allowed him to live in a decent neighborhood in near anonymity. As his father had been such an infamous wastrel, he'd decided he was far better off being a simple solicitor, rather than a man who was the son of the disgraced future Baron Alford. The chaps at Oxford were horrified by his embrace of middle class life, but then again, most of them had a substantial income from thriving properties. Nathaniel, though he had grown up in a sprawling ancestral home, had been poor nearly his entire life. His grandfather couldn't even afford to buy him a commission and besides, no one he knew in his new life was aware he was in line for the barony. He was plain Nathaniel Emory to them.

All that changed when he'd met with his grandfather's solicitor two days after the old baron's funeral. He'd known things were bad, but he had not been prepared for the utter hopelessness of the situation. His grandfather had authorized his father to sell every bit of unentailed property in a desperate effort to avoid the very financial ruin that was now facing Nathaniel. He had two choices—allow the estate and the title to fall into total ruin or find the diamond.

As he stood in the Andersons' garden watching the owner's annoyingly cheerful daughter head to the kitchen for some balm for his hands, he realized how precarious his position was. No one who heard him speak would for an instant believe he was a gardener. Some might have the talent for accents, but Nathaniel did not. He'd tried and failed dismally, even to his own forgiving ears. Thankfully, the lady of the house hadn't noticed his clipped, aristocratic manner of speaking. Perhaps because he was speaking so low, the poor woman likely hadn't heard a word he'd uttered.

As a matter of fact, no one who saw him garden would believe him to be a gardener either. He knew next to nothing about the profession, though he'd been poring over books on the subject for the past week. The main reason he hadn't shown Miss Anderson the plants was because, other than the roses—he knew those were the ones with the thorns—he had no idea what any of them were. Taking out his *Pocket Guide of Flora and Fauna of England*, he walked to the collection, grimacing when he noticed more than one seemed to be withering. No doubt the things needed watering; at least he knew that much. He flipped through, trying to identify a few of the other plants, to no avail.

He'd been in enough parks to know that ornamental gardens were not planted in neat little holes like the ones he'd dug looking for the diamond. When he'd begun his systematic search by spearing the soil with a draw hoe, he hadn't realized just how rocky the earth was. His plan had been to spear the dirt, and if the hoe hit something, voila, he would have the diamond. Unfortunately, nearly every time he speared the blasted dirt, he struck something and was forced to dig a hole to determine just what it was he was hitting. During his search, he'd cursed his grandfather nearly as much as he'd cursed the rocks and roots he'd hit—both rather a waste of his breath.

If someone should come upon him looking as if he were trying to murder the garden with his hoe, he would simply tell them he was "cultivating" the earth to prepare it for the plants. He'd hoped he would find the diamond within a few days, but already it had been a full week and all he had to show for his labors was a grid of holes and bleeding hands. It was beginning to look as if he would actually have to start some gardening or be fired, and then where would he be? He'd have to sneak into the Andersons' garden at night, not a pleasant prospect.

As he looked over the ruined landscape, he felt slightly ill. Though he'd never been a man who shirked his duty or avoided work, hard manual labor was not something he had a great deal of experience with; his damaged hands were proof of that.

A rustling sounded behind him and when he turned, he was surprised to see the older Miss Anderson and not one of the kitchen maids. Since he'd begun work, one maid in particular, Sara, had been making eyes at him and had come up with one excuse or another to visit him while he worked. She was a pretty thing, but such extracurricular activities were definitely not on his agenda. He might be acting the gardener, but he was a baron, and as such, it was important that he carry on with a certain amount of honor and dignity—if digging holes and disguising oneself as a laborer could be considered honorable or dignified. Still, he refused to entertain the idea of a dalliance.

"I've brought you some balm and some gloves." She thrust out one hand and in her palm was a small red pot filled with a pungent substance that he could smell from several feet away. He took a step back and she let out a delighted laugh. "Cook says if the smell doesn't nearly kill you, then a balm won't do the job."

In her other hand was a pair of slightly soiled white gloves. He took the items warily, then looked up and straight into the face of an angel. Nathaniel was not a whimsical nor a poetic man, and so he was unable to put into words the effect she had on him. It was a bit like jumping into an icy cold lake and having the very breath taken from you. Surprise. Astonishment.

Lust.

Yes, *that* was the word he was looking for. It coalesced inside of him as if it were some fast-moving, fatal illness. Hale and hearty one moment, then on death's door the next. That was how quickly his body began to burn. He was struck dumb by it.

He hadn't even realized he was staring until it was obvious his stillness was making her uncomfortable, and she cleared her throat. "The balm is for the blisters," she said, looking from the pot to his hands, as if he were touched in the brain.

Before, he hadn't truly looked at her, had wanted her to simply go away so he could continue his search. Now, though, here she was, the most beautiful girl he had ever seen in his life—and he had seen many beautiful girls in his day. Her eyes were the blue of a summer sky, her skin flawless, her lashes uncommonly long and curling, her hair burnished gold. He forced himself to look away.

"Thank you," he said low, then turned away, feeling like some sort of ignorant buffoon. Here was a man who had won debates against the greatest minds at Oxford, had attended balls in London and charmed beautiful ladies, acting like a bumpkin who had never seen a pretty girl before. It occurred to him that perhaps it had been far too long since he'd kept company with a woman if he could be nearly paralyzed by one pretty, country miss.

"You'll have to replace those gloves with something more utilitarian, I'm afraid," she said to his back. "Those belonged to one of our footmen."

Nathaniel blinked and looked stupidly down at the thin, white cotton gloves. "Yes," he said.

"There is an emporium in the village."

Go away.

"Thank you." He dipped a finger into the balm and put it on the worst of his torn blisters, letting out a loud curse when the stuff seared his skin.

Instead of being insulted by his language, Nathaniel heard her laugh. "I promise you, once the stinging goes away, your hand will feel better." It seemed that every time she spoke, there was laughter in her voice. It ought to be annoying, but he found it was not. He tugged on the gloves, wincing, then took up his hoe and plunged it into the earth.

"I do apologize—if my mother told me your name, I have forgotten it. I shouldn't like to call you 'hey, you there' or 'gardener.'"

He couldn't stop the smile from forming and was grateful only that he was facing away from her. "Emory. Nathaniel Emory." He had little cause to believe she would recognize the name, not in this tiny village so far from London.

"I'm pleased to have you as our gardener, Mr. Emory," she said, without even a pause at hearing his name.

"Thank you," he said, then thrust his tool into the ground. It made a satisfying *clink* and once again Nathaniel's hopes were raised that he might find his grandfather's treasure and remove himself permanently from St. Ives.

"I'll let you get on with your work, shall I?"

Nathaniel nodded and doffed his cap, nearly smiling when the girl frowned and wrinkled her brow adorably, then went to retrieve his spade, hope blooming in his chest that he would finally find the diamond.

"Well, Mr. Emory. Good day," she called behind him. "I should like to see your garden design. Perhaps tomorrow you can show it to me."

Still with his back to her, rudely, to be perfectly honest, he said, "Yes, miss." Garden design? He hadn't given that a single thought, but he knew one thing—whatever his design, it would require endless holes.

"Clara, come on," called the younger sister.

He listened as the sound of her rustling skirts grew dimmer until he was left with only the sound of birdsong and his raging lust.

"Whatever were you talking about to our gardener?" Harriet asked, clearly vexed that Clara had taken so long.

"Gardening, of course," Clara said, then tweaked her sister's nose. "Horticulture is a ladylike pursuit and I was thinking that perhaps I should get involved before Mother turns the garden into a miniature version of the Royal Botanic Gardens." They'd visited the gardens last year, and while they were lovely, Clara had been hoping for something a bit simpler. A curving gravel path lined with all manner of flowers, leading to a lovely bench where she might read. Topiaries were all the rage at the moment, but Clara did not care for them. Something about carving bushes into animal shapes seemed somehow undignified—for both the plant and the animal it depicted. She did hope Mr. Emory was not planning on any topiaries.

"I think Mother would much rather you practice the pianoforte," Harriet said.

"That is a lost cause and you know it. You simply want to torture me by saying such a thing. What did Cook give us?"

"Beet salad," Harriet said, then took off with a screech as Clara gave pursuit. She stopped when she was out of breath, still laughing, and Clara pretended to be angry.

"If there is even one speck of beet salad in that basket, I shall steal all the dessert and feed it to the gulls."

"No, I swear. Not one speck. I asked for some, but Cook said there was none, more's the pity," Harriet said with an impish grin.

It was times like this when Clara didn't understand how anyone could think Harriet plain. She was a little like that odd misshapen paperweight Harriet kept on her writing desk—ordinary at first glance, but with intriguing depths on closer inspection. To Clara, her sister was lovely in every way.

"I think I will get interested in gardening too," Harriet said, "and tell him that beet greens are the latest rage in English gardens."

Clara gave her sister a friendly shove, then continued down the long road to the beach.

"What shall I tell the gardener to plant? Other than beets, that is," Clara asked. Harriet shrugged, and Clara playfully pressed down on her sister's shoulders. "No shrugging, Miss Anderson. It is a gesture of the lower classes," Clara said, mimicking perfectly their teacher at Mrs. Ellison's Seminary for Young Ladies.

Harriet shrugged and shrugged until she was laughing so hard she could not shrug anymore. "We are the lower classes," she said, still shrugging. Harriet stopped suddenly, then spun around, her eyes wide with mock horror as they turned a corner and saw a man ahead of them on horseback. "It's the murderous earl," she whispered frantically.

Clara widened her eyes to match her sister's. "Do you think he means to murder us too?" Clara asked, giggling when Harriet narrowed her eyes.

"No, but Mother would love to hear that you met the earl by chance," Harriet said.

Alas, the earl took a turn away from the road to the beach, and the girls trekked on.

In the beginning of her mother's quest to find her a husband, Clara was careful never to let any gentleman know she favored him, mostly because she did not want to incite anyone's interest in something that was a futile cause. When the baker's son, Alfred, a young man Clara had admired, had come around asking for her to ride out with him, Hedra had been outraged by his audacity. She'd had a footman physically remove him from their house, humiliating him in the process. Clara would never forget the look on Alfred's face, and she never wished to see another friend treated so.

"You will marry a titled gentleman or not at all," Hedra had declared.

Now, six years after that unfortunate event, it appeared Clara would not marry at all. At twenty-four, she was not very far from being put to the back shelf; most of her classmates had already married, and many had children. Suitor after suitor was rejected out of hand, simply because he didn't have the word "lord" as part of his name—or at least as part of his sire's name. More than once Clara had hinted that no titled man would want to marry her, but that only resulted in copious tears and handwringing from her mother—and more than a bit of guilt from Clara.

When Clara was eighteen, after a particularly heated discussion at the breakfast table about the latest lad turned away, Harriet had said, "We should put an advertisement in the newspaper: Wanted: Titled gentleman in need of pretty girl with large dowry." Hedra's face had turned nearly purple with rage, and it wasn't until Clara laughed and made as if it were the greatest joke that her mother's color returned to normal.

Clara quickly learned it was better just to go along and hope that one day her mother would give up the quest to find her a husband.

When she was Harriet's age, she allowed herself to take flights of fancy and imagined that a prince or duke might fall instantly in love with her, as her mother insisted would someday happen. Six years of being paraded in front of every titled gentleman that the Andersons could manage to get within a mile of had taken its toll. All the years of finishing school, her substantial dowry, her pretty face, meant nothing to a titled man who was looking for a suitable wife. Breeding meant more than anything, and if there was one thing Clara was missing, it was blue blood. Hers was about as ordinary as a girl's could get, for it wasn't all that long ago that her father was working as a tin miner and her mother was working in a bakery—when she wasn't helping her parents at their pig farm.

Still, Clara could not bring herself to tell her mother that her efforts were futile. It hurt so much to see Mother sad, so Clara did what she could to make her happy. And if that meant going along, that's what she would do and what she had been doing since she'd returned from finishing school, that bastion of manners for upper middle class girls who had heightened expectations.

"Oh, there's Rebecca," Harriet said, then lifted her skirts to hurry and catch up to her friend. She'd gone perhaps twenty feet before she realized Clara was still walking sedately toward the beach.

"Go on," Clara called, smiling at her sister's enthusiasm. Her shy sister seemed to break out of her shell when she was with her friends. Clara, on the other hand, had few close friends, mostly because there were few girls her age that her mother considered suitable. Her mother's ambitions for her had the unfortunate result of making the local girls think Clara was a social climber, which she was, she supposed, even though she did not truly care if she married a gentleman—or know if she wanted to marry at all.

Clara stopped at the top of the stairs that led down to the beach, watching her sister's progress, and wondered if there was something wrong with her own heart. She'd never been the least bit interested in any boy she knew, never mind finding herself in the throes of love. From what she'd seen, girls made complete cakes of themselves when they were in love. When she'd been in finishing school, her classmates had spent endless hours giggling about this man or that man, describing how their hearts beat faster and their stomachs went all aflutter. No one had ever made Clara's stomach do anything but twist in worry or revulsion. Perhaps it was the sorts of men her mother had pushed toward her—widowers or men desperate to get their hands on her dowry.

She shook her head and pushed all those thoughts away. It was a lovely day, warm and sun-filled, and she was on her own without a chaperone to make certain she didn't laugh too loudly or lift her skirt up too high so she could feel the cold sea wash up against her. She spied a perfect wentletrap and bent to pick up the shell, all thoughts of husbands and falling in love erased from her head.

With endless reluctance, Nathaniel realized that if he were to continue his ruse, he would actually have to begin planting…green things. St. Ives had no lending library and no bookstore, so Nathaniel had to travel to Penzance to procure a copy of *My Garden, Its Plan and Culture* by a bloke called Alfred Smee. He couldn't help thinking that a man named Smee would certainly be the type who would enjoy gardening enough to write a book about it. Nathaniel much preferred books of adventure, so it was with great unwillingness that he opened the thick tome and began reading about how to create the perfect garden. Lord knew he had no experience with it.

As he picked up the book, he winced in pain from the blisters that were just starting to heal on his hands, and questioned, not for the first time, the sanity of his scheme. No matter how long and hard he thought, however, finding that diamond seemed to be the only way to begin to restore his properties and make sound investments that would ensure the future of the barony. The sun still shone brightly outside and he positioned himself by his quarters' only window. It was a cozy little place, tucked behind a large storage shed on the edge of the property, and one he was glad to have. He had no desire to sleep on the third floor with the other servants. As it was, he could tell the others on the staff looked at him suspiciously and with a small bit of hostility, mostly because he spurned all offers of friendship. It wasn't that he was unfriendly or a snob—Lord knew he had no right to any snobbishness given his current situation—but rather that it was safer all around if people let him be.

Part of him wished he was the sort of man who could allow all the Alford holdings to fall into complete ruin. More than once he wished he'd had the chance to ask his grandfather why he'd allowed his son to nearly decimate all they had. Rents had not been raised in more than twenty years, mostly because no improvements to the properties had been made. Nathaniel's tour of their holdings shortly after his grandfather's death had been more than depressing. The few tenants they had were ancient and no longer able to pay their rents at all; their children had left to work in mines or factories. More houses and farms lay fallow than were worked, and the income generated from rents hardly paid for the interest on the debt his father and grandfather had incurred. Any investments his grandfather had made had been divested by his father—with the blessing of his grandfather. He had vague recollections of his father urging his grandfather to take money away from one investment to put into another, the heated arguments, his grandfather finally relenting. When Nathaniel had turned twenty-one, he had gladly signed the deed of settlement, which in effect prohibited him from selling the last of their holdings. Everything was entailed for another two generations and there was absolutely nothing he could do about it.

It was his intention to systematically search every inch of the garden until he found the diamond, whether it took days or weeks, though he prayed it would not take nearly that long. The only alternative to finding the diamond would be to marry an heiress. Frankly, he'd rather have blistered hands and an aching back for a few days than marry. He was only twenty-five and hadn't nearly had enough bachelorhood freedom to tie himself for life to some girl who could only attract a man because of her dowry. Just the idea of it, of selling his heritage to the highest bidder, was extremely distasteful. As long as he still had hope of finding that blasted diamond, by God, he would look for it.

Now, flipping through the gardening tome, he wondered if he had made a mistake. The Andersons' garden now seemed endless—at least he could be certain he was searching on the correct property. His grandfather, for all that he'd died before giving him an exact location, was quite clear about the property on which he had buried the diamond.

He flipped to the dedication page of the gardening book and read: *To Elizabeth, who had ever promoted my studies, shared my anxieties and cares, and participated with me in the delights of My Garden.*

"What a load of hogwash," Nathaniel muttered. He could not imagine anyone getting so enthralled in growing plants that he felt compelled to write a massive book—the thing held 736 pages—and enlist the help of his spouse. Poor Elizabeth, Nathaniel couldn't help but think, tied to a man who likely cared more about fertilizer than her. Then again, perhaps "participated with me in the delights" held a naughty meaning. The book had just been published, which meant his friend Alfred Smee was likely still alive. If he discovered the diamond, he just might visit Mr. Smee and his lovely wife and thank them.

Scanning the contents, he skipped the boring stuff and went straight to the chapter titled, "The General Plan of My Garden." Nathaniel had no guilt at the idea of copying precisely, inasmuch as he could, the gent's plan. But it was soon obvious that what he was reading about was far beyond his capabilities; he would require an army of gardeners working on the Anderson property to accomplish one-tenth of what Smee's garden held. And he was not about to allow an army of gardeners onto the property, where one of them might discover the diamond before he could.

Smee, it appeared, had planted vegetables in and around all the pretty stuff—not a very practical plan, Nathaniel thought. What was a maid to do if she was told to fetch a bunch of carrots? Fight the thorns of a rose bush to get to the edible bits?

He was beginning to think he might be in over his head, and his promises—made when he'd thought he would be in and out of the Anderson property in a matter of hours—had been a tad overstated.

Still, Nathaniel kept reading, hoping he would be able to muddle through long enough to fool the Andersons into thinking he was an actual gardener.

"Hello? Mr. Emory?"

He whispered a curse. He had hoped Miss Anderson hadn't meant to oversee the construction of the garden, but it seemed she was paying him a visit as promised.

He went to his door and opened it to find her standing in silhouette just outside the shed. "Yes?" he asked as he made his way toward her, trying not to notice how the setting sun behind her only accented her shapely form. Instead, he thought about how very annoying it was that this young miss was interested in the garden. He did not want anyone in the household interested in anything he did, and so by the time he was standing in front of her, his expression was wholly uninviting. She came only to his chin, if one were to press down on the mass of hair piled on her head.

She looked at him warily, her eyes going from his hair, now uncovered and still damp from dunking it beneath the water pump, to his eyes, which were narrowed. He imagined he was quite a frightening sight to a young woman. "I thought I could look at your plans for our garden," she said uncertainly. "I've given it quite a bit of thought."

He stared at her, wishing he could tell her to go away, but there was something about her expression that made it difficult to send her off. Besides, she was the daughter of his employer; he could hardly be rude. "Let me get a pencil and paper," he said, then turned and was surprised when he heard her following behind him. How very bold and improper of her. He turned and stared at her, and she pulled up short as if just then realizing she was walking toward his private quarters.

"I'll wait outside," she said, then smiled, and he tried hard not to be stunned into immobility by that smile.

He took up a piece of paper and pencil and, as an afterthought, the thick gardening volume. A footman had delivered the paper and pencil the day prior, but Nathaniel hadn't thought to do anything with them. He had hoped he would not need to actually design a garden, that he would be on his way to London to find a gem expert and a buyer for his diamond. The girl was outside, sitting on the garden's only bench, when he returned. Lord, she was a picture. The sun shining on her hair made it seem spun from gold; her skin held the blush of a perfectly ripened peach. Nathaniel stopped dead, and if he were alone, he might have laughed until he cried at the thoughts that had just gone through his head. Try as he might, he couldn't stop himself from thinking about what her skin would be like beneath that fashionable gown of hers, smooth and soft and warm to the touch. And perhaps as tasty and sweet as that peach.

"What have you in mind?" she asked.

If only he could tell her, she'd likely run from the garden and never bother him again. Actually, if not for the threat of losing this position, he might have done just that. But the thought of her running, screaming into the house to get her father stopped him cold. He mustn't forget why he was here. No dalliance, even with a girl as lovely as Miss Anderson, was worth losing the diamond. Then he realized something. He was not a man to her, he was a servant, and even the hint of a flirtation would be deemed not only improper but grounds for dismissal. He had to remind himself that he was not a baron, far above this girl's station, but a gardener speaking to a girl who was far above his.

A soft floral scent teased him, and he stiffened, realizing she was close enough that he could smell whatever perfume she had applied that morning. The bench they sat upon was quite small, forcing them in close proximity, far closer than would have been deemed proper had he been a man calling on a lady. He pushed himself as far away as he could, but was still too close for comfort.

"Would you be more comfortable in my father's office?"

"No," he said, staring at the blank page before him. Nathaniel tried to recall something he'd seen in the book, then drew a square and pointed, using the book as a desk. "This be your house," he said in an awful attempt to sound like a working man. He drew a winding path and little misshapen globs that in his mind were shrubbery and plantings. At the far end was the small pond, so small that it had only attracted an errant mallard or two since he'd begun. A few rectangles, a circle, and he was done.

"What are these?" she asked, pointing to two rectangles he'd place by the pond.

"Benches."

"Oh." Her expression was not one of approval. "May I?" She took up the book, pencil, and paper and placed it on her own lap, her brow furrowing as she thought. "I thought an arbor would look lovely at the entrance to the garden. I saw some vines by the plants Mother picked out that I'm sure you could train to climb up the lattice-work." She looked up at him expectantly, as if he'd have some opinion on that, so he nodded. "Excellent. I'll have Mr. Billings—he's a local woodworker—create something for you."

As she went through her requirements for the garden, it seemed her enthusiasm grew with each sentence she uttered, and Nathaniel almost felt sorry for her. She would never get the garden that grew in her imagination, unless the Andersons hired another man after he'd found what he'd come looking for. He took the time to look at her, to appreciate the delicate curve of her jaw, the soft outline of her lips, her gold-tipped lashes, which almost seemed to glow in the light of the setting sun. He rarely got the chance, he realized, to sit next to a lovely woman and just stare at her without her knowledge or the added strain of intentions. His one experience of officially courting a girl had been an awkward and eye-opening affair. While that particular girl had been pretty enough, she'd also been interminably boring and rather stupid. Their meetings were so fraught with tension, he could hardly take the time to really look at her.

But Miss Anderson was so enthralled with her garden, she was completely unaware of his perusal. It was very nearly like staring at a fine work of art, knowing that one would never have the money to purchase it, but allowing one's mind to drift to that place where owning such a masterpiece was a possibility.

"Oh," she said suddenly, and Nathaniel was jarred from his mental wanderings. "We should have a fountain, don't you think?" She drew a circle and little dots that Nathaniel assumed were supposed to be water droplets. "Later, perhaps," she said, obviously taking his silence as reticence. "I suppose we should concentrate on planting everything before it dies. I noticed some of the plants are getting a bit wilty."

"I noticed that myself, so I watered them this afternoon. I do believe they've bounced back a bit," Nathaniel said, and immediately realized he'd allowed himself to forget where he was—and who he was supposed to be. Miss Anderson snapped her head around and stared at him wide-eyed.

"Where are you from, Mr. Emory?"

"Cumbria."

Her brow crinkled prettily. "A long way from home, aren't you?" Then she looked out at the garden, at the mess of holes, then at the bundles of plants that were still sitting above ground. He could almost see her mind working, and prayed she was not as intelligent as she was pretty, but it would likely take a dull person, indeed, not to have heard the culture in his voice.

"I need this position, miss," he said, his voice low. He could feel his entire body tense. Everything depended on this girl letting the discovery go, throwing away her curiosity, allowing him to stay. For an instant, he wondered if he should tell her the truth, that he was looking for treasure that was rightfully—if not legally—his.

"I'm sure you do," she said softly. "Else why would an educated man such as yourself be working as gardener for a minor estate such as ours." She let out a small laugh. "I should have realized when I saw your shoes."

"My shoes? Not my blistered hands?"

"You can tell everything about a man by the shoes he wears, Mr. Emory. And no gardener I have ever seen wears the sort of shoes you are wearing."

Nathaniel looked down at his shoes, a pair he'd spent precious money on at one of the finest shoemakers in London. Even though funds had always been quite low, he had acquired a taste for the finer things—and a deeper appreciation than most of his peers because he actually had to work for whatever he purchased. Now, sadly, they were scuffed and dusty, but there was no hiding the fact they were not the type of shoes a lowly gardener would wear. "I need this position," he repeated, feeling as if the world were about to drop out from underneath him.

"I'll not tell your secret, Mr. Emory. I have no doubt you do, indeed, need this position." She smiled gently. "If only to pay for your expensive shoes."

He let out a low laugh. "Thank you."

"Someday, perhaps, you'll tell me your story. I've no doubt that it's an interesting one. For now, though, I'll bid you a good evening. I am looking forward to seeing our garden when it's completed."

She stood and walked to the house, leaving Nathaniel there feeling out of sorts and strangely irritable, but not knowing why. Then it hit him; she *pitied* him. Just that realization caused his cheeks to flush in humiliation. Pity was something he'd grown quite used to, having had a father who was the scorn of the aristocracy and a grandfather who was considered eccentric at best. Poor, motherless child with a wastrel father who was scorned by nearly everyone in the ton. He sat there, hands fisted, as he watched the setting sun and fervently wished he could return to his old life, where no one knew who he was. The only problem was, he'd always lived under the threat of discovery. If the other men he worked with had known he was a baron, they would have immediately treated him differently. And when they realized who his father was, how famously disgraceful he had been, that would have been far worse.

"What can you tell me about our gardener?" Clara asked that evening as her maid, Jeanine, was fixing her hair for dinner. She found herself slightly disturbed by the man, and for obvious reasons. Hadn't her mother found it odd that an obviously educated man would answer an advertisement for a gardener?

Jeanine stepped forward holding a blue gown for Clara's approval, and Clara nodded, for she didn't really care what she had on her back as long as it kept her warm and covered. The Andersons always "dressed" for dinner, a habit that Clara found tedious in the extreme. Hedra insisted on acting like quality even though they were nothing of the sort. Unlike Harriet, who had only vague memories of their old life before their father's tin mine began producing scads of tin, Clara remembered with great fondness a time when the Andersons lived in the village and were part of life there. They'd had a tiny cottage on a narrow, cobblestone street, where neighbors would drop in unannounced for a bit of tea. No one stopped by their house now; it was far too grand for their old friends to step inside. Or so they said.

While Clara tried to act the lady, in her heart she knew she was nothing of the sort. She secretly preferred ale to that nasty sherry her mother insisted she drink and she much preferred a walk to the beach than a day playing pianoforte or working on her needlepoint, though she was more than proficient at both. Harriet would get quite cross with her, for Clara found such things easy to achieve but had no interest, whereas Harriet practiced for hours daily and didn't seem to improve at all.

"I could hold up a potato sack and you'd nod your head," Jeanine said, laying the dress on her bed.

"A potato sack would likely be more comfortable." Clara sighed. "My hair is perfectly fine. It's not as if we're expecting company."

Jeanine came up behind her and pretended she was going to muss it up, making Clara screech in protest. "Scoundrel," she shouted.

"Harridan," Jeanine returned without missing a beat.

Jeanine was far more than her maid; she was her best friend, her confidant, though in front of her mother, Jeanine was the perfect lady's maid.

When Clara had been younger, the two of them made a great game of it, giggling hysterically when Hedra left the room. Now, they accepted their roles but kept their friendship a secret from all, including Harriet.

"You haven't answered my question," Clara said when she stopped laughing.

"About the gardener?" Jeanine wrinkled her nose. "A fine looking man but a bit of a mystery. Not at all friendly. He comes into the kitchen to eat with the rest of us, then leaves without saying hardly a word. Something about him isn't right, though I can't put my finger on what."

"Oh."

"Is he giving anyone trouble?" Jeanine asked, her eyes narrowing. Jeanine, being three years older than Clara, acted more like an older sister and was extremely protective of Clara. "That Sara has been making all sorts of eyes at him but he doesn't give her the time of day. I hope she doesn't get into any trouble." This last was said darkly, and Clara immediately understood what sort of "trouble" Jeanine was referring to. Another of their maids got into "trouble" with a stable hand and the two had to get married. Jeanine let out a laugh. "You should see her, mooning after him as if he were some sort of Greek god. Which he may be, given his fine looks. But he doesn't give her the time of day. He doesn't give any of us the time of day."

"Sounds like you're the one smitten," Clara said, then ducked when Jeanine threw a hair pin at her. "You'll take out an eye someday."

Jeanine retrieved the hairpin, laughing. "You know I'm soft on Charlie. That gardener's too big, too moody. George said he looks like he's got something to hide. Prison maybe. I don't care for him a bit, for all his good looks."

Clara shrugged—something she would never do in front of her mother—and said, "He doesn't seem so awful to me." Though Jeanine was her best friend, she wasn't about to tell her how she felt about their new gardener. He was, as Jeanine so succinctly put it, like a Greek god. Tall, of fine form, handsome in a breathtaking way, with thick dark hair and a perpetual dark shadow on his jaw. Indeed, Clara wasn't certain she had ever seen a more handsome man than their new gardener. As the elder daughter of the household, she knew she shouldn't think of a servant in such a way, but it was difficult not to when looking at the man.

Jeanine was correct, though. He might be handsome, but he did not appear to be particularly intelligent. What sort of man of culture would settle for a gardener's position? Either a stupid man or...

...one who was in terrible trouble.

Chapter 2

Roger King looked up from his desk as a middle-aged man of apparent means walked through his door, and he immediately set aside the report he'd been working on—the dealings of a man who wanted to marry a bit above himself. The girl's family was not going to like what he'd found.

Standing, he said, "How can I help you, sir?"

The man looked around the room as if searching for another person. As Roger's office was only slightly larger than a wardrobe, it was a futile search. "You're the detective?"

"I am," Roger said, nodding his head and indicating a seat in front of his desk. Roger studied the gentleman, noting the fine cut of his suit, one that was well-made but seemingly tailored for a slightly smaller gent. Or a gent who had gained a few pounds and did not have the cash to purchase another. This could be a problem. His shoes were highly polished, which meant he had a valet, and the signet ring on his finger was thick and gold. This could be his payment should the fellow not have the available cash, and he found himself relaxing.

The newcomer had deep brown eyes that assessed him nearly as thoroughly as Roger assessed the man. "How old are you?"

Roger smiled slightly. It was a question he got often, for he looked a bit younger than his years. Sixty on the inside, twenty on the outside. "Thirty."

"And you have experience?"

More experience than a man should have. When he was twenty-three, he married, and his darling wife had twin girls just one year later. They were slaughtered while he was at work. He'd come home from his job as a bank clerk to find them together on a blood-soaked bed, throats cut. One daisy had been laid carefully on his wife's chest in a macabre contrast to the ugliness of the scene. His family's murder was his first case and the only one he'd yet to solve. His grief had been so overwhelming, the constables never doubted his innocence and his alibi was easily corroborated. After a year of watching the police bumble about, then forget his family's murder, Roger decided to take things into his own hands. He'd been searching ever since.

"I've plenty of experience, sir. And I've never not solved a case for which I was hired." To be honest, most of them were solved in a single afternoon. People, he realized soon after he'd begun his work, were bloody stupid, particularly the criminals. "And plenty of work." Now, this was a lie. Weeks could go by without his office door opening, and other than the small case he was wrapping up, it hadn't opened in a while. He pretended to look in his ledger on the ruse of searching for time in his schedule.

"I'll double your normal fee," the man said.

Now, this was interesting. Most people found his normal fee, two pounds a day, exorbitant. Roger gave the man another assessing look. "I'm afraid I cannot take the money of a man whose name I do not know."

"Jonathon Belmont."

"Are you a relation to…"

"Viscount Heresford. Yes. My uncle."

Roger suppressed his excitement. "My fee is five pounds a day," he said, feeling only a twinge of guilt for asking slightly more than double his fee.

"Ten pounds then?" His brows snapped together and Roger was just about to clarify what he'd meant, when the older man said, "Done."

Roger swallowed and clenched his fists in his lap. Ten pounds a day would pay his rent and feed him for weeks if he took a few days to solve whatever it was he was solving.

"I'll pay you fifty pounds in advance, for you'll need to travel." Belmont took out his billfold and counted out five ten-pound notes. "I don't want this to take more than a month."

Roger just about fell off his chair. That was *three hundred pounds*. Enough money to allow him to concentrate on his family's murder for months. "This must be exceedingly important to you."

"Mr. King, you have no idea. My father was betrayed by his best friend. An item of great worth was stolen from him by the scoundrel, then hidden. I want it found. Not only for its value, but as retribution for what was done to my father."

"Are you certain this object has not already been found, sir?"

"We would know." He let out a low chuckle. "Everyone in England would know."

His curiosity piqued, Roger asked, "What is this object?"

"A diamond. A blue diamond worth a king's ransom."

Chapter 3

"Mother, what are your plans for the garden?"

Hedra looked up, her face registering her surprise at her daughter's question. "I've hired a gardener. I expect he'll plant one."

"I was wondering if I might take that on as a special project. You know, Mrs. Pittsfield mentioned that gardening was a lady's venue, and I am getting terribly bored with painting and the pianoforte. Harriet is the artist in the family." Beside her, Harriet snorted in an attempt not to laugh. Harriet was an abysmal artist and she well knew it. That snort earned Harriet narrowed eyes from Hedra, but for once their mother let it lie.

"I suppose that would be all right. A lovely garden is something we could show off when we entertain. I approve," she said, dipping her spoon into their fine pilchard stew. For all that the Andersons had heartily embraced everything upper crust, Hedra, unless they had company, ordered their cook to prepare good old Cornwall cuisine.

"What is your obsession with gardening all of a sudden?" Harriet asked.

Clara laughed. "It's hardly an obsession. But I do adore being out of doors and I don't want to take long, boring walks like you do." She gave her sister a nudge. "It's a ladylike pursuit that I find interesting."

"Just as long as it does not interfere with your pianoforte, voice, and dancing lessons," Hedra said. "A lady must apply herself to the finer arts if she wishes to attract a husband."

"Yes, Mother," Clara said, ignoring the kick her sister gave her beneath the table. It did seem as if every conversation they had at the dinner table somehow circled back to the fact that Clara was expected to find a husband. It was, she knew, her only true purpose in life, according to her parents. Clara was their ticket to true respectability, and though it was a role Clara did not cherish, she hated to disappoint her mother and did try her best to emulate the ladies her mother so wished her to become.

"Speaking of which," Hedra said, wiping her mouth delicately, "we're off to London in the autumn for the Little Season. While we're there, we can order dresses for next Season. Isn't that right, Silas?"

Her father looked up as if surprised to be addressed. "Dresses? Oh, yes. Our Clara needs 'em."

Clara pressed her lips closed, trying not to think about the disaster London had been last Season. They'd rented a townhouse at a fashionable address, and her mother thought this was all that was needed for them to be admitted into London's ferociously guarded society. They'd driven in Hyde Park behind a pair of outrageously decorated horses, bearing bright red plumes and jangling collars—another dubious recommendation of Mrs. Pittsfield. Clara had tried to gently steer her mother away from the older woman's recommendations, but Hedra would not hear of it. Mrs. Pittsfield, having been a lady's maid to the now-deceased Dowager Duchess of Canton, was as close to the aristocracy as her mother was likely to get, and she listened to every bit of advice as if the duchess herself had written it.

Clara didn't much care for Mrs. Pittsfield, who seemed to relish her role as arbiter of all that was aristocratic a bit too much. Her poor mother sat on the edge of her seat every time the old termagant opened her mouth. Hedra had a small notebook that she would feverishly write in whenever they returned from a visit, and Clara's stomach coiled in dread whenever she saw it in her mother's hands. Mrs. Pittsfield was to blame for Clara's having to suffer through finishing school and practice the pianoforte until her fingers were numb. The dance lessons, the lessons in elocution, painting, needlepoint, voice. If a lady did it, then Clara must excel in it.

When Clara was younger, she'd relished the attention and took to her lessons with enthusiasm. Now, though, it all seemed like an exercise in futility. She would never be accepted into the aristocracy, would not marry a duke or an earl, as Hedra had fervently wished. What her mother had done was make her entirely unmarriageable—an overeducated, overpolished country miss. No local man would look at her and no man of the upper crust would consider marrying her. Unless, of course, he was desperate for money. For if there was one thing a desperate aristocrat could overlook, it was a low birth when it came with scads of money.

Thus far, however, Clara had managed to steer clear of such men, much to her mother's deep dismay. If she had found one such man who didn't make her stomach twist in fear or revulsion, then perhaps Clara would have put in a small amount of effort. As it was, though, she had not—and was now beginning to believe she never would.

She sat on the bench, with Mr. Smee's book on her lap, looking like a Monet painting and the sort of distraction it was difficult for a man like him to ignore. But ignore her he did—or tried valiantly to. Every once in a while, she would let out a small sound, a *hmm*, when he assumed she'd read something interesting. To him, though, that *hmm* was the sound she might make when she was being touched by a man, a finger trailing up her thigh, a mouth on one breast, tongue on her lips. Swallowing heavily, he shoved the rich earth around the roots of a rose bush and patted it firmly.

"Mr. Emory, do you believe there could be a treasure beneath our garden?"

And just like that, his blood ran cold. "I hardly think so," he said after a moment, a moment when his heart nearly exploded from his chest.

"Our Mr. Smee discovered all sorts of Roman artifacts in his garden, as well as the remains of a Gothic chapel. Wouldn't it be great fun if we discovered something in our garden?"

Nathaniel nearly choked. "Yes, it would." And then, under his breath, "I'm counting on it."

As the sun grew higher, the sounds of his spade against the rocky soil meshed with the sounds of insects, birds, and pages turning, along with an occasional *hmm*. Despite the fact he didn't want her there, he found he rather liked seeing her sitting on that bench, the picture of femininity in her lemon-yellow dress. She wore a large straw hat, which kept her face in the shadows; a parasol lay unused on the bench beside her. He had a feeling should anyone from the household venture out to the garden, that parasol would be hastily unfurled.

"Listen to this: 'It is a common notion that gardens should be laid out for one general effect; but the result of such a plan is to produce a single view, and the whole can be seen at a glance. This is, however, monotonous, and my liking is to have many pictures; so that my visitors have to walk a long way before they can see the many beautiful views which my garden affords; and little spots of cultivated wildness, or of special cultivation, are found where they are least expected.'" She looked up expectantly. "Doesn't that sound lovely? I do wish we could visit his garden."

Then she looked around the Andersons' relatively small plot of land and frowned. To Nathaniel's thinking, it was an enormous property, considering he was faced with digging up nearly the entire three acres. But as compared to many fine gardens in England, it was tiny.

"Perhaps we could do a miniature version of Mr. Smee's garden." Her attention was brought back to the book that he had only opened once, and her lovely lips formed a frown. "Oh, he suggests planting carrots and other vegetables amongst the decorative plants. That seems impractical to me, does it not, Mr. Emory?"

"Exceedingly so, particularly for the kitchen maids." She frowned even more fiercely at that and darted a look toward the door that led to the kitchen before returning her attention to the book.

"Goodness, Mr. Emory, this isn't a book about a garden, it's a book about a park. I fear our little patch of earth will never rival Mr. Smee's creation. It's no wonder he's so full of himself." She closed the book and set it aside. "Still, perhaps there is something noteworthy in it."

She stood and walked toward where he was working, touching the pointed rose leaves of the bush he'd just planted, a small smile on her lips. There he was again, staring. It was a dangerous thing to look at her too long, like staring at the sun. He would be blinded by her, and then someone would discover him gazing at her like some lovesick teenage boy. Or a randy young man. Nathaniel forcefully turned his head away and wondered what he could do to make her leave.

She hunkered down next to him, heedless of her lemony confection of a dress, and studied the rose bush he'd just planted. "Do these little holes in the leaves mean we have some sort of pest eating my garden?" She pointed at one leaf that was, indeed, riddled with small holes. She turned the leaf over and there they found miniscule white insects. "How awful. We must find a way to get rid of them."

Nathaniel made the mistake at that moment of looking up directly into her eyes. The rush of desire he felt at that moment was stunning, and he stood abruptly, startling her so much, she lost her balance and ended up on her bottom. Instead of getting angry, as many women would, she laughed, then extended a hand to be lifted up.

Now here was a conundrum. Should he grasp her pristine gloved hand with his dirty work glove, or take off the glove and grasp her hand with his ungloved one? What would a servant do? he wondered. To hell with it, he thought. He was a gentleman and a gentleman would never soil a lady's glove. He stripped off his glove and grabbed her hand, hoisting her to her feet and stepping back, using so much force, she stumbled toward him a few steps before gaining her balance.

"My, what a ride," she said with a nervous laugh. As she brushed off the back of her dress, Nathaniel increased the distance between them and pulled out his small pocket gardener book to see what it said about leaf-eating insects, and was shocked to find that his hands were shaking.

"Endelomyia aethiops Hymenoptera," he said in perfect Latin born of ten years of private schooling. Miss Anderson looked at him blankly. "Rose slugs."

She wrinkled her nose prettily. "Does it say how to kill them? Besides crushing them with one's fingers, that is."

He read briefly, then lifted his head and grinned. "Crushing it is. Or leave them be and let the birds have a nice meal. The holes are a bit unsightly, but don't truly hurt the plant overall."

Miss Anderson worried her bottom lip for a moment, a small crease appearing between her eyes as she thought about the problem, and Nathaniel simply could not bring himself to look away from her. What was it about her that he found so entirely compelling? Perhaps it was knowing he could never act on his desire that made him want her so. No. It was simply that she was lovely and charming and held something extra he could not quite name, but that unnamed something was affecting him more than he would like.

"I shall crush them," she said like a ruler promising to crush his enemy, and Nathaniel laughed. "But not with these gloves. It appears I shall have to purchase something a bit more utilitarian."

"I could crush them, miss."

"Oh, no. I shan't have you spending your time crushing tiny insects. That would take you away from building our garden. I don't mind. I'm not a bit squeamish. Besides, those tiny slugs are eating my roses and that is something I cannot allow."

Nathaniel looked at the long row of rose bushes he'd already planted, all with tiny holes on their leaves. It would take hours to remove all the slugs from the leaves. Didn't she have things to do other than murdering insects and torturing men? And what if he found the diamond when she was out in the garden? He supposed he could manage to keep it a secret, but having her out in the garden with him only made things all the more difficult.

"Miss Clara, your mother has asked that you get ready for your visit to Mrs. Pittsfield." The Anderson girls' maid, Jeanine, stood ramrod straight at the edge of the garden. Charlie, who was the Andersons' driver, was sweet on her and had already staked his claim on the maid, much to Nathaniel's amusement. Jeanine was tall and thin, with dull blond hair, a narrow nose, and thin lips that seemed to rarely turn up into a smile— unless, that is, Charlie was teasing her about something or other. At this moment, those lips were pressed together in what Nathaniel could only guess was disapproval. When he'd first started at the Anderson estate, he hardly thought he'd need to endear himself to the staff, and he also feared discovery, given his inability to rid himself of his cultured accent. Now it was clear his taciturn nature had fostered suspicion and dislike. He gave a mental shrug. He'd be gone long before any of them knew who he was or what he was about.

"You seem to have developed a sudden interest in gardening," Jeanine said, and Clara could tell by her tone that she was more than merely curious.

"It keeps me out of the house. And would you like to know something? I quite like it." She shook her head, baffled by her new interest. She'd always appreciated a pretty garden, and they'd toured several in London during their visit, but she hadn't had any burning desire to create something like what she saw in her own property.

"I may like a garden, but I don't much care for the gardener," Jeanine said darkly.

Clara looked at her friend as they walked down the long hall toward where her mother was waiting in the main parlor. "I don't find him all that onerous. Then again, I'm sure you see him more clearly than I do."

"Well, Sara asked him where he was from. And would you like to know what he said?"

"Certainly." Clara pressed her lips together to stop from smiling.

"Not here. That's what he said. 'Not here.' Now what is that supposed to mean, do you think?" She let out a small snort. "Not here."

"Perhaps he simply likes his privacy. Or is shy and doesn't like talking at all." Or perhaps he has something to hide, more than his cultured accent.

"'T'isn't natural, is all."

"Jeanine, you are all from St. Ives. It only makes sense that someone not from here would arouse your suspicion."

"Not if they were friendly. Poor Sara was in tears last night because she asked if he might walk her home and would you like to know what he said?"

This time Clara remained silent, knowing Jeanine would tell her whether she wanted to know or not.

"He says, 'No, thank you.' Just like that. What sort of man says 'no thank you' when a pretty girl asks to be walked home?"

"I suppose a man who doesn't want to go for a walk," Clara said, then let out a small laugh. Jeanine laughed with her, stifling her mirth when they saw the housekeeper, Mrs. Randall, walking toward them with her stern countenance. The older woman gave the two an assessing look as she passed but said nothing.

"All the maids are making fools of themselves over him," Jeanine said.

"All of them but you," Clara said, teasing the maid, who was quite taken with Charlie, their driver.

When they reached the main stairs, Jeanine went up and Clara continued to the parlor, where she found her mother sitting impatiently.

"Really, Clara, you know how Mrs. Pittsfield is about promptness."

"Yes, Mother. I do apologize. I was out in the garden. It's coming along very nicely. Some of the roses are already beginning to bloom and there are so many buds. We'll have a lovely rose garden in no time."

Hedra smiled. "I am so happy to hear you are finally showing enthusiasm for a ladylike occupation. When the gardener has completed it, we'll have a garden tea. What do you think about that?"

"That would be wonderful," Clara said, wondering whom they could invite. Mrs. Pittsfield, of course, and perhaps the Smythes and the Chatsworths. They were landed gentry and had attended other functions the Andersons had put on, and Harriet would be thrilled to have her friends over.

"The carriage is ready, Mrs. Anderson," their footman said from the door. Clara spun about, ready to go out, but a shriek from her mother stopped her.

"Your dress! What happened to it?"

Clara craned her neck to see, but as the offending stain was on her backside, she could only make out the edge of the damage. "I fell in the garden. Is it that noticeable?"

"Come here," Hedra said, then proceeded to wipe at the dirt. "It'll have to do. I'd rather not be late. Mr. Baker will be there today."

Clara stifled a groan. Mr. Baker was the third son of a local viscount and a more pompous fool Clara had never met. The only reason he was attending such a low event was because he wanted to get his skinny hooks on Clara's dowry. He made no secret of his distaste for her family or her origins.

"Mr. Baker is horrid, Mother. I do wish you would strike him off your list of possible suitors."

Hedra sniffed. "He is the son of a viscount."

"And I'm the daughter of a tin miner, something he likes to remind me of at every meeting. Besides, his hair has tiny flecks of white everywhere, as if he's just been caught in a snow storm."

"You could do worse," Hedra said cheerfully. "You aren't getting any younger, you know. Why, most of my friends' daughters have long since married."

This was true, but Clara did not plan to rectify the matter by marrying someone who made her want to gag each time she saw him.

Three hours later, Clara was home and back in her garden, happily murdering slugs and imagining they were Mr. Baker.

"You seem to be taking unwarranted pleasure in killing our little friends," Mr. Emory said, laughter in his voice.

Clara tucked her head and smiled. "I'm imagining they are an awful man I was forced to keep company with this afternoon."

"Ah."

"I'm twenty-four," she said, then looked up at their gardener to see if he knew what she'd meant by that. He started whistling the Wedding March in answer as he thrust his spade into the ground, striking yet another rock; yes, he understood. Clara watched as he bent and fished around for the offending stone, picked it up, gave it a quick look, then thrust it into a growing pile at the edge of the garden.

"Yes. Marriage."

"And you are opposed?"

"Not at all. I'm opposed to marrying onerous men who have snow in their hair in October."

He let out a laugh, deep and masculine, and Clara's stomach responded with the oddest flutter. She looked over to him and watched him work for a time. He really was a handsome man, tall and brawny but somehow refined. The day was growing old and casting a warm glow on the tanned skin of his forearms, and Clara noticed for the first time the corded muscle there. Broad shoulders tapered to a slim waist, and his workman's thick trousers hugged his backside in an oddly appealing way. Swallowing, Clara quickly averted her gaze, horrified where her thoughts had gone. When she looked up, he was looking at her with the oddest expression on his face, one filled with amusement and something she prayed was not recognition. How mortifying to get caught admiring a servant's form. She felt her cheeks flush as she ducked her head so that her hat hid her expression.

"Do you plan to build a wall with those stones?" she asked, glad her voice sounded normal when she did not feel normal in the least.

"I may, once the garden is in." Clara relaxed when she heard the sound of the spade digging into the soil. "When I am done here, I thought I could build a foundation for a small hothouse. That way your mother would have flowers in the winter as well as the spring and summer."

"That would be lovely. Shall I ask her this evening? I shall," Clara said, answering her own question. "Mr. Smee's garden has quite a large hothouse. Ours shall be much smaller, of course, but perhaps I can get some ideas of what to plant."

"What is your favorite flower?"

As Clara worked to remove the slugs, she decided that roses were not her favorite, though they were the most common type of flower to be found in an English garden. "When I was a young girl, my favorite flower was the bluebell. There was a field near my grandfather's farm that would turn blue in the spring. He used to say I had bluebells for eyes." Her voice had grown wistful, for she hadn't seen her grandfather in far too long, and she missed him terribly.

"Let me see," Mr. Emory said, straightening and coming over with the obvious intent of judging for himself whether her eyes were the color of bluebells. That's how Clara found herself gazing up at him, noting things about his face that she hadn't taken in before, simply because she hadn't truly looked at him. Now she saw he had lines from the sun near his eyes and the tips of his eyebrows were slightly lighter, nearly blond, and that his lashes were thick and shadowed eyes she'd thought were brown but that were a deep, green-gray. Those eyes studied hers, unwavering, filled with mild amusement before suddenly flaring with some other emotion.

"That's a fair comparison," he said blandly before turning back to the roses, leaving Clara feeling strangely disappointed, though she couldn't say why.

"And what is your favorite flower?"

"I haven't one," he said curtly. "All the ones that don't die are my favorites."

Clara felt suitably dismissed, and she could tell from his tone that he'd grown bored with the conversation. Why was she even talking to him at all? He was the gardener, nothing more. A man whom her mother had employed. She was done killing bugs for the day.

"I'll continue my bug-killing tomorrow. Good evening, Mr. Emory." She started walking from the garden feeling unaccountably hurt, and confused that she should be hurt at all. Lifting her skirts, she made her way out of the torn-up ground toward the house. Just as she reached the edge, where the lush green grass began, she heard him say, "Orchids. They were my mother's favorite, I was told, so I suppose they shall be mine."

Clara didn't turn, but she felt so much better as she made her way to the back entrance. When she reached the door, she turned back to wave, just in case Mr. Emory was looking up, and felt a ridiculous surge of happiness when she saw him standing there, hands resting on his spade's handle, watching her progress. She waved and he gave her a small bow, which made her laugh, for it was such a gentlemanly thing to do.

Someday, she vowed, she would learn all of Mr. Emory's secrets.

That night, she looked out her window at her garden with a new and strange sense of satisfaction. Her whole life had been learning and studying ladylike pursuits that would make her more marriageable. This garden was hers. Yes, the hard labor was being done by Mr. Emory, but the inspiration came from her. And Mr. Smee, if she were completely honest. She'd surprised herself how fascinated she was by his work, his passion for his garden, and she hoped that someday she might tour it. His book sat on her bed, and although she felt a bit foolish for it, she was greatly looking forward to reading it this evening.

Of course, her little patch of land was hardly worthy of his note, but wouldn't it be wonderful to exchange ideas and learn from such a man? For now, reading his book would have to do.

The sun was low on the horizon, giving a soft yellow-orange glow to the landscape. Clara adored this time of day, when it seemed the whole world was soft and quiet. Below her, two maids rushed out of the house, whispering frantically to one another, and Clara smiled at them, envying them their friendship. Clara watched, curious, as the two walked along the perimeter of the garden, then proceeded toward the small pond that Clara hoped would one day be part of their garden plans. For some reason, the pair stopped, appearing to be looking at the back of Mr. Emory's small quarters. For goodness' sake, Clara thought, these women were shameless, just as Jeanine had said.

One waved, and Clara assumed Mr. Emory must be back there enjoying the pretty night. The two giggled and chatted for a time before finally, seemingly reluctantly, returning to the house, huddled together and talking too quietly for Clara to understand what they were saying. It wasn't until they were directly beneath her window that she distinctly heard one of the maids—Sara perhaps?—"He's a right Adonis, he is." And the other one, "And don't you think he knows it."

Poor Mr. Emory was indeed being hounded by the maids, just as Jeanine had said.

The next night and the one that followed saw other maids taking similar strolls just before dusk. Apparently, word had spread that Mr. Emory liked to enjoy the evening air. Each night, a different set, although Sara appeared twice. And each time, the girls would stand near Mr. Emory's quarters and flirt and chat for several minutes. This could not continue, Clara decided. The poor man was getting no peace.

After the third visit, Clara decided to catch the maids in the act and make it clear that they were not to bother her gardener anymore. No doubt Mr. Emory was far too polite to tell them to shoo.

Gathering up her wrap, Clara headed to the back of his quarters directly after dinner. It was another lovely evening, though a bit chillier than it had been. With determined steps, she headed for the small outbuilding where her gardener lived, looking back once to make certain she would arrive before the silly maids. She turned the corner and stopped cold. Then let out a small squeal before covering her face with her hands.

Mr. Emory was unclothed.

Well, very nearly so. He wore no shirt, only a pair of trousers, open at the waist and revealing far more than a girl ought to see, a flat torso and thin line of startlingly masculine hair that disappeared beneath his waistband. Though she'd managed to cover her eyes quickly, it was not so fast that she missed seeing his sheer beauty, his sculpted torso, wet from his bath.

"You are unclothed, sir," she said from behind her hands, then gave a little peek through her fingers. Goodness, he was lovely. His skin glistened in the soft light, the waistline of his trousers was damp from the water, and he was looking at her with a decidedly amused expression and without a hint of embarrassment.

"Did you get a good enough look? Shall I put on my shirt now?" he asked, laughter in his voice.

"I am not looking," she said, spinning around so she would not be tempted. "And the very last thing I expected when I turned the corner was to see an unclothed man."

"I am not unclothed," he pointed out logically.

"You are far too unclothed. And now I know why those maids have been going for nightly strolls. Have you no shame?"

He was silent for a long moment, and Clara thought he *was* ashamed of his behavior, but it didn't take long to realize he was laughing softly; she could hear the huffs of air behind her. "Who am I to deny the women their nightly entertainment?" he asked, the devil.

Clara couldn't stop the laughter that bubbled up but she did her best not to let him know she found him amusing. He was shameless, but in such a charming way, she could hardly be angry.

After a bit of rustling, she heard him say, "You may turn around, Miss Anderson. I am fully clothed."

She did, cautiously, and found to her relief—at least she told herself she was not disappointed—that he was now clothed, though hardly respectable. His shirt was not fully buttoned and it clung to his damp skin in a most enticing manner. As she watched, he tucked the tails into his trousers and lifted his braces onto his shoulders. For some reason, that simple movement made her feel strangely warm.

"I wonder if you could bring yourself to stop entertaining the female staff," she said, trying to sound stern. "I do not want to bring this to the attention of Mrs. Randall or Mr. Standard. No doubt they would not be pleased."

Mr. Emory crossed his arms in front of his muscular chest and stared at her for a long moment. "My quarters are small and I don't have the room to bathe properly without getting everything wet."

Clara let out a small huff of frustration. "Yes, but do you need to bathe every night?"

He chuckled. "As a matter of fact, I do. I dislike going to bed with dust on my face and grime on my hands. Or smelling like some common laborer."

She raised one brow, tempted to remind him that he *was* a common laborer, but then decided there was nothing common about Mr. Emory. Her raised brow apparently spoke volumes, for he laughed aloud.

Behind them, they both heard the sounds of at least two women out in the garden, chatting excitedly, no doubt in anticipation of that evening's show. "Ah, my audience is arriving right on time," he said, smiling at her in a maddening way. He actually did enjoy putting himself on display, she thought.

Clara spun around to face the maids—Matilda and Susan—and placed her fists on her hips. "Good evening," she said, and nearly laughed aloud when the two stopped as if they'd walked into a wall.

"Oh," exclaimed Matilda. "Miss Anderson. Good evening, miss. We were just—"

"I am aware what you were 'just,' Matilda," Clara said pleasantly. "Would you mind informing the other maids that Mr. Emory enjoys his privacy and no longer wishes to be disturbed in the evenings?"

"Don't seem to mind all that much," muttered Susan, and behind her Mr. Emory let out a choking noise that sounded very much like stifled laughter.

"Yes, miss," Matilda said, giving her companion a glare. Next to her, Susan stretched her neck so that she might get a glimpse of Mr. Emory, who stood behind Clara, no doubt grinning at the two women. Clara gave Susan a glare, which the maid cheekily ignored, before the two turned around and, with obvious reluctance, returned to the house. Clara could almost imagine the maids all gathering and hearing the news that their nightly forays into the garden to view the half-naked gardener were now over.

When they were gone, Clara turned again to Mr. Emory and gave him a curious look. Her mother had taught her (Hedra had been informed by Mrs. Pittsfield) that one of the most important responsibilities of an employer was to make certain employees behaved in a respectable manner. If a young maid were to "get into trouble," it reflected badly on the employer. Clara in no way felt comfortable discussing such matters, but was reluctant to involve her mother, who might find it necessary to fire their gardener. The thought of Mr. Emory being fired did not sit well with her; they'd only just begun their work and who knew how receptive a new gardener would be to her plans?

"I do not encourage them," he said, growing serious. "And I have no intention of going down that path. I am here to do a job and that is my only reason for being here."

"Very well," Clara said, vastly relieved that she would not be forced to discuss such a delicate matter. She looked back to the house. "They are quite young and you are a stranger. I daresay they know every man within fifty miles and you are a novelty to them. A mystery. I'm surprised Harriet hasn't solved you yet." She laughed.

When Mr. Emory gave her a curious look, she explained. "My sister loves a mystery and has a remarkable memory. Quite extraordinary. Have you heard of a Lord Berkley? He was accused of murdering his wife not long ago and is now rumored to be taking up residence at his estate not a few miles from our house. My mother is in a tizzy because, well, he's an earl and Harriet is in a tizzy because he was accused of murder."

"Your mother likes earls, does she?" he asked, seeming to find this amusing.

"My mother likes anyone with a title," she explained. Wincing, she said, "She thinks I can draw their interest. Or rather, she thinks our fortune can."

He had been cleaning up, neatly folding his wash cloth and putting his soap atop it when he paused and turned to her. "You've a fortune?"

Clara knew she should not discuss such things, and normally she would not, but Mr. Emory seemed only mildly curious and Clara didn't think there would be any harm in telling him. It wasn't as if anyone in their household didn't already know her mother was trying to entice titles with a hefty dowry.

"Twenty-five thousand pounds and five thousand a year after that," she whispered. It seemed a scandalous amount of money for a marriage contract. "My mother is convinced that will attract all number of titled gentlemen."

He made an odd expression, almost regret, before saying, "And you do not think so?"

Clara let out a snort of a laugh, then bit her lip, knowing that snort was telling enough to explain why an earl would not be interested in her. "Do you not understand the aristocracy?" she asked.

He chuckled softly. "More than you would suppose."

"Then you must know how impossible it would be to expect that I would draw the attention of anyone other than, perhaps, a very old or very poor titled gentleman without an heir. At least those are the types whose attention I've drawn thus far. Though, thankfully, not the attention that results in a proposal."

They were silent for an awkward moment before Clara gave a sharp nod. "As long as we're clear," she said, which Mr. Emory seemed to find amusing, for his eyes turned to half-moons even though his mouth remained set.

"As I said, Miss Anderson, I have no interest whatsoever in any of the staff."

Clara smiled hesitantly, because there was something in his tone, something in the way he looked at her that made Clara flush. "Very well. Good evening, Mr. Emory."

Nathaniel watched her go, trying not to feel too disappointed by the dowry that Miss Anderson thought was a fortune. For many men, twenty-five thousand pounds would be a fortune, but that would hardly touch the amount he needed. While he might feel a stab of shame for his sudden interest in Miss Anderson when she mentioned the fortune, and his equally sharp stab of disappointment when she gave him the amount, he must remain pragmatic. Lion's Gate and the Alford title must be saved and twenty-five thousand pounds would hardly do that. He needed the kind of fortune the blue diamond would bring.

Too bad, really. He rather fancied Miss Anderson and he certainly would welcome her into the marriage bed. She might not come from a strong lineage, but a man had to overlook such things when great fortunes and great beauty were involved. Alas, Miss Anderson's dowry was not a vast fortune, so it would appear when he woke the next morning, he would still be pretending to be a gardener and would continue to search. The blasted diamond was on this property, of that he was certain. It was only a matter of time before he found it.

Despite himself, he looked at the house, his eyes drawn to the room he knew was the elder Miss Anderson's. A soft light glowed, and he could picture her getting ready for bed, slipping on a silky gown, brushing that glorious golden hair of hers. He could feel the tug of arousal and turned away, forcefully, and with a sharp shake of his head. It would do no good to allow himself to think such things, would only serve to torture him when he tried to sleep.

The next morning, Nathaniel woke up early, dressed, and headed to the kitchen for his breakfast. The Anderson household was not, by most standards, a grand household. Though it was clear the Andersons aspired to grandness, their estate was fairly small and their staff adequate at best. The females were run by the awful Mrs. Randall, the housekeeper, and the men by Mr. Standard, the butler. At breakfast, the long, scarred wooden table where the servants ate was surrounded by ten people, seated in accordance to their rank. Nathaniel found it ironic that he, a member of the peerage, had been seated across from the Anderson's only scullery maid, a young girl with buck teeth who tended to drool when she ate.

Most mornings, Nathaniel sat quietly, shoving food into his mouth, and listening to the gossip. He never contributed to the conversation and responded only when asked a direct question—even if the subject around the table was him.

"'e thinks 'e's better n' the lot of us." This from Ralphy, one of the footmen, whose greatest dream was to work in a fine house. Nathaniel made a mental note not to hire him when he had found his treasure and was able to restore his estate. He knew Ralphy was speaking of him, and though the footman had lowered his voice from his usual nasal pitch, Nathaniel still heard the comment clearly, which he supposed was the intent.

Nathaniel did look up the table to where Ralphy sat with a rather feral expression on his pinched face. The footman looked startled to find Nathaniel staring at him, and when Nathaniel graced him with a smile, the man looked downright confused.

"It wasn't a compliment," Ralphy said, his cheeks turning ruddy.

Nathaniel went back to his meal.

"Leave 'im be, Ralphy. 'E's just shy."

Ralphy let out a snort so violent, a small bit of ham flew across the table and landed on the other footman's plate.

"That's quite enough," Mr. Standard intoned, glaring at Ralphy, who immediately looked chagrined. Then Mr. Standard did something quite unexpected. "Mr. Emory, I would like to speak to you privately following breakfast."

As one, the other servants looked at Nathaniel, who curled one side of his mouth up and nodded. He would do nothing to jeopardize his position and he had a feeling Mr. Standard was going to lecture him on proper social behavior amongst the Anderson staff. Bloody hell, he would probably have to be friendly and have conversations. Perhaps he would simply stop eating entirely and rely on Cook to bring him food. He sighed inwardly, cursing his grandfather again for not living quite long enough to tell him precisely where the damned diamond was buried.

After breakfast, Nathaniel headed to the butler's small office and braced himself for whatever it was the man was about to say.

He knocked on the door and the butler bade him enter. "Close the door, please."

Nathaniel did, then looked around at the cozy, dark-paneled room, thinking this was a far better accommodation than his own mean room, with its rough planked floor, uncarpeted, and bed that was too small for his tall frame.

"You've been here three weeks, I believe?"

"Yes, sir."

Mr. Standard waved his hand at a leather chair. "Please take a seat." Nathaniel did, his curiosity growing exponentially. "I have a bit of a dilemma and I was hoping it would be resolved by now." He let out a long, beleaguered sigh, the kind men let out when they are faced with a terrible task. Like firing someone.

"This position is quite important to me," Nathaniel said quickly, and was slightly relieved when the man shook his head, dismissing his concerns.

"Lord Alford," the butler said boldly. "Why are you here?"

Chapter 4

Nathaniel tried to school his features, but apparently had not been quick enough. The butler's use of his title was so unexpected, he could not hide his surprise. Mr. Standard seemed delighted.

"I knew it," he said excitedly, then sat down slowly opposite him, as if Nathaniel might make his escape if he moved more quickly, staring at him in disbelief all the while. Then, realizing he was sitting in the presence of a baron, he leapt to his feet.

"Please, do sit, Mr. Standard. I am impressed. How could you have possibly made the connection?" Now that the game was up, it didn't make sense to hide his real identity; his reaction had sealed his fate.

"I didn't at first. The name jumped out at me—Debrett's, of course—but Emory is not such an uncommon name. Then I noticed your speech, your mannerisms and your, pardon me, lack of gardening skills and I could only come to one conclusion." The butler leaned forward, excitement in his eyes. "I am thirty years old. Do you know how many butlers are as young as I? Granted, the Andersons are not an important family and one could argue that working for such a family actually hurts my career. It is a gamble, and one I pray pays off."

"Ah. You are an ambitious man, I see."

Mr. Standard smiled. "I am. I know, for example, that you inherited the title just four months ago when your grandfather passed away. My condolences. It's all here, in this notebook." He produced a small leather-bound book. "And I also know that your grandfather's butler was an ancient man, who retired and whose modest pension is a bit of a drain on your limited accounts." His smile was triumphant more than smug.

"And how do you know all this?"

"I make it my business to know. Working for an impoverished baron is far better than working for a wealthy tin miner." He paused, his entire body tense, and Nathaniel stared at the man, still shocked by the amount of knowledge he had about what was a fairly obscure and unheralded title. "I shan't tell anyone your secret," he said finally. But Nathaniel thought he detected an unspoken and subtle threat.

"You do know you are attempting to extort a peer of the realm," Nathaniel said dryly. When the other man blanched, he held up a hand. "And I will allow it, of course. It is imperative that you keep my secret and, as it happens, I will be in need of a butler, and from what I can see, you've done a fine job with a staff that isn't particularly well-trained."

Nathaniel watched as the butler attempted to maintain his dignity, but it was a losing battle, apparently, for his face split into a grin. "I shall be honored, sir, to work for you whenever whatever you are doing here is completed." He hesitated a moment. "Might I be so bold to inquire why you are here working as a gardener?"

"No, you may not," Nathaniel said, and appreciated it when the man looked slightly sheepish but not at all insulted. "Suffice it to say, I am doing nothing illegal and nothing that will hurt anyone in this household. I hope that alleviates your concerns, Mr. Standard."

"Thank you, sir, it does. As much as I would like a better position, I will remain loyal to the Andersons for as long as I am in their employ. How long do you think that will be?"

Nathaniel let out a sigh. "I have no idea. Pray that it will not be long."

"Is there any way I can be of assistance?"

Narrowing his eyes, Nathaniel said, "You are aware of the state of Lion's Gate, are you not? It will not be nearly as luxurious as your current surroundings."

"Creature comforts are not important to me," he said. "Position is. Beg pardon, sir, but I have my eye on Clarendon. Their butler is in his sixties. By the time he retires, I shall be in a much better position to apply there."

Nathaniel barked out a laugh. "And here I believed working for a barony would make you happy. You do have lofty goals if you wish to gain a position with the Duke of Chesterfield."

"As you said, my lord, I am a man with ambitions."

Standing, Nathaniel offered his hand to the butler, which the other man shook, his expression solemn. "It will be a pleasure working for you, my lord. And I would like to apologize in advance for any disrespect I will have to show you until our positions are put to rights."

"Of course. I promise I will not take offense."

Nathaniel left the butler's office and maintained his composure until he reached the gardener's shed. There, he grabbed the first tool he could find and threw it as hard as he could against the wall, smiling grimly at the large chunk of wood that flew back at him, nearly hitting his head. "Bloody *fucking* hell," he shouted.

Behind him, he heard a feminine gasp. Miss Anderson, no doubt, and he closed his eyes, wishing himself back in London and as far away from this picturesque village as he could get. St. Ives was beginning to annoy him. It was too quaint, too quiet. He was beginning to loathe the clean smell of the sea and the pretty trees that reminded him of pictures he'd seen of tropical places. And he loathed gardening. "My apologies, Miss Anderson," he said without turning around.

"You obviously didn't know I was standing here," she said, and he thought he heard laughter in her voice. Did nothing offend the girl? He was sorely tempted to find out. "What has you so upset, sir?"

"I...stubbed my toe," Nathaniel offered lamely.

"Are you all right? Shall I have Cook take a look at it?"

"No. It's fine, thank you." He turned and wished he hadn't for she was simply lovely and the sort of woman who would tempt the strongest of men. The early morning sun bathed her in a soft light, making her ethereal, a nymph come to tempt him to sin. God, what he wouldn't do to find out what she tasted like. To hear the sounds she would make when he gave her pleasure. Nathaniel had never been much of a carnal creature, but there was something about this girl that called to his baser side and made desire rush through his blood like some mad beast. A peachy light shined softly on her, making her already fine features even more beautiful. How had her parents created a creature as lovely as she? They were both short, squat people, and here stood their offspring, slim and willowy and breathtakingly beautiful.

"I've brought back Mr. Smee's book. It really is remarkable what he's done." She stepped forward and held out the volume, a shy smile on her lush lips. He wondered if she had the remotest idea what she was doing to him. Likely not. This girl was far too innocent and he had been far too long without female company to withstand her lure. Self-preservation kicked him hard in the gut. He had little doubt it would take only the smallest effort to seduce her, but that way led to disaster.

"Are you planning to hang about today and supervise me?" he asked harshly, wanting her to run away. Instead, she smiled.

"You are grumpy today, Mr. Emory. Have you eaten yet? Had your morning tea?" She smiled at him and damned if he didn't smile back.

No doubt Miss Anderson had learned at an early age that honey attracted more bees than vinegar.

"Just don't expect conversation," he said, pulling on his gloves.

"Oh, I shan't. In fact, I don't mind at all if you do not respond to my inquiries or opinions. I shall continue to murder insects whilst you continue to murder the earth with that spade of yours." She smiled again, her eyes merry half-moons. "I've had my mother order gravel. I should like a gravel path, one that winds toward our little pond. And Mother has spoken to Mr. Billings—he's the local builder, you recall—about building a hothouse this autumn. It's all very exciting."

"Yes, I'm filled with rabid anticipation."

Miss Anderson giggled and spun around, the floppy straw hat she liked to wear nearly falling off. Nathaniel followed her, pausing to look around at the hated garden in an effort to gauge his progress. Doubts had begun to fill him that his grandfather might have been wrong. What if he dug up the whole garden and never found the damned diamond? What if he missed it? What if he found it and it wasn't worth nearly what his grandfather had thought it was worth?

As he stood there, watching the lovely Miss Anderson begin to crush tiny insects, he decided he would give it one more month. If he hadn't found the diamond by then, he would leave and good riddance. He would save the estate some other way. A sick dread filled him when he realized his options were woefully limited. His job as a solicitor wouldn't make even the smallest dent in what was needed to make Lion's Gate livable again. Nathaniel had never been averse to hard work, but the debt, the funds for sweeping repairs, was insurmountable without a large influx of cash that was only available two ways: the diamond or an heiress. Before he went down the route of hunting for a rich wife and throwing his pride and life away, he would try to find the diamond.

One month. Perhaps two. He looked out over the sweeping lawn that ended at the small pond and smiled when he spied two ducks swimming about.

"Oh, we have visitors," Miss Anderson said. "Wouldn't it be lovely if they had some ducklings? Though we hardly have room for a full family of ducks. I do believe I shall ask Mother about the possibility of expanding the pond."

Miss Anderson's vision of the garden seemed to be getting grander by the day. It might be best for that vision if Nathaniel left sooner rather than later.

The two worked in the garden, Miss Anderson fussing over her roses— which Nathaniel had to admit were looking quite a bit healthier than they had been—and he outlining the curving path to the pond. Every once in a while, Miss Anderson would look up and he could tell she was envisioning the garden as what it might be one day. The straw hat let in tiny pinpricks of light, giving her small sunshiny freckles, and Nathaniel wondered if those dots of sun would result in real freckles. They worked in companionable silence until Clara's sister came looking for her.

"Mother sent me to remind you about the luncheon. Some titled gentleman is supposed to be there and she's all atwitter."

Clara smiled brightly. "Tell Mother I'll be in shortly to prepare."

As soon as her sister was gone, however, Clara frowned heavily and let out a sigh.

"I take it you don't want to meet the gentleman?" Nathaniel asked, amused by her reaction. A normal gardener likely would not have made that inquiry, but Nathaniel was not an ordinary gardener. Besides, he was curious.

"Lord Foster. He's the third son of the Marquess of Piedmont. Boring. Ancient. Odiferous."

Nathaniel tried to hold it in, but failed terribly by barking out a laugh. "Odiferous?"

"I do believe he has not bathed in years. His fingernails are black, his teeth green, his skin strangely yellow. And my mother would like me to marry him. I would rather marry a toad. A toad smells better and is far handsomer."

Just the thought of some old man pawing at Miss Anderson caused Nathaniel's blood to boil. "If he is so objectionable, why would your mother consider such a man?"

She looked at him as if he were daft. "*I* am the daughter of a tin miner. *He* is the son of a marquess. Marriage to such a man would be considered quite the coup. You see, it is my mother's fondest wish that I marry a lord, one with a title preferably. Lord Foster has no chance whatsoever of becoming the marquess and his income is barely adequate to finance his love of French brandy—he always seems to have a glass of the stuff in his hand—which is probably why he'd even consider sitting in the same room as us. I come with that impressive dowry, which Mother believes will entice a titled gentleman to ask for my hand." She let out a puff of air, which caused an errant curl to dance on her forehead. "You have no idea how lucky you are to not have to worry about such things."

"Can you not simply tell your mother you refuse?"

She screwed up her face charmingly. "I could, but it's so difficult. She gets so excited each time there is a prospective husband and I do adore her, so it's nearly impossible to tell her no. And Lord Foster…" She let her voice trail off. "Mother says that he is old and would likely die and then I'd be left a widow and would forevermore be known as Lady Foster." She plucked off a bug. "I'd be a lady."

"And that's what you want? To be a lady?" His words came out more harshly than he'd intended, and she snapped her blue eyes to his. He had no idea why, but dash it all, how could she be so foolish as to marry some old goat?

"I want my mother to be happy," she said after a long silence. Nathaniel was about to argue that marrying someone simply to please a parent was foolish in the extreme, when she said, "And it would pave the way for Harriet. My mother has spent all her efforts on me and quite forgotten that Harriet is of age to marry. If I were to marry well, Harriet would have an easier time of it, I think."

"Perhaps you could convince Lord Foster to bathe. You might unearth a dashing fellow."

She burst out laughing, then, apparently belatedly, realized a lady did not laugh with such gusto, and pressed her mouth closed, but not before she let out a small, adorable snort. "He's seventy-three. His dashing days are quite over, I'm afraid."

"Really, I picture myself dashing at that age," Nathaniel said.

She smiled and looked at him in a way that made his blood heat. "I think you shall be dashing at seventy-three." They stared at one another for far too long before Nathaniel turned away and went back to work with frenetic energy.

Clara felt herself flush, a strange heat that started in her center and flew through her like a hot wave. It was so startling, she let out a small gasp and froze when Mr. Emory's head snapped up. He turned and glared at her, his eyes stark and almost frightening. "A bee," she said, and smiled. His dark eyes darted about, looking for the fictitious bee and Clara found herself stifling a laugh and wondering why she felt so incredibly happy.

"Clara! Mother is getting impatient," Harriet called from her second-story window.

"Good-bye, Mr. Emory. Do take care of my garden whilst I'm away."

He sketched a small bow. "I shall, Miss Anderson."

Clara spun about, feeling odd and wonderful. Even the thought of spending an afternoon charming Lord Foster didn't fill her with the dread it usually did.

When Clara entered the house, her mother was there looking frazzled, her cheeks slightly flushed. "My goodness, we have to leave in fifteen minutes, Clara Anne. You will never be ready in time."

Clara waved her mother's concern away. "If we are a bit late, Mrs. Crocker will not mind. Besides, you know Jeanine can have me ready in the shake of a lamb's tail." Clara lifted her skirts and ran up the stairs, ignoring her mother's puff of displeasure. Three years in finishing school had not been enough to remove all her unpolished bits. Clara still laughed too loudly, walked too quickly, and ate with too much enthusiasm to ever be mistaken for a true lady, though when in lofty company, she did a much better job of it. Her mother, bless her soul, only knew what Mrs. Pittsfield told her—that well-bred young ladies were seen and not heard, sat up straight, and smiled vacantly and charmingly whenever addressed. Clara did her best to emulate that ideal, if only to please her mother, who had sacrificed so much for her.

The Andersons might have all the trappings of wealth, but they had far fewer funds than anyone knew. Too much was spent on appearances—gowns, fine carriages and cattle, lessons on dancing, elocution, singing, and painting. Endless money spent all to one end: finding a titled gentleman for Clara.

Until recently, Clara had been more than happy to go along with her mother's lofty plans. Lately, though, she'd found the idea of marrying for position far less attractive.

Jeanine was nearly as flustered as her mother when Clara flew into her room, out of breath and laughing. "Your mother is in a lather," she said, immediately tackling the buttons on the back of her gown and stripping it off in record time. "Lord Foster is attending the luncheon, you know."

Clara wrinkled her nose as she removed her corset cover and Jeanine laughed as she tossed Clara's everyday dress on the bed before returning to undo her stays. Once the corset was removed, Jeanine hurried to the wardrobe to retrieve the corset that would enhance her afternoon dress, a fitted green silk gown that showed off her small waist. The dress was by Worth and had a slight military construction that contrasted nicely with the feminine train. It was one of Clara's favorites and had been one of her mother's more lavish expenditures. She'd worn it just once.

Once the dress was on, Jeanine stepped back and grimaced. "Your hair. I haven't a hope of getting it done in time." Her thick, wavy hair was currently in a long braid down her back.

"Just pin it up," Clara said, tugging on a clean pair of gloves.

"I'll hear about it when you get home," Jeanine grumbled as she pulled Clara over to sit before her vanity. In a matter of minutes, her simple braid was wound up at the back of her head and pinned in place. Turning her head to see what her maid had done, Clara smiled.

"Perfect, Jeanine. Mother won't say a word, and if she does, I'll be quite cross with her."

Jeanine laughed. "You are never cross with your mother. As a matter of fact, I've never seen you cross with anyone."

Clara smiled. "Being cross never solved anything," she said, and Jeanine rolled her eyes.

Jeanine grabbed her hat, a jaunty number that looked like a miniature bonnet embellished with excessive ribbons and a small green ostrich plume, and quickly attached it to her head. "Shake, please," she said, and Clara shook her head to make certain the hat stayed in place. Pulling out her pocket watch, Jeanine let out a sigh. "With two minutes to spare," she said, letting out a breath of relief.

"One minute. I want to say good-bye to—" She stopped herself. Jeanine might be a friend, but she would never approve of Clara's befriending their gardener. "—my garden. It's so lovely. Have you taken a look? It's coming along quite nicely." Clara half ran to the window and looked out, her eyes not on her roses but the man digging holes nearby. She willed him to look up, and when he did not, she opened the window rather loudly. Mr. Emory looked up then, and Clara held her breath for a long moment, only releasing it when he tipped his hat and smiled.

Behind her, Jeanine said, "Your mother, miss."

With great reluctance, she closed the window softly and turned away, her heart beating a bit faster than it should. Her gardener had tipped his hat, not blown her a kiss. Not that he ever would. And not that he ever should.

But wouldn't it be thrilling if he did?

Clara dipped a deep curtsy, glad only that Lord Foster had not condescended to come over to kiss her hand. As usual, the man held a snifter of brandy, and Clara wondered if his frequent visits to Mrs. Crocker's home were due to Mr. Crocker's great love of fine French brandy. Mr. Crocker was first cousin to Viscount Pellingham. Mrs. Crocker came from a family with obscure ties to the Duke of Windsor, whom she had never met but whom Mrs. Crocker managed to bring up in most conversations, calling His Grace "my relation." The woman had a perpetual smile, her prominent cheeks rounded, as if she was delighted with every aspect of the world. Clara had no idea why Mrs. Crocker regularly included Hedra on her guest list, for her mother had no connections. Harriet suspected it was because Mr. Crocker, who owned several tin mines, was interested in purchasing the Andersons'.

Clara didn't care about the whys of their invitations, she only knew that receiving them made her mother ecstatic and so she was on her best behavior when they visited the Crocker estate. Conversation drifted, as it often did, to people and places Clara did not know, and so she plastered a polite smile on her face and let her mind wander to more pleasant topics. At the moment, that would be her garden. Or rather, her gardener.

It was wrong of her, she knew, to admire a servant's physical attributes, but it seemed she couldn't help herself. The odd flutter she felt inside when she looked at Mr. Emory seemed to be growing daily and she could only recognize it for what it was: She was getting a bit spoony over him. It would probably be a good idea to stop spending so much time in the garden, but the thought of that was quite depressing. And it wasn't only that Mr. Emory was so fine looking, but that she quite liked gardening. Not only did it allow her to be out of doors, but she gained a great deal of satisfaction when she returned to the garden and saw the results of her hard work. Her roses were lovely and the garden itself was getting more beautiful each day.

"I would love to walk in the garden with your daughter, Mrs. Anderson."

The reed-thin voice of Lord Foster sliced through her thoughts and brought her back to the room where she sat pretending to listen to the conversation around her. Clara forced herself to keep her smile.

Lord Foster stood and offered up a wrinkled, rather yellow-looking hand. "Shall we, Miss Anderson?"

"Of course, my lord." She stood sedately and walked toward the leering old goat, willing him to look up past her breasts and into her eyes. Then, perhaps, he might read what she was thinking behind her smile. Alas, no, he continued to stare at her breasts, even though her dress was quite modest. "If you will excuse us," Clara said to the small gathering.

Lord Foster, snifter still in hand, accepted a refill from a footman before offering his arm, which Clara took. When Clara had told Mr. Emory that Lord Foster was odiferous, she was not simply trying to be amusing. He did stink, an odd assortment of old, unwashed flesh and awful cologne that was meant to mask the smell of him. Clara swallowed and tried to breathe as shallowly as possible until they were out of doors.

"How are your children, my lord?" she asked as they stepped out the door and into the Crockers' expansive garden. The last time she'd been to the estate, she hadn't paid much attention to the flora, but now she examined it with keen interest. It was an appealing garden, she thought, but too structured. Too English, she supposed. And, like so many English gardens, the poor shrubbery had been chopped into topiary. Statuary was placed strategically and predictably, fountains gurgled, spouting water from cherubs' pitchers, and paths were well-tended and pleasantly positioned. It was, she couldn't help thinking, exceedingly boring, and she decided that Mr. Smee's vast wild garden would be far more interesting.

"My children? Greedy." He laughed at his own jest, then ended up hacking weakly into a handkerchief.

Clara hated the thought, for she wasn't a mean person, but she couldn't help hope that Lord Foster would meet his maker before he decided whether to court her.

"And then he keeled over, just like that. The physician said his condition was very grave. I feel terribly guilty."

Miss Anderson had rushed into the garden shortly before he was quitting for the day, clearly bursting to tell him about her visit. Though he'd told himself he was glad for the privacy that afternoon—he had made great progress in the area he'd covered—he found he was unaccountably pleased that Miss Anderson had decided to visit him. Apparently, just as Lord Foster and she were approaching a cherub pouring water from a pitcher, Lord Foster had stopped and clutched his chest, then stumbled toward the fountain. If it hadn't been for the cherub, it was almost a certainty he would have fallen in. As it was, Lord Foster landed heavily on the edge of the fountain, she said, then slid to the ground.

"Why would you feel guilty? Surely, you had nothing to do with it," Nathaniel said, pausing in his work to hear her response, the smallest of smiles on his lips.

"Because just before he suffered the attack…" She paused, then moved closer and whispered, "I was hoping he would meet his maker before he could ask my father to court me."

Nathaniel was quiet for a long moment before barking out one loud laugh, followed by a stretch of silent laughter, his shoulders shaking with mirth. She looked so adorably horrified, he felt compelled to put her mind at ease. "Ah, I can understand why you are racked with guilt. But look at it this way, if God heard your wish and then acted on it, then He must have rather liked the idea."

"That shouldn't make me feel better, but I confess it does." Again, they found themselves staring at one another, smiling stupidly, until they weren't smiling, they were just staring. Her lips parted slightly and her eyes took on that look he was already beginning to recognize. The surge of lust that hit him was intoxicating, unlike anything he had ever experienced before, at least whilst having an ordinary conversation. She was so innocent, she likely didn't even know how she was looking at him, but Nathaniel knew.

Just like the last time, it was he who looked away first. "Miss Anderson," he said gravely, "I wonder if perhaps you've been spending too much time in the garden."

His entire body was on edge, a bowstring pulled taut and ready to snap. This lust he felt was making him think things he never should, not about an innocent girl and certainly not the daughter of his employer. Keeping focused on his mission was imperative, but it was damned difficult with her standing there looking at him with drowsy eyes and parted lips.

"I rather like spending time in the garden," she said after a long silence. "And I rather like talking to you, Mr. Emory. I know I shouldn't think of you as such, but I do think of you as a friend. For some reason, I can tell you things I cannot tell anyone else. How many people would have laughed when I told them I wished for someone to die?"

He let out a low chuckle. "I just...I don't want you to..."

"What?"

"I don't want a friend," he said finally, praying she knew what he truly meant. He didn't want the sort of friend he dreamed of kissing, who kept him up at night thinking about how she would feel beneath him. Whose body enticed him and made him wish he was the sort of man who could take advantage of a simple country girl.

"Oh," she said in a small voice.

"We are from two different stations, you and I. It is important that we, both of us, understand that." He felt a prick of guilt for saying that, but it was a reminder to him, as well, and was nothing but the truth.

For some reason, that made her smile. "Mr. Emory, you are being silly. We are of the same class. If anything, your background is likely far better than my own."

"You shouldn't spend so much time alone with a man," he said desperately. "What if someone were to notice? They might think things they oughtn't."

She let out a small laugh, but then her cheeks flushed, and he wondered, dumbfounded, if such thoughts had never entered her head. Perhaps he'd been wrong about the way she'd looked at him; perhaps his own lust had muddled his brain so much he was imagining she felt the same way. "No one would think such things," she said, sounding slightly baffled that he would have suggested anyone would.

"I believe you would be surprised what people would think."

Her eyes grew wide. "Has someone said something? One of the staff?"

"No," he said quickly. "Nothing like that."

"There, it's settled. I will continue to garden and entertain you with my stories and you shall pretend not to listen and pretend you wish me to go away."

"But I really do wish you to go away," he said, then immediately regretted his words when he saw her face. "Only because I wish you to stay." Damn. He prayed she didn't realize what he'd meant.

They began another staring contest and when her eyes dipped to his mouth, he had to fight not to pull her into his arms. "Miss Anderson," he said, exasperation tingeing his voice. Surely she knew what she was doing to him.

She curled her lips inward and furrowed her brow, unable to meet his eyes, making him wonder if she was finally recognizing the danger she was in.

Letting out a sigh, he thrust his spade into the earth, then tilted it to dig up yet another stone. "Please," he muttered as he bent over to pick it up, then, realizing it was just another rock, threw it into the pile.

Clara turned back to her roses, then stilled, her eyes on the small grouping of plants he'd put in just that day. Bluebells, or at least they would be in the spring. She turned and smiled, and damn if his heart wasn't warmed by that smile. He'd been walking from town and saw a field full of them; it wasn't as if he'd done much more than dig them from the ground.

"Thank you, Mr. Emory," she said.

"There was a whole field of them."

"And now I have some here." She looked at the bluebells as if he'd planted her a garden worthy of Mr. Smee. That she was so delighted shouldn't have pleased him quite so much, but it did. And that was, perhaps, worse than lusting after her.

"I'll probably kill them."

She grinned. "I know, Mr. Emory." After letting out a giggle, she turned and left, leaving him completely confused about what had just transpired.

Before entering the house, she called back, "See you in the morning, Mr. Emory." Then she spun about and rushed inside, leaving him staring after her. After a time, he started laughing.

That night, Clara sat in front of her mirror combing out her hair and humming beneath her breath while Jeanine set out her dress for the next day. She and her mother were lunching with some "important family" who had ties to some earl and her mother wanted them to create a relationship with them so that they might be invited along when they went to visit the earl. Hedra was an expert on forming relationships with families who had vague ties to the aristocracy that she so wanted Clara to be a part of. For the past week, she'd been all atwitter about Lord Berkley, who was rumored to be coming home to St. Ives to permanently take up residence at Costille House, an historic old castle not three miles from their home.

"You're in a fine mood tonight," Jeanine said.

"I do believe gardening has lightened my disposition. Who knew toiling in the dirt would be so beneficial to my constitution?" It was true, but Clara worried that the thing that lightened her mood the most was not gardening, but their gardener. It was wrong and silly but she couldn't help it when her heart sped up a beat when she saw him, or when he smiled, or when he threw a rock into the growing pile. Or when he looked at her as if he was thinking he might kiss her. Was he? Or was she simply wishing?

A long silence ensued, the sort of silence that was filled with meaning. Clara glanced at Jeanine and something about her expression made her believe her maid had some deep thoughts brewing in her head.

"Mr. Emory has been making eyes at Sara," she said finally, and Clara paused momentarily in her brushing before continuing on, with slightly more force than before.

"She's a bit young for him, is she not?" Clara asked, striving to keep her tone neutral, trying to ignore the fact that Mr. Emory's looking at anyone bothered her a bit.

"She's just a few months younger than you," Jeanine said, snapping open a petticoat and laying it next to her gown.

"I'm sure they'll make a lovely couple," Clara said. Really, what business was it of hers whether their gardener and one of their kitchen maids made googly eyes at one another all day long? Perhaps he was one of those men who flirted with all girls, and she was one of those girls who thought he only flirted with her. Now, that was a sobering thought.

"I don't trust him," Jeanine said. "There's something about him that's off. You spend a lot of time with him. Haven't you noticed he hardly speaks a word? I thought perhaps he was touched in the head, but then I heard him talking to Mr. Standard, all friendly like. I'm wondering if he's got his sights on some position in the house. I think Mr. Gregory is worried about his job. That gardener is a head taller than Mr. Gregory and you know how footmen are supposed to be of a certain height. It's a wonder your mother hasn't thought of it herself yet."

"I hardly think Mr. Emory has designs on Mr. Gregory's job."

"But have you heard him talk? We all think he's taken diction lessons, and why would he do that if he didn't have ideas about bettering himself?"

Jeanine rarely annoyed Clara, but at this moment, Clara was feeling a bit of annoyance creep into her.

"He's causing problems," Jeanine said, lowering her voice as if someone might overhear.

This got Clara's attention. "What do you mean?"

Jeanine stopped her work to come over to where Clara sat. "Whenever he's in the room with the rest of us, well, it's just not the same. Mr. Standard acts like he's something special and Mr. Emory sits at the table like he owns it."

"Is he rude?" As much as she enjoyed Mr. Emory's company, if he was disruptive with the other members of the staff, he would have to go.

Jeanine furrowed her brow. "It's not like that. It's difficult to explain. Just a feeling, small things that make me think he doesn't belong here. Most of us grew up in St. Ives. Where's he from? What's he doing here? Who is his family?" Her maid worried her hands together in her lap, and Clara knew Jeanine was upset, but without a specific complaint, there was little she could do.

"Would you like me to speak with him?"

"No. I'd like you to sack him."

"On what grounds?"

"He's not much of a gardener, for one."

Clara laughed aloud. "That is true. But my mother hired him, not I, so I'm not certain what I can do. I suppose I could speak with my mother about it, though to be honest, I rather like Mr. Emory. I find him to be a pleasant fellow."

Jeanine narrowed her eyes slightly. "It's like that, is it?"

To her horror, Clara felt her cheeks redden, though she wasn't even certain why. "What can you mean?"

"He's handsome enough," Jeanine said with a shrug.

"Are you implying that I have set my cap for him? Because I can assure you, I have not." Clara rarely spoke sharply to anyone, and for her to do so to Jeanine was highly unusual, but for some reason her maid's words touched a nerve.

"I'm sorry, Miss Anderson." Jeanine squeezed her eyes shut, clearly mortified. "Of course you would never carry on with a member of the staff." She put her hands on each side of her face. "Sometimes I forget who you are and who I am."

Clara stood and gently grasped Jeanine's wrists, bringing them down so that she could look into the maid's eyes. "You are my *friend*," she said, giving Jeanine's hands a gentle shake. "I confess I have noticed how handsome our gardener is. Like every other female in this household. But he is only our gardener, nothing more." In that moment, Clara made a silent vow to herself not to become spoony over Mr. Emory, something she knew she was on her way to becoming. Perhaps she should stay away from the garden for a while, just so she could clear her head.

Jeanine let out a long sigh. "I am relieved," she said, then laughed. "I must say one would have to be dead not to notice how handsome he is. And I do worry about Sara. She's beginning to make a cake of herself, inventing all sorts of reasons to go out to the garden. Of course we all see through her."

"Why would it be so bad if Sara and our gardener fell in love?" Clara asked, ignoring the twinge she felt in her stomach that protested against the idea of Mr. Emory falling in love with anyone.

"Because, like I said, something's off with the man."

"Does anyone else feel the way you do?"

Jeanine made a face and Clara laughed. "We're all a bit suspicious of him, to be honest. But it could be only that he is a stranger here."

"Let me know if something happens beyond your imagination," Clara said, teasing her.

"If I wait until he murders us all in our sleep, it will be too late," Jeanine mumbled darkly, but Clara just laughed.

"The man can hardly bring himself to kill garden pests. I do not think any of our lives are in danger."

Jeanine seemed slightly appeased, but said ominously, "I'll keep an eye on him."

"Chicken and dumplings tonight, Mr. Emory," the cook said, beaming at Nathaniel. Mrs. Ellesbury was the only member of the staff who had been kind to him. He felt more comfortable in her company than anyone else's, perhaps because as a young boy he'd spent long hours in the kitchens watching the family cook work. She'd been the only woman in his life when he'd been young, the one who had bandaged his scrapes and given him hugs. Mrs. Ellesbury, with her rosy cheeks and dandelion-fluffy hair, reminded him of those long mornings when a bored young boy had watched his cook make berry muffins just for him.

"Now I have something to look forward to all day," he said, grinning. "That and your beautiful company."

She blushed and waved a hand at him. "I'll be telling Mr. Ellesbury that you've been flirting with me again," she said, placing in front of him a plate heavy with browned potatoes and a thick slab of ham. This simple fare and the hard physical labor was agreeing with him, for he could feel himself growing stronger, leaner. Though he'd never had much fat on his bones, laboring in the garden had trimmed him down so that he'd noticed his trousers were getting a bit loose in the waist.

He sat at the table and nodded when Mr. Standard entered. The butler's eyes widened and he jerked his head, indicating Nathaniel should stand, which he did as soon as he realized his error. It was something he often forgot to do since he was so used to servants hastily standing when he entered a room, he'd hardly noticed them actually doing it. Perhaps he ought to pretend Mr. Standard was a woman, he mused, as he gave the butler an apologetic smile.

"You're late for breakfast this morning," Mr. Standard said, then shot a look at Mrs. Ellesbury so that Nathaniel would know he was giving him a lecture only for the cook's sake. "Don't let it become a habit. Mrs. Ellesbury works hard enough and this is not a restaurant where you may stroll in any time you'd like."

"My apologies, Mrs. Ellesbury," Nathaniel said, trying to ignore Mr. Standard's reddening cheeks. Chastising him did not come naturally to the young butler, but was a necessity given Nathaniel's predicament. If anything, he was grateful for Mr. Standard's guidance in these matters, because he was completely ignorant about servant etiquette.

"Oh, don't you fret, Mr. Emory." Then she winked and said, "But perhaps you should pay more attention to the time."

Nathaniel had been purposely late, an attempt to avoid the staff, particularly the female members. He could not honestly say he did not like the attention they gave him; it was rather uplifting to find himself the object of their adoration. Why not have a bit of fun while was here? As long as it did not move into the physical, a bit of flirtation would be harmless enough. But one girl, Sara, seemed to have moved from friendly flirtation to something more fervent, though he'd really done little to encourage her. He'd look up at odd times and there she would be, preening, batting her eyes, giggling. Someone ought to tell the girl that such behavior did not work on men—most men, rather. He'd waited until he was sure the other servants had departed the kitchen before making his way there, guessing Mrs. Ellesbury would still give him a hearty breakfast, and he'd been correct.

"How goes the garden?" Mr. Standard said, drawing Nathaniel's attention back to the butler.

"Well enough. I think in a few weeks it will be near to complete. I hope." The butler smiled, understanding that Nathaniel was talking more about his becoming butler to Lion's Gate than about the garden itself.

"And you have everything you need? Equipment and such?"

Nathaniel thought for a moment, then nodded. "Yes. For now. I may need something more when we begin preparing for the hothouse, but I'll know better after I begin. Miss Anderson mentioned a local man would be building it?"

"That would be Mr. Billings. He does most of the odd building around these parts." Mr. Standard gave a furtive look to Mrs. Ellesbury and, noting she was busy, leaned forward and whispered, "Is there anything else you need? Something to make your time here more pleasant? I know your room is mean and not at all—"

Nathaniel held up a hand. Mr. Standard's earnestness was heartening, and Nathaniel gave him a grateful smile. "A prayer, sir, that I will finish my work here in a timely manner. That's all I need."

The butler smiled. "Oh, I nearly forgot. A letter arrived for you yesterday." He seemed mortified to have forgotten. "One moment."

Mr. Standard disappeared, leaving Nathaniel to finish his breakfast, and returned just as he was taking his last bite.

"It's from London," Mr. Standard said, the same way someone might say, "It's from the queen."

A quick glance told Nathaniel it was from his solicitor, and he tucked the letter into his pocket, much to the obvious disappointment of Mr. Standard, who had clearly wanted him to open it in front of him. "Thank you, Mr. Standard," he said, then got up and left the kitchen to start his day.

Back in his quarters, Nathaniel withdrew the letter. He was quite curious what could have been so important that Gordon had seen fit to send him correspondence. He'd been quite clear with his solicitor that his identity needed to remain a secret and that correspondence from a solicitor would only arouse suspicion.

"Dear Mr. Emory,

I have learned that a Mr. Belmont has been inquiring about a certain item that his father lost. I thought you should know that your name and that of your grandfather were mentioned more than once. He is looking for you, sir. Be aware.

Kindest regards,

Samuel Gordon, esq."

"Be aware?" Nathaniel said, as he read the cryptic note again. So, Belmont's son was looking for the blue diamond. Why, after all this time?

It would have been easy enough for the man to find his grandfather when he was still alive—unless the son was just now learning of the diamond. Nathaniel thought back on what his grandfather had told him about Belmont. His old friend had died decades ago and no one from that family had made any inquiries. It was possible they didn't know of the diamond; he hadn't known until his grandfather had told him, after all. How was it possible after all these years that a Belmont was now searching for the same diamond?

Gordon had written "Be aware" not "Beware," so perhaps it was nothing to worry over. Nathaniel tucked the letter into his traveling bag, wondering what this could mean. Did Belmont think he had a claim to the diamond? Was it possible that he did? If what his grandfather said was true, then it was plausible that Belmont did have some sort of claim on the diamond, but he'd be damned if the family got a penny from it. His grandfather had suffered for years, unable to walk, his days filled with endless pain, all because of a Belmont. No, they wouldn't get a sixpence of the money—if he ever found the blasted thing.

Chapter 5

"Checking out today, Mr. King?"

handed over his room key.
eren't for the large sum of
given up his search quite
ffice more than a month
ost of which had been
his had been Roger's
re solid information.
sit the current Lord
idated estate.

learly documented
rd son of Viscount
d a massive blue
tune once cut up
absconded with
rly penniless in a
d on as crew to a
at the hands of the
ment for his own
this point, it was
ing on the ship. *I*
ds. He blamed his

ite madly obsessed
liamond had been
ading the journals

and being paid three hundred pounds to find the diamond, Roger had been more than willing to work for no fee for at least a month, maybe more. He was becoming nearly as obsessed with finding the diamond as Mr. Belmont had been.

Best of all, he'd found another daisy. While traveling to Cumbria, he'd stopped at an inn, and as he did in every village and city he'd ever been in, he'd begun asking questions related to his family's murder. This time, he'd struck gold. Fifteen years prior, a woman had been brutally murdered in her home and a daisy had been carefully laid upon her body. Her twelve-year-old son had found her. His twin ran to get their father to help, but it was far too late for the poor lady, whose throat had been efficiently cut. When he'd heard the gruesome details, his heart had nearly stopped. It was far too coincidental, the details of this murder that had taken place hundreds of miles from London. A woman, a daisy, and twins.

Alas, this was another unsolved murder. The local constable had determined that it was some sort of attempted robbery, that the woman had perhaps interrupted a burglar and had paid the price with her life. Before leaving that tiny village, Roger sought out the constable and told him of his family's murder.

"This is the third case I've discovered involving twins and daisies," he'd said.

The man's face had paled markedly. That particular case had hit him hard, for the constable was the father of twins himself, and he could not imagine his own sons finding their mother thus. Now, he had another reason to fear. Two cases might be a coincidence. Three meant there was a monster in England, one that must be stopped.

If only Roger could find the bloody diamond, he could spend all his time searching for his family's murderer. He had a feeling that finding the current Baron Alford would lead him directly to the diamond, so for now, his search had turned from the diamond to Nathaniel Emory. He had a feeling if he found the baron, he would be significantly closer to finding the diamond.

Chapter 6

Clara looked out their carriage window, bored and restless, as her mother prattled on excitedly about how they were to go to London in the autumn. Her father, his large hands folded over his stomach, his hat shoved over his eyes, pretended to sleep, Clara suspected, so he would not be forced to participate in the conversation. She gave her father a fond look before returning her gaze out the window.

Hedra seemed unusually restless. "Mrs. Gardener said the baron might be visiting. *Might*. All this traveling and he might not even be there." A hefty sigh. "I s'pose we can return later in the autumn. He always visits in the autumn, she says, and this was just a chance. She's a second cousin, you see." Clara was well aware of Mrs. Gardener's relationship with the baron. Mrs. Gardener was a curiosity, to be honest, for Clara could not understand why she had issued the invitation to their home in the first place. They had met her in Bristol; Mrs. Gardener and her daughter, Susan, had been staying at the same hotel and they had struck up a conversation. The two families had lunch together, and Clara had felt Mrs. Gardener was assessing them, or rather, assessing her. Long, thoughtful looks, as if Mrs. Gardener was wondering what she was doing amidst the rest of the Andersons, who, Clara had to admit, seemed an awkward bunch. Clara, recently graduated from Mrs. Ellison's Seminary for Young Ladies, was meticulous about her social interactions, being careful to put into practice all she had learned.

Hedra, so her grandmother had said, had been a lovely girl, with thick, chestnut hair and brilliant blue eyes. Her face was, perhaps, a bit too square, her jaw too strong for real beauty, but Hedra had been pretty enough, her grandmother said. Now, Hedra was a blocky woman, with iron-gray hair and a bit more bulk on her bones than even a matron should have. Clara and Harriet had gotten their height and hair from their father, their eyes from their mother, and who knows where everything else came from. It would look to an outsider as if Clara and Harriet had been plucked from a cabbage patch and placed with this ordinary couple. Harriet, reed thin and pale, and Clara, a beauty unmatched in all of Cornwall (those were her grandmother's words as well).

People could be cruel. They seemed to think that Clara would not care if they insulted her parents directly to her, by asking her how two such common people could have produced her. More than once when she was attending the finishing school her mother had insisted she enroll in, a girl had made unkind comments about her parents.

"You must admit it is a curiosity," one girl had said to another, as if Clara hadn't been standing with them.

"The only curiosity is why someone would be so rude to say such a thing," Clara had said, feeling her entire body heat. She disliked confrontation but she would not stand for someone directly insulting the family she loved. The girls seemed mostly confused that Clara would be angry and were not a bit remorseful.

"Clara, are you not listening?"

With an apologetic smile, she said, "I fear I was not, Mother. I was lost in thought."

"This is an opportunity," Hedra said, stressing the last word.

"I understand."

Hedra worried her hands together, clearly not convinced that Clara understood the importance of this visit. Mrs. Gardener was quite a bit higher in social status than they and it was a bit of a coup to have been invited to her home—and with the possibility of meeting a baron. She was someone who could open doors for Clara, put a cloak of respectability on the family.

"Mother, all will be well. You know I comport myself like a queen when I am with company."

Hedra reached over and patted her hand. "I know. You will charm them and they will ask you to accompany them to all sorts of amusements when we go to London. It shall be lovely."

Clara gave her mother an indulgent look. "They'll do no such thing and you know it. But it shall be a lovely visit, and if the baron is there, I shall be my most charming self. I do hope he is not an octogenarian."

Hedra gave Clara a playful slap to her wrist, then, seemingly satisfied, she closed her eyes and was soon napping. Looking across to where her father sat, Clara noticed that he was indeed sleeping, no longer pretending to sleep. She hoped this visit went well for their sakes. They had sacrificed so much so that she might marry well. Harriet, lucky girl, got to stay home—she always got to stay home whilst Clara was paraded about. Harriet loathed social engagements and her mother had taken pity on her and finally stopped forcing her to join them. Abandoning Harriet to her own devices left Clara alone with her thoughts far too often, and lately her thoughts inevitably drifted to her garden and her gardener. It was quite telling that every time her mother said "Mrs. Gardener," her heart sped up just a bit, simply at the word "gardener."

Closing her eyes, a small smile on her lips, she pictured him even now, working on the hothouse foundation. He would be warm, his shirt clinging to his heavy muscles, his hair dark along the edges from his labors. Every once in a while he would stop and survey his work, then frown because she was not there to give him cheer. Did he even note her absence? Was he relieved?

Ugh, should she care? Clara pressed her lips together, angry at herself for dwelling on Mr. Emory. She could have no future with such a man, for Clara had no desire to cause her mother a fatal attack. A giggle nearly bubbled up past her lips at the thought of telling her mother that she and their gardener were planning to court. Hedra would no doubt faint dead away and her father would lock her in her room. Her father might not say much, but he was just as adamant as her mother that she marry well.

"What is all this money if I can't use it to secure my daughter's future?" he'd said more than once. Her father had spent a fortune on travel, dresses, lessons on comportment. How ungrateful would she be if she threw it all away on a whim simply because her mother had hired a handsome gardener? Surely she had more self-respect than that!

As the Andersons' well-sprung carriage made its way to Chatford Manor, Clara vowed that she would no longer look at Mr. Emory as anything other than what he was: a servant.

Chatford Manor was a charming and ancient home, built in the sixteenth century, with a sharply peaked roof and dark gray stone walls, nestled amidst a well-groomed landscape. Clara, who wouldn't have noticed such a thing three weeks before, looked at the garden with new, appreciative eyes. She amazed herself by recognizing several of the flowers they passed as they traveled down the long drive: the blue ceanothus, its rounded blooms looking much like lilac, swords of delphinium, and a feathery yellow border of thalictrum. Clara had asked that Mr. Emory include the yellow flowers, such a cheerful color, along the path that led to the hothouse.

"Do you think we'll have time to tour their gardens?" Clara asked her mother, who was still a bit groggy from her nap.

"Only if his lordship asks you. If he's here, that is."

Clara looked longingly at the gardens, but nodded. "Perhaps tomorrow," she said.

Mrs. Gardener stepped out of the door as the Andersons departed from their carriage and greeted the family warmly. "Welcome to Chatford Manor," she said. "I do hope you find it agreeable." The older woman looked directly at Clara when she said this last, and with such meaning, she felt a flash of alarm. When she had met the family in Bristol, it had only been Mr. and Mrs. Gardener and their daughter, Susan. Was there a son? One whom they hoped she would find agreeable?

It soon became obvious, when Mr. Gardener and Susan exited the house, that no other family members would be appearing, so Clara assumed she had imagined that telling look. Still, the feeling that the Gardeners had an ulterior motive for inviting them persisted until they were introduced to Baron Longley, a tall, distinguished gentleman of perhaps forty years with thinning dark hair plastered to his head with pomade and a thin, rather dashing mustache. He was not entirely unappealing and seemed genuinely interested in getting to know her, so Clara thought perhaps this trip hadn't been entirely a waste of time.

The first evening was pleasantly spent with dinner and music afterwards. Hedra had a tiny bit too much wine with dinner and was slipping into her Cornish dialect, but no one seemed to notice or care. Once they were all in the parlor, Mrs. Gardener convinced Susan to play the piano, and Hedra announced that Clara "sings like an angel" so the group urged them to put on an impromptu performance. Clara, who loved to sing and had been complimented many times for her talent, was more than happy to oblige the request, even when she noted a bit of hesitance from Susan. That hesitance was soon discarded when the two began to perform a Mozart duet, and she could tell by Mrs. Gardener's expression that she had done justice to the song. Even Susan warmed up to her and the two forged a fledgling friendship, formed through their love of music.

Following their final performance, Baron Longley clapped heartily. "You should spend some time in London, Miss Anderson. I would be more than happy to make the introductions."

Clara smiled warmly, excited about the prospects of a season in London, something she would never be able to achieve without a well-placed sponsor. She looked around the room, noting her mother's beaming face, and then Mrs. Gardener, who was looking at Baron Longley as if he'd grown another head. It was such an odd look, but Clara dismissed it when the baron repeated his invitation with even more enthusiasm.

When everyone was retiring for the evening, Mrs. Gardener drew Clara aside, and she remembered that odd look she'd given the baron.

"You are such a lovely girl, Clara," Mrs. Gardener said kindly.

"Thank you, Mrs. Gardener."

"And intelligent. You must have realized by now that I had an ulterior motive in asking you and your parents here."

A slight bit of alarm passed through Clara, but she managed to smile politely. "I hadn't thought you had any motive at all, Mrs. Gardener," she said.

The older woman frowned briefly, then smiled. "Baron Longley is a generous fellow, but I would not put any stock in his comment. I daresay by tomorrow morning he will have forgotten he issued the invitation and would no doubt be mortified that he had done so. I have known the baron for a very long time, my dear, and I can assure you no invitation will be forthcoming." The kind way Mrs. Gardener was looking at her, the pity in her tone, was humiliating, but Clara continue to smile gently, to breathe, to stand still when she wanted nothing more than to run to her room and hide.

Mrs. Gardener continued, "My mother lives in a pretty little house on the property. She was unable to attend this evening as she was not feeling quite up to it." Mrs. Gardener paused. "I think that, yes, you would be perfect for her. You are educated, and despite your circumstances, appear to be quite charming and refined."

Clara shook her head slightly. "Forgive me, Mrs. Gardener, but I fear you have me at a loss."

She let out a light laugh. "I do apologize. I have asked you here because I am considering hiring you as a companion for my mother. I wanted to see you in a social situation, and I must say, Miss Anderson, you have passed muster. I do believe you would be a perfect companion to my mother. She's a pleasant lady and has few wants or needs other than good company and perhaps someone to read to her. I fear I am far too busy and cannot give her the attention she would wish."

Clara could feel a blush of humiliation stain her cheeks. This was the real reason her family had been invited to the Gardeners' and it had nothing to do with meeting the baron. The woman had simply been sly enough to lure her mother with the baron's presence. Clara could almost imagine the conversation she'd had with her daughter as they'd schemed to get her to come to Chatford Manor to better get to know her.

"Thank you, Mrs. Gardener. I do appreciate your thinking of me. Would you mind very much if I gave it a bit of thought and spoke with my parents about it?"

"Not at all," Mrs. Gardener said warmly, seemingly unaware of how she'd humiliated Clara with her offer.

"Good night. And thank you for a wonderful evening," Clara said. No one would *ever* say she was not poised or ungracious. If there was one thing she'd learned in finishing school, it was to maintain one's dignity at any cost.

At breakfast the next morning, Clara did her best to hide the sadness that seemed to have enveloped her body overnight. The baron ate a hearty meal but did not re-issue his invitation, much as Mrs. Gardener had predicted. Next to her, Hedra craned her neck trying to get the baron's attention, but he steadfastly ignored her, even when her mother asked if he were staying another night. The Andersons were not. Mrs. Gardener apologized profusely, but she had dear friends arriving that afternoon. Would it be too much of an imposition for the Gardeners to cut short their visit?

Hedra, of course, not wanting to upset Mrs. Gardener and ruin Clara's chances of being introduced in London, readily agreed. Before they boarded their carriage, Mrs. Gardener pulled Clara aside.

"I do hope you will consider the position, Clara," she said.

"I will, thank you, Mrs. Gardener," Clara said, through a throat that ached. Up until this point, all this traipsing around England in search of a husband had been a bit of a lark. Clara had known, of course, that her low birth would not be seen as desirable to most aristocratic men, but she'd never before been so pointedly—and kindly—reminded of this fact.

They were a joke. An amusement at best, pitied at worst.

Clara climbed aboard the carriage, across from her parents who were in unusually high spirits. "Imagine," Hedra said once they were under way. "A baron sponsoring you. Oh, Clara, I do believe he has an interest in you. A widower with children needs a wife." Hedra clapped her hands together, unable to contain her exuberance. "I am so proud of you, Clara. Imagine, you, a baroness. Or at the very least, attending balls during the little season. A dream come true after all our efforts."

Hedra was so happy, Clara didn't have the heart to tell her the true reason they'd been invited by the Gardeners. Why make everyone miserable?

"That's wonderful, Mother," Clara said, giving her mother a happy smile to hide her pain. As they rumbled down the long drive, Clara gazed out the window at the gardens, knowing now she would never get the chance to tour them. At least if she had seen the garden, this trip would not have been a complete waste of time. As they drove through the arched entry to the property, Clara heaved Mr. Smee's thick volume upon her lap, ignoring her mother's look of exasperation.

"A book that large is hardly a ladylike pursuit," she said with a sniff.

Clara pointedly ignored her mother and opened to a chapter on glass houses. Their glass house, of course, would be diminutive compared to Mr. Smee's, but Clara could hardly contain her excitement at the thought of growing exotic plants year-round. Imagine growing oranges and lemons.

"I wish you were as enthusiastic about finding a husband as you are about your garden," Hedra complained, but Clara could tell she wasn't angry with her. Nothing this day could make Hedra angry with her elder daughter.

"I am always exceedingly pleasant whenever we are near a potential husband," Clara said, reluctantly returning her attention to her mother. "Perhaps we ought to double my dowry, as that seems to be the only characteristic the men we have met are interested in."

Hedra narrowed her eyes as if assessing whether her daughter was jesting or being snippy. "Perhaps we will," she said, daring Clara to object.

"Triple it then," she declared with a laugh, and Hedra giggled.

"If I thought it would work…"

"Mother! Really, if that is all a man is interested in, then I am not interested in him."

"Unless he has a title," Hedra sniffed. "At any rate, I do have the feeling Baron Longley will be visiting St. Ives quite soon. I issued an invitation, you know. And I know once he sees our estate, he will better understand what a fine investment joining our family would be."

Clara reached deep inside to stop herself from rolling her eyes. Mrs. Pittsfield had expressed horror that Clara had rolled her eyes and ever since that occasion, the gesture was strictly forbidden.

"Papa," Clara said, "did you marry Mother for her money?"

"For her peach pie, it was," he said without hesitation, earning him a playful kick from his wife.

"Even with the best peach pie in all of England I could not have attracted the men who are eyeing you, my dear," Hedra said.

Clara did not possess a vain bone in her body, but she was aware God had gifted her with several fine features: her thick, golden hair; her delicate chin and nose; her brilliant blue eyes (the color of bluebells); her womanly curves. But when she looked in the mirror, she did not see a rare beauty; she saw herself, an ordinary girl who wanted more than anything else to live an ordinary life.

"Clara had to get 'er looks from someone," her father pointed out. "And it sure as rain wasn't from my side of the family. Bunch of ogres." That was, Clara realized, her father's attempt to say he thought his wife pretty.

Clara leapt from her seat and gave her father's cheek a quick kiss. "You do not look like an ogre, Papa. You only act like one."

He growled and Clara squealed, hurriedly returning to her seat. It was so rare that her father jested about anything, the small exchange left Clara feeling strangely melancholy when it should have just brought happiness.

"Did you meet your baron?" Mr. Emory asked the next day. Clara had gone to the garden directly after breakfast, brimming with excitement about their planned glass house. Mr. Smee offered excellent advice and she could hardly wait to share what she'd learned. Mr. Emory had begun the foundation, creating a large rectangular outline on the far corner of their property. They had debated its location before she'd left, deciding it should be as unobtrusive as possible.

"He is not my baron, and yes, I did," she said, nipping off a rose whose petals were turning brown. Now that the pests were mostly gone, she'd become rather obsessed with the appearance of the roses. They were fully in bloom, and the scent of them filled the air. Clara hadn't really liked the smell of roses; they had seemed so cloying when inside. But out of doors, with a soft breeze making the blooms dance, the scent was purely wonderful. "He was far too old for me and I told my mother I would reject his suit even if offered. It was a waste of a trip."

She heard the deep sound of his chuckle and looked up at him from beneath the brim of her straw hat. "What is so amusing?" she asked, laughter in her own voice.

"I suppose it's seeing the other side of things. I must confess, I had no idea." He shook his head and continued raking the newly laid gravel that snaked its way to the pond. Eventually, they would plant shrubbery and trees that would one day provide needed shade. Their garden had started as nothing more than a large expanse of green. Apparently, the family who'd lived in the house before them had been avid cricket players and had used the lawn as a playing field. Now, though, Clara could see the beginnings of something wonderful, something lush and pretty and magical.

"What do you mean, 'seeing things from the other side'?"

"The side of a female who is looking for a husband. I must confess, I believed it all happened much more naturally, rather than like a well-planned assault. Your mother would have been a great military leader."

Clara laughed, for that was an apt description of her mother. Every appointment, every entertainment, every trip was carefully planned and executed. This latest trip, though a failed campaign, was a great victory in Hedra's mind and Clara would never correct that misconception. Mr. Emory stood as he often did, hands resting on the top of the rake's handle, chin resting on his hands, looking at her with a smile. She ought to commission a painter to capture him thus, for he looked so uncommonly handsome. When she realized where her thoughts had wandered, how her fancies were creating a turmoil inside her, she lowered her gaze and turned around. Had it not been only a few hours since she'd vowed to stop thinking about Mr. Emory in such an inappropriate manner? But how could she help it, the way he smiled at her, the way he looked at her as if...

As if he were thinking the same thing. Clara drew in a sharp breath. Surely, Mr. Emory did not think of her in that way. He'd done nothing untoward, hadn't looked at her the way she was used to men looking at her. And yet...the air seemed electrified whenever she was with him. Was it all her imagination? What if he did think of her, want to kiss her? What good would it do to acknowledge such a thing when she could never, ever act on it? Mr. Emory, for all his fine diction and charming ways, was their *gardener*.

Swallowing heavily, she chanced a look in his direction and was disappointed to see that he'd gone back to work. Had she expected him to be staring at her like some lovestruck fool? Really, she thought, could she get more ridiculous? He was working his way toward her, the sound of the rake getting louder, and she could almost feel his presence, like some magnetic pull. When he was by her side, she couldn't move, couldn't breathe, because she swore she felt the heat of him. The sound of the rake ceased, and her senses were filled with the scent of warm man and soap. And that made her recall his naked torso, his gleaming muscles, that tantalizing bit of hair that disappeared beneath the waist of his trousers.

"Excuse me, Miss Anderson," he said softly.

She managed to turn her head to look at him, and he moved back a bit so the brim of her wide hat would not smack him in the face. His dark green-gray eyes regarded her and she felt herself drawn to him as if she truly was being pulled toward him. *He wants to kiss me. I know he does.* "Yes?" A breathy syllable.

"I need to rake where you are standing, miss."

Clara was momentarily confused. Rake? "Oh, rake. Of course. I am in your way." She let out a nervous laugh, feeling her blood heat, but this time in mortification. "I'll just move, shall I? So you can rake."

He gave her an odd look. "Thank you."

Clara turned away and squeezed her eyes shut briefly, silently chastising herself for her foolishness. It was bad enough to have the maids gawking at him; certainly she shouldn't count herself in their numbers. A thought occurred to her then, a cold dash of realization, that perhaps Mr. Emory was so uninterested in the maids because he had someone back home that he'd already set his cap for. The maids, Sara in particular, were pretty enough and had made it abundantly clear they would be open to his interest.

The sound of a wagon drew her attention and when she saw what it held, her mortification was completely forgotten. It was filled to overflowing with shrubs and small trees, trees that would one day grow and give her garden little spots of shade.

Whirling around, she gave a small sound of delight and was glad to see Mr. Emory grinning back at her. "Elm trees and poplar cuttings. Geraniums and some other flowers I thought might look nice. Your garden will have lovely shade in about twenty years."

"Oh, that one in the middle will give shade today," she declared, lifting her skirts and hurrying over to the wagon. "Hello, Joseph," she called to the driver. Joseph lived not far from her grandmother's farm and she'd known him most her life. If her father hadn't discovered tin, he was just the sort of man she might have married: strong and honest, with a ready smile and a lovely Cornish accent. He set the brake, then swung down with the easy grace of a man who has jumped from his wagon a thousand times.

Clara ran to the wagon and clutched the rough wood, peering inside to see what it contained. Marigolds, feverfew, sweet woodruff, their scents mingling together to create such a tantalizing aroma. Breathing in deeply, she could hardly contain her excitement at what her garden would look and smell like when they were all planted in the earth.

Behind her, she heard Mr. Emory approaching. "This is wonderful, Mr. Emory. Now we shall have a true garden, not only a rose garden. It shall rival Mr. Smee's."

"A small version of that esteemed gardener's creation," he said.

A particular scent touched her then. "Lavender. Oh, it's my mother's favorite scent. She'll be so pleased when I bring in a bouquet from our garden." Without realizing it, Clara had clutched his wrist in her excitement, giving it a little shake. When he looked down, she followed her gaze and dropped her hand, quickly mumbling an apology.

"No apology needed," he said, bending down, whispering. "If Joseph wasn't here, I'd swing you about in celebration."

"And I just might let you, Mr. Emory," she said saucily.

Joseph dropped the back of the cart and Mr. Emory was drawn over to assist in the removal of the plants.

"Goodness, Mr. Emory, where did all this come from?"

He hefted out a large clay pot containing a small tree, letting out a brief grunt. "Here and there," he said with a mysterious smile. That smile was intriguing, for it seemed to hold a secret.

"Where, specifically, here and there?" she asked, hurrying to follow him as he trudged toward the garden.

"Here, do you think?" He nodded his head to an area near where the gravel path began.

"For now," Clara said distractedly, looking around and wondering where all those lovely plants would go. "We should remove everything and then decide. Oh, is that a pear tree?"

"And a plum," Joseph said, pulling another small tree from the back of the wagon.

Clara watched the two men going back and forth from the wagon to the growing collection of plants, too many varieties to begin to name. When they were finally finished with their task, Clara slowly toured the plants, feeling like a child on Christmas morning. With all these varieties, they could, indeed, create a pretty little garden that would be worthy of showing off. Behind her, Joseph's wagon rattled away, and Mr. Emory came up beside her.

"There's another load coming next week," he said, taking out a handkerchief and wiping his brow.

"From where?"

"An estate up north, I believe."

Clara stared at the plants, her eyes wide, her mouth slightly open in disbelief. "Mr. Smee?"

"The very same," Mr. Emory said with odd hesitation.

For some silly reason, Clara's eyes pricked with tears. She'd been carrying around that thick volume for weeks, reading and studying, and imagining what it would be like to create such a masterpiece as Mr. Smee had done. And here before her was his garden—or at least bits and pieces of it. All hale and hearty and filling the air with the sweet and rich aroma of Beddington, a tiny town in Surrey, where Mr. Smee had created his wondrous garden.

"I shall have to thank him," she said softly.

Next to her, Mr. Emory was silent, a heavy sort of quiet that caused her to look up at him. "Mr. Smee died in January. I dealt with his son. I am sorry, Miss Anderson. I know you'd hoped to meet him one day."

Tears sprang to her eyes and she quickly dashed them away, embarrassed. "So silly of me. I didn't even know the man." And yet, reading his book, she felt she had come to know him as an old friend who was imparting his horticultural wisdom. How sad his wife must be to look out and see what her husband had done, knowing she would never watch him toil in his garden again. "I thought perhaps I might invite him to see our garden, or at the very least write to tell him about it, how he inspired it."

"These are still things he grew, that were part of what he planted."

Clara nodded. "Yes, and so we must honor them and not allow them to die," she said fiercely, giving Mr. Emory a challenging look.

"I shall do my best to make certain all of these plants and the ones to come will be cared for to the best of my abilities."

"That, Mr. Emory, is what I fear most," she said, teasing him.

He laughed, a warm, melodic sound that did odd things to her insides. "I shall have to borrow my book back, then, so I may learn from Mr. Smee's great gardening wisdom."

"I am happy to return it to you once I am done with it. Who could have known I would find such reading so riveting? He wrote that he hadn't much success with his plums because of the soil. Perhaps the St. Ives climate and soil will be better." She touched a plum, its rich purple skin smooth beneath the pad of her index finger. It seemed miraculous to her that she was looking at plants grown by Mr. Smee himself; there was only one way this could have transpired. "You wrote to him."

"Yes. I hadn't any idea how to go about procuring plants." He gave her a sheepish grin, for a gardener should certainly know something as basic as that. "His son was apparently moved by your passion and your interest in Mr. Smee's garden and writings. These were his gifts to you. I think it gave him great pleasure to know that something of his father is growing so far away from Beddington."

"I shall have to write and thank him. Profusely." She let out a small laugh. "It's odd, isn't it, that I have had gifts far more valuable than this, and yet I think this is my favorite gift of all. Thank you, Mr. Emory."

He shook his head, and she could tell her words had embarrassed him. "I did nothing but write a letter of inquiry. The younger Mr. Smee is the man you need to thank."

Clara bent and inhaled the lovely scent of a lavender plant. "I am going to design a plan straight away," she said, feeling more excited than she had before her first ball. She turned to run inside to gather up her sketch book and pencil, then stopped. "You don't mind, do you, Mr. Emory? If I create the plan?"

"I am certain whatever plan you devise will be far and above better than mine."

Clara smiled at him, her heart full, her entire being filled with excitement. For her garden. Not, certainly, for her gardener.

Nathaniel worked six days a week, with Sundays off. The entire staff and the family, when they were at home, attended church in the mornings and then most went off to visit their own families. If it were up to him, Nathaniel would have continued to work the seventh day, but it would have drawn undue attention. Every time the spade slipped into the earth, every time he bent down hoping to find the diamond and came up holding a bit of Cornish rock, his gut tightened. But there was something worse happening of late. Much worse.

He found himself forgetting, for long stretches of time as he toiled in the garden, what he was there for in the first place. He found himself, much to his surprise, falling in love with creating a place of beauty. Each plant tucked into the earth and watered gave him a strange sense of satisfaction, as if he were honoring Mr. Smee, carrying on his mission, creating a monument to a man he'd never met. Miss Anderson gave him the book each evening, and each evening he found himself immersed in the writing, recognizing plants and ideas and strategies. Understanding.

Miss Anderson's plan was simple, yet elegant, and clearly influenced by Mr. Smee. The meandering path that led to the pond would be lined with a variety of shrubbery and flowers, with a tree and bench here and there, so that one might rest or simply gaze upon the flora. Small, hidden paths would eventually lead to an unexpected feature, a cluster of lavender, a flowering tree, or a patch of berries. As he toiled, Miss Anderson was there, talking or working, a constant presence that he was coming to look forward to. When she was not there, when she was off with her parents husband hunting, the garden was a lonely place. Even though her absence meant he could concentrate on his search, instead he found himself working on new parts of the garden to please her. While it was easier then to remember why he was in St. Ives, what the ultimate goal was, he still found himself missing her. At night, after a long day, he would think about Lion's Gate and hope his manager was handling his duties in his absence. He wrote to his manager weekly, letters posted by Mr. Standard so as not to elicit curiosity from the staff. He longed to return, to set thing to rights, to let his tenants know that he had not abandoned them. Not entirely. At night, when he wasn't torturing himself with images of Miss Anderson, he was torturing himself thinking of all that needed to be done to restore his estate, his title, to something he could be proud of.

Lately, it was far easier to push thoughts of Lion's Gate away than thoughts of Miss Anderson. Clara. It was what he called her in his head, it was how he thought of her when he let his thoughts drift where they shouldn't. When he touched himself and imagined it was her hand. He burned for her in a way he had never burned for a woman before. Those few times when her eyes had gotten drowsy and her lips parted slightly, when she looked at him like a woman who wants to be kissed… Good God, there was a special place in heaven for chaps like him who resisted beautiful women like Clara.

How could he ignore the sweet curve of her breasts, the fullness of the bottom lip that begged to be kissed, the gently rounded derrière that he'd found himself imagining naked beneath his palm? Beneath his lips. He'd never gone so long without the comforts of a willing female and his body was shouting for him to ease his need. Shouting? It was more like screaming. Even though she'd looked at him more than once, desire clear in her gaze, he would not act for more reasons than he could count. Knowing he could not touch her did not make not touching her any easier.

His mind returned to that day in the garden, when he'd been raking and she'd been dead heading. He'd stood there, inhaling her intoxicating scent, woman and sunshine, and thought he might die if he didn't touch her, if only to gently move her out of the way. And then she'd looked at him, and he'd known. It hit him, fierce and hard, like a blow to the head, that she wanted him too. Damn girl was so innocent, she probably didn't even realize what was happening between them. But he knew.

It didn't matter how many times he told himself to stay away, to drive her away if need be. He couldn't. He missed her when she was gone. The loneliness of this place was nearly suffocating. Though he'd taken to having a pint or two at a local pub, Nathaniel couldn't shake the knowledge that if he were to disappear or die, no one on earth would even take note. When God had taken his grandfather, He had taken the only person who loved him.

Thanks to his father's misdeeds, young men had been directed not to befriend him lest they be associated with one of the most notorious wastrels in the ton, and it was almost amusing how quickly a mama could move when she saw her daughter speaking with him. "Bad blood," he'd heard more than once. His lack of fortune likely played an even greater role in his lack of female interest.

Two days after the wagon of plants arrived at the Anderson house, Nathaniel found himself sitting in the White Hart Tavern looking at a fetching barmaid who had the sort of curves a man dreamed of. She was either new to the place or hadn't been working the nights he'd attended in the past; he would have noticed her.

"She's my daughter." A low growl near his ear.

"A lovely girl," Nathaniel said, looking up into the face of the massive barkeep. He had blacksmith arms, an anvil for a jaw, and a scowl that could make most men quake—including Nathaniel. Given that one of the man's large hands could probably crush his skull, Nathaniel kept his eyes on his pint for the next few minutes, looking neither left nor right so as not to incite the man's ire.

After several long, tense minutes, the man said, "You're not from here." A statement of the obvious. "I'm from Cumbria."

"You're the Andersons' gardener." It sounded like an accusation.

"I am."

"Sam Parsons," he said, holding out his hand for a shake. Nathaniel held out his own hand, inwardly relieved when the man's shake was firm but not brutal. Sam eyed him a long moment, and Nathaniel met his gaze with unrelenting focus, knowing this handshake was some sort of test of his character. Seemingly satisfied by what he saw, the barkeep poured him another pint. "On the house."

With a grin, Nathaniel thanked him before taking a long drink. And he nearly spit it out when he heard from the table behind him, "Blue diamond." He slowly lowered his pint, his entire focus on the men behind him.

"I heard the same," came a gruff response. "Can't say I put much stock in him. If someone buried a diamond here, don't you think we would have heard about it by now?"

"More like he's got rocks in his head." The other man's response earned him a chuckle, but Nathaniel found nothing amusing about the fact that there was a sudden interest in a diamond that hadn't been seen in more than fifty years.

"He's gonna have everyone in St. Ives diggin' up their gardens. I tell you what, if I found a diamond in my garden, I sure wouldn't hand it over to some bloke from London. Dumb sod."

Nathaniel slowly spun on his stool, debating whether he should admit to have been eavesdropping on their conversation. The two men looked up as he turned, their eyes filled with mild hostility. "I can say for certain it's not at the Anderson place," he said with a laugh. "If it was, I surely would have found it by now and be living in a mansion."

The larger of the two men, a grizzled older fellow with a thick gray beard that likely held the remnants of his last few meals, narrowed his eyes. "You're that gardener?"

Nathaniel nodded.

"You sound just like that bloke from London what's looking for the diamond." The two men exchanged glances, as if silently acknowledging that there must be some sort of connection between him and the man who had been making inquiries about the diamond.

"My apologies, gentlemen, but my father insisted I be educated, then dropped dead, leaving me to fend for myself at age thirteen. He left me with excellent pronunciation, no money, and few skills."

The two stared at him for a long beat before the bearded man started laughing. "Poor sod," he said finally, then shoved out his hand for Nathaniel to shake. "That's the worst story I've heard today." Nathaniel found himself gripping another work-worn hand, then another when his companion offered his own to shake.

"I'm Alan and this here is Jory," the bearded man said. "Join us if you like."

Nathaniel slid off his stool and pulled out a chair so he could join the two men at their table, grateful for the chance to find out more information on whoever was inquiring about the diamond. It was more than worrisome that after so many years of silence, whoever was searching for the diamond had tracked it to St. Ives. Would it only be a matter of time before they learned where it was buried or that the current Baron Alford was working as a gardener at a local estate? He had little concern he would be recognized, but he'd had little concern that anyone else would be looking for the diamond either. Now, he realized it had been a mistake to keep his name, for if whoever was looking for the diamond knew the full story of what had happened, it would certainly seem suspicious that a baron should be in St. Ives working as a gardener.

"I imagine news of a treasure buried somewhere in the village is causing quite a stir," he said, trying to bring the conversation back to the diamond.

Jory shrugged, his bony shoulders moving up and down in an exaggerated way. "We've had plenty of tales of buried treasure in St. Ives. I don't think anyone is going to get too riled up about this one."

"I saw Jack poking holes in his garden this afternoon," Alan said. "And I say, why not? Maybe there is a diamond buried somewhere."

Jory looked at his friend, aghast. "You've been lookin', haven't you?"

"Why not? If it's worth as much as the bloke says it is, I don't know why I wouldn't. Says it could be worth ten thousand pounds. Imagine that."

Now this was interesting, for the diamond was worth far more than that. "Gentlemen," Nathaniel said, stopping their argument. "Alan made a good point, which should make you wonder why someone who is looking for a treasure would let everyone know he's looking for it."

Alan gave a sharp nod. "Go on."

"Think. If you thought some treasure was buried somewhere, but you had no idea where, what would be the most efficient means of finding that treasure? In a village as large as St. Ives, one certainly could not find it alone." And when someone found it, he had no doubt he or she would be offered slightly more than ten thousand pounds, a pittance compared to the diamond's true worth. A diabolical plan but a good one.

"That scoundrel," Jory said. "He's lookin' for free labor."

Alan let out a laugh. "What he don't know is that if someone here found the damned diamond, they sure wouldn't tell any fancy pants from London."

"They wouldn't have to," Nathaniel said, sobering the two men up. "Small village like this wouldn't be able to keep a secret for long." He looked each man in the eye. "Am I wrong? Look how fast news of the diamond spread."

Jory let out a curse. "He's right. If it was found before breakfast, everyone would know by lunch."

Although the news that someone else was looking for the diamond was disconcerting, realizing his competition had no idea where the diamond was hidden was a bit of a relief. Nathaniel had no doubt that he if found the diamond, no one would know about it—until he started making inquiries about its true value.

"You thinking there is a diamond?" Jory asked him.

"Could be. Could be it was hid in some other village. Why St. Ives? Seems an odd place to hide something like that. No seaport nearby, no rail up until a year ago. Perhaps this is simply an elaborate hoax, someone having a bit of fun with you fine folks, amusing themselves."

Alan snapped his generous brows together. "Who would do such a thing?"

Nathaniel shrugged. "Some bored bloke from London? Is he still in town?"

Jory looked up at the ceiling. "As a matter of fact, my friend, he is."

Bloody hell. Nathaniel suppressed the urge to leave the pub immediately, but he wanted to learn more about the gent before he did. How in God's name had he tracked the diamond to St. Ives? Either he was a damned good investigator or one lucky bastard. Perhaps whoever was looking for the diamond had an agent in every county spreading rumors about a lost treasure.

Nathaniel thought back to his grandfather's story, to the day he was brutally beaten and left for dead. Could it be that he had still been in St. Ives?

"You know, I hear St. Ives is a cursed place. Seems unlikely someone would have buried a treasure here."

"Cursed, you say?" Alan asked, and Nathaniel could tell he'd touched on a nerve.

"Just stories. People dying unusual deaths."

Alan and Jory exchanged looks. "There was Lady Greenwich, but her death was ruled a suicide, so that doesn't count," Jory said with a sharp nod. "Most other unusual deaths were ruled accidents, they were."

Alan let out a sound that told Nathaniel he didn't believe Lady Greenwich's end was all that innocent. "Just because the earl bought himself clear of the charges don't mean he didn't kill her. Everyone says he did. Even now."

"And now supposedly there's a secret diamond hidden somewhere worth a king's ransom. I would think that would be the type of thing that would pit neighbor against neighbor. Cursed, I say."

"Maybe he's got something there," Jory said, giving Alan a sidelong look.

"And I heard a baron was nearly murdered here. Would have died if not for a miracle. Shot in the head, he was."

"And he lived?" Alan asked. "Don't sound like much of a curse to me."

"I know that story," Jory said, and Nathaniel silently congratulated himself for his cleverness. "Old man Jenkins found him. You remember, Alan. Poor sod was bleeding like a stuck pig out his head. And he was a cripple after that."

Alan furrowed his brow as if trying to remember. "Out on St. Ives Road, it was? Near Carbis Bay, just outside the village."

"That's the one. We were just wee cheldern then. I remember, though, 'cause he gave Jenkins a fat purse as a thank you. That's how he got that fleet of fishing boats of his that his ungrateful son is leaving to ruin."

Jory gave Nathaniel a suspicious look. "How'd you hear about that way up north?" He looked him over. "You weren't even born then."

"Baron Alford was my neighbor," Nathaniel said easily. "We lived on one of his properties."

"How about that?" Alan said, seemingly pleased that the three of them shared some common story.

"I was not aware of the other murders," Nathaniel said with a chuckle. "I only knew the baron's tale. Perhaps St. Ives truly is accursed."

The three men had a laugh, and Alan waved to Sam Parsons, calling for another round. Though it made Nathaniel a bit on edge to stay, he agreed. Hell, he hadn't had this much fun in a long time. And as long as he was here at the pub spinning tales with these men, he wouldn't be in his room, alone, dreaming of a pretty girl with golden hair.

Chapter 7

"'And hour by hour, when the air was still, the vapors arose which have strength to kill. At morn they were seen, at noon they were felt. At night they were darkness no star could melt.'"

"Why are you quoting Shelley to me?" Nathaniel asked without thinking. A gardener, even a bad one, would likely not have a working knowledge of the famous English poet.

Clara looked at him askance and he held his breath. "Because I'm worried about our plants." It was a chilly day with the wind blowing hard over the Atlantic, creating whitecaps on the sea that were visible even from this distance.

"I thought the temperatures rarely went below freezing here."

"They don't. Still, I would be greatly saddened should something happen to destroy our garden when it is just now beginning to, well, look like a garden."

Clara put the book aside and stood, pulling her wool coat closer around her. Her cheeks were rosy from the chilly air and wind, and she looked particularly beautiful. Nathaniel clenched his jaw, aware of her moving closer to him.

"Are you angry with me?" she asked.

He darted a look to her and found himself clenching his jaw again. It was either that or take her hand and drag her into his lair and ravish her. These past few weeks, the lust he'd been feeling had not dissipated. Indeed, it, along with his affection for her, had grown even stronger. Even with her bundled up in a shapeless old wool coat of a nondescript color, she was far more appealing than any woman he had ever known. Angry? No, he was not angry. He was mad with lust. And maybe just a little bit in love.

"I am not angry," he said through clenched teeth.

"Hmph. Then perhaps you should stop clenching your jaw incessantly. I daresay you will shatter your teeth."

As she moved past him, he stared at her a long moment before finally giving in and letting out a huff of laughter, which won him a classic Clara smile. "There," she said impishly, looking back as she walked along trailing her fingers lightly over the hydrangeas that would soon need trimming. "That is much better than frowning all the time."

She paused, as if just noticing the once-colorful blooms were now more brown than vivid blue. "We shall have to prune these," she said, and for some reason, her use of the word "we" made his heart do a strange thing in his chest. There was no "we" nor would there ever be. He wondered what she would do if he kissed her the way he'd dreamed of doing since that first day in the garden when he realized how extraordinary she was. Thoughts like that only led to one thing, and that was disaster, for he was quite certain he would not be able to stop at one kiss. As a man of honor, he would have to be certain such an indiscretion never happened. Clara was young and exceedingly innocent, and despite drowsy eyes and parted lips that begged for his kiss, he was aware she truly did not know what she was wishing for. At least he prayed not. That one thought—that she was an innocent and wanted to remain so—was an invisible but impregnable wall, one he would not climb. Based on their conversations, no man had done more than plant a chaste kiss on her lush lips. He hated those men who'd had the pleasure of hearing her sigh when he knew he never would. Despite his deep sense of honor, he knew he was racing against time. He must find the diamond soon lest all his defenses and good intentions crumble at his feet. Impregnable wall? Indeed, he feared he was kidding himself. All she needed to do was let him know she wanted his kiss and all would be lost.

Christ, just the thought of kissing her was making him aroused; he shifted uncomfortably.

"We're leaving for London at the end of the month for an extended time," she said, her words acting like a bucket of cold water. She looked up as if gauging his reaction, which he was quick to mask. Was it only two months ago that he'd promised himself to give up his search after one month? And yet he was still here, still searching, still creating her garden. At some point in the past weeks, he'd abandoned his self-imposed deadline. Why?

Long hours passed when he didn't even think about the diamond, when all his focus was on the garden. Or on her.

"Your garden will miss you," he said, and she grinned.

"But not my gardener."

"That would be presumptuous, do you not think?" he asked, aware they were flirting. So much for honor and sacrifice.

"I shall be brave enough to say I will miss you." She raised one saucy brow. "You are the only person in the world I can tell my secrets to without receiving a lecture."

He let out a chuckle. "I cannot recall any secrets told, Miss Anderson."

"Here's one, then. I loathe the aristocracy and its rules. The thought of pretending I am something I am not for the rest of my life makes me ill. My happiest memories are of being a child helping my grandparents on their pig farm. This," she said, indicating her lovely gown, "is uncomfortable and still, after all these years, feels like a costume."

Nathaniel swallowed, staring at her with an intensity she must feel. "Then why do you do it? Why do you parade yourself in front of those titled gentlemen like some sort of mare for sale?"

When her eyes filled with tears, he cursed himself for his callousness. "Because my mother is so very proud of me, of our accomplishments. I cannot break her heart." She blinked, and the hint of tears he saw in her eyes was gone; he wondered if he'd imagined them.

"What of your own heart?"

She shook her head. "I have never been in love, so it's not something I shall miss. I don't expect to love my husband. Isn't that what all girls of good breeding are taught? That to fall in love is the height of foolishness? What of you? Have you ever been in love?"

"No. Never." My God, it looked like her heart was breaking and he could do nothing, say nothing, to give her comfort. Never had he felt more helpless.

"Why?"

"I suppose I am in a similar position as you, Miss Anderson. Caught between two worlds and not belonging to either one."

She took two steps toward him and he tensed. "Who are you, Mr. Emory? Truly?"

"I'm just a man looking for something I haven't yet found and probably never will," he said, glad he could tell some sort of truth. Lying never had sat well with him.

"I will say this, sir. You have found this garden. Look at it. It's lovely, is it not?"

"The most lovely garden in all of…" She raised her brow as if challenging him not to lie. "…St. Ives."

"Sadly, even that is not the truth. Costille House has a much grander and much lovelier garden than ours."

"Costille House?"

"Lord Berkley's estate. He's the earl I mentioned, and my mother is beside herself with joy that he has taken up residence. He's coming to luncheon tomorrow," she said, as if it was the worst possible news.

"To meet you, I take it?"

"Oh, we've already met. He's a nice enough gentleman, but…"

"Yes?"

She smiled sadly, then looked away, out toward St. Ives Bay. "He doesn't hold my heart." She seemed to gather herself together. "And besides that, he's an earl, for goodness' sake. No earl is going to be interested in courting a commoner. He certainly doesn't need my dowry. And he's rather handsome. So far, the only titled gentlemen who have even glanced twice at me are those who are as ugly as a toad or poorer than a church mouse. Even with their flaws, they will not have me. They believe they would be soiling the purity of their family line, no doubt. You have no idea how the aristocracy works, how a man with little intelligence and little worth can think himself better than a great man like my father who made his own fortune with brain and brawn."

Her cheeks pinkened when he just stared at her. Frankly, it was difficult to keep a straight face when she'd just insulted him and his peers. "You think I am talking like a Progressive. Perhaps I am. Perhaps after all this time I've realized that aristocrats, except for the chance of birth, are no better than I am. I might even say they are less. What do they do but prance around and wallow in their own importance?"

To say Nathaniel was stunned would be a vast understatement. He wondered, with a sickening twist of his gut, what Miss Anderson would say if she knew he was a member of the aristocracy she seemed to so loathe.

"Surely not all members of the aristocracy are so disagreeable."

She tilted her head as if going through a catalogue of people she'd met. "Perhaps you are correct, Mr. Emory. I'm certain there are one or two with pleasant dispositions who do not believe God put them on this Earth to lord it over everyone else."

He barked out another laugh. "Perhaps one or two," he said, grinning.

"The Earl of Berkley is rather pleasant. And, as I said, quite handsome."

"Handsome, is he?" Nathaniel fought the ridiculous jealousy that burned in his blood. Any man would find Clara far too tempting, no matter her low birth.

That thought lingered in his mind for far too long before he shoved it away. He was *any man*, was he not?

"Too handsome. Though I do believe if I were to dress you in an expensive suit, you would look just as handsome as he." She looked at him and laughed. "I've embarrassed you."

"Indeed you have, Miss Anderson."

"I suppose I should not notice such things," she said on a sigh.

"Or say them aloud."

"Are you chastising me, sir?"

"I am." She looked so beautiful at that moment, with the breeze picking up the brim of her ever-present straw hat and exposing her entire countenance to his hungry gaze, he could not have looked away if the blue diamond had struck him in the head.

And there it was. That drowsy look. Those lush parted lips. He could tell by the rise and fall of her breasts that her breath quickened. *Step away, Nate. For God's sake...*

"Miss Anderson..." He nearly choked out her name and his gaze, as if he had no control, settled on her lips.

"I've never been kissed."

Clara took a step back, as if increasing the distance between them would make what she'd just said go away. But it had come bubbling out, pushed by this terrible, wonderful feeling that boiled in her stomach whenever she was near to him. He was looking at her the way a man looks when he wants to kiss a girl. She knew that much, at least.

"That, Miss Anderson, is a tragedy." His voice was low, rumbling through her, making the desire she felt—for she knew that was what it was—only increase. It was very nearly painful, this ache that before had only been hinted at, a pleasant feeling that would touch her when she saw a particularly fine-looking gentleman. With Mr. Emory, though, it was a constant, heavy thing, something that had her touching herself at night, imagining her hand was his. Oh, God. What was wrong with her that she should do such things, think such things?

Nothing could come of such feelings. He was her *gardener.* Oh, Lord, how had she let this happen?

She dropped her head and stared at the ground. "I'm sorry—"

"Perhaps I should—"

They spoke at the same time and she snapped her head up. "Perhaps you should what, Mr. Emory?" she asked, sounding breathy, sounding not at all like herself.

He took a deep breath. "I..." He closed his eyes briefly and his entire body went taut, as if he were about to make a dash for it. "I could kiss you," he finally said, as if those words were wrenched from deep within. "If you'd like."

"I would. Perhaps. If you wouldn't mind, that is."

He laughed low, so softly she hardly heard the rumble. "I would be honored to be the first man to kiss you," he said with a small smile. "But nothing more. One kiss."

Clara swallowed, then looked around for a safe place for the kiss to take place.

"Behind my shed perhaps?"

"Now?"

He shrugged. "I suppose it's a good time. No one is about. I'll go in, then you can wander around back and I can give you that kiss."

Clara giggled, nervously, then pressed her mouth tightly. She hated the way she sounded when she giggled; it seemed so undignified. "Very well." She turned back to the hydrangeas and began decapitating them, her nerves getting the best of her. When she dared look up, he was gone, presumably around behind the shed waiting for his kiss. Oh, good Lord, what was she doing?

Taking a long breath, she let it out slowly, trying to calm her nerves. It was just a kiss. What harm could come of it? Just a silly kiss that she would one day look back on with fondness and a bit of pride. Imagine, kissing her gardener. How very naughty of her. Clara, who tried and tried never to do anything that would upset anyone, found it rather nice to think she might have a naughty memory to store away amongst all the others.

Oh so casually, she wandered toward the shed, pretended to be fascinated by a butterfly, then dashed behind the small building, only to run right into a hard, manly chest.

"I didn't realize you were in such a hurry for this kiss," he said, laughing as he looked down at her. When she'd collided with him, he'd placed his hands around her upper arms to steady her, but now, his hold loosened, drifting up and down. Clara stared into his chest, at the white button that held his shirt together. "Miss Anderson?" He dipped his head in an attempt to make eye contact, and her body began to shake from silent laughter.

When she dared look up, he was smiling at her and looked uncommonly handsome. She had never been so close to him, never noticed how beautiful his dark green-gray eyes were, the way a dark blue rimmed them, how his lashes spiked straight out and were far longer than she'd realized. Lifting a finger, she trailed it over his cheek, a spot where he'd missed shaving, and wished she'd taken her gloves off so she might know what his beard felt like. He bent his head, his intent clear, and she placed her finger on his lips and watched as he smiled.

"Second thoughts?" he asked.

Instead of responding, she lowered her finger slowly, watching with mild fascination how his firm lip moved and snapped back into place when she released it. Then, standing on tiptoe, she pressed her lips against his and waited, for this was as far as her imagination had brought her, to this simple and wonderful feeling of her mouth pressed against his. He increased the pressure, moving his lips against hers, producing a sharp sensation of need with that simple caress. She could hear their breaths, feel his, harsh and hot, against her lips. His hand, gloveless, cupped her jaw and he let out a deep sound, a moan, a growl, a sound that was purely male.

With a tilt of his head, the kiss deepened, and Clara gasped. This was just a kiss, one kiss, but it was lasting far, far longer than she'd thought it would. Did it count as one kiss? His tongue darted out, tasting the seam of her mouth, demanding entrance.

"Open," he whispered.

And she did, allowing him to taste her, for her to taste him, all dark and delicious. It did something to her, ignited the thing that had been brewing inside her for weeks, made her body ache and feel as if she were going to burst out of her skin. This was desire, raw and hot and wonderful. She let out a sound of pure want, not caring that he would hear her, not caring that he would know how much she wanted this, wanted him. The hand that had rested on her jaw moved to the back of her neck, and his other hand pressed her against him, splayed just above her bum.

He stopped suddenly, letting her go, causing her to stumble thanks to knees that had grown decidedly weak. Their kiss—their one kiss—was over.

Mr. Emory stared at her, his eyes dark, almost angry, his fists clenched fiercely by his sides. "All right, then. We're done."

Clara raised her eyebrows in question. "Very well. Thank you, Mr. Emory." She bit her lip and saw his eyes dip once more to her mouth. She swore he took a small step toward her but perhaps it was just her imagination. Or wishful thinking. Smoothing down her skirts, she gave him a quick, business-like nod and turned away, only to have him grab her around the waist and pull her back into him. She could feel his heaving chest, warm against her back, and his mouth on her neck. He embraced her like that for perhaps ten seconds before letting go and disappearing into his room, leaving her there, panting for breath and wondering what she had just done.

* * * *

"Mother, where is Harriet? Lord Berkley shall be here within the hour and I cannot find her anywhere."

Hedra was sitting at her vanity while her maid put the finishing touches on her coiffure. "She's out somewhere," Hedra said, flitting her hand in the air. "Walks are good for one's constitution."

"Did you not tell her of the earl's visit?" Clara asked, aghast.

"I didn't want to put her through it. You know how nervous she gets, and it's not as if the earl is coming to see *her*."

Clara sighed. "He's not coming to see me, either, Mother. As a matter of fact, I cannot imagine why Lord Berkley deigned to accept our invitation at all. Really, Mother, Harriet could have managed one simple luncheon with one important visitor. Do you not think Harriet's feelings will be hurt when she finds out Lord Berkley was here?"

"She'll be relieved," Hedra said, brooking no argument.

Luncheon was a tedious affair until Harriet showed up, wearing a dew-dampened gown that was more fit for cleaning a house than luncheon with the highest ranking peer they had ever entertained. Lately, Harriet had taken to allowing her hair to curl rather wildly, and Clara believed it was some sort of silent rebellion against their mother. Secretly, Clara thought Harriet looked lovely with her hair natural, but at that moment, windblown and disheveled, she did not look the part of a young woman receiving a high ranking member of the aristocracy into her family home. Despite her appearance, Lord Berkley was exceedingly charming and insisted Harriet join them, which Harriet seemed to revel in, the scamp. Few people knew that Harriet had a bit of the devil in her, and Clara liked to see that side of her sister come out.

In the end, her mother was tipsy and embarrassing, her father was stoic and silent, Harriet was charming and Lord Berkley amusing. Clara was not present at all. Instead, her mind was firmly on her garden—or rather with her gardener behind his shed.

After their kiss, Clara could not bring herself to go out to the garden and she wondered if she would ever find the courage to do so again. What had he thought of her, agreeing to kiss him like that, allowing him to take such liberties? Allowing? No, she had begged for his kiss and relished every moment of it. Would she ever forget the feel of his mouth on hers, the hard planes of his body, the way he'd pulled her against him as if he didn't want to let her go? That long, hard ridge she'd felt, that could only be one thing, mean one thing. He'd desired her as much as she'd desired him.

She'd hardly gotten a moment's rest last night, lying in bed and reliving every touch, every sound that had come from his throat. Should she be ashamed of herself? She found that shame was the least of the emotions that warred within her.

"...garden?"

Clara looked up from her plate to see all eyes on her, including his lordship's. "Please forgive me, I was lost in thought. Did you ask a question about our garden?"

Hedra let out an impatient sigh. "I was wondering if you and 'is lordship wanted to take a stroll around the garden. And 'is lordship agreed."

"Oh," Clara said, forcing a smile. Then a terrible thought hit her. Mr. Emory would likely be in the garden, working. How awful for her to be walking about their garden on the arm of another man, and an earl at that. "Of course."

Lord Berkley stood and looked at her politely. Bored. He had no more interest in touring their garden than she did, but it seemed they would. The earl darted a look at Harriet, as if silently asking her permission to step out with Clara, which seemed a bit odd, but Clara thought rather sweet of him. Did he think Harriet should have been included in the invitation?

The earl held out his arm and Clara took it obligingly. "It's not much of a garden as we've just begun to plant it. But I've heard Costille House's gardens are lovely and perhaps you can offer some advice on our small plot."

"I fear my knowledge of gardening is likely far less than yours, Miss Anderson."

When they stepped out the door, Clara held her breath, giving a silent prayer that Mr. Emory was not still at work. Of course, he was. He looked up when he heard the door open, and froze for a moment when he saw she was not alone. Clara felt her cheeks heating.

Mr. Emory was a servant, and as such, Clara should not acknowledge him as they made their way around the garden. She'd been taught by her mother that the divide between staff and employers was sharp and never should be crossed. Kissing one's gardener had certainly been crossing that divide. Headfirst. Without hesitation. One day ago, she'd been behind the shed in a passionate embrace with Mr. Emory, and today she would hardly acknowledge him as she strolled arm-in-arm with an earl. Her entire body was filled with a sickening heat. It felt almost as if an imaginary string tethered her to Mr. Emory, and as they drew closer and closer to where he worked, that string only tightened until it was a painful thing.

Mr. Emory, after that one, long glance, continued to work, but Clara sensed he was intensely aware of the couple as they walked down the path he'd raked not a few hours prior. Everything was neat and well-kept, not a weed in sight, not a dead petal or brown leaf to be found. He must have suspected their fine visitor might be viewing their garden and had made the necessary preparations. It must have taken hours, and Clara felt her heart clench at the thought of him rising before dawn to make certain her little garden was perfect for their visitor. A visitor he must know had come to see her.

"A lovely patch," Lord Berkley said, but Clara sensed he was merely being polite. "What is your favorite flower, Miss Anderson? I shall be certain to send you and your sister a large bouquet."

"Bluebells," she blurted out, and nearly laughed at the earl's expression. "I'm afraid they are long past their bloom, so I shall forgive you for the lack of a bouquet."

He nodded and smiled at her, but his eyes flicked back to the house.

They moved past where Mr. Emory worked, and Clara noticed that despite the chill in the air, his back was wet with sweat and his hair damp along his collar. His jaw was tense, sharp, and he kept his eyes shadowed by the brim of his cap. He moved aside and bowed his head in deference to the earl, his boots sounding overloud on the gravel, and of course Lord Berkley didn't acknowledge him. Earls did not engage in niceties with gardeners—unless it was their own gardener perhaps. As they passed, he looked up at Clara and winked, and just like that, the heaviness in her heart lifted.

And just like that, she fell just a little bit in love with her gardener.

Nathaniel had not met the current earl, but had met his father when he was younger, under less than desirable circumstances. His father had gotten blind drunk and barged into a meeting of the London Historical Society, thinking he was at another meeting entirely. A lad had been sent to their townhome with a note asking him to come and fetch his father, who was "indisposed." His father was not just a drunk, he was a loud, obnoxious, and vicious drunk, who had made many an enemy among the ton. Nathaniel both feared and loathed him, for at times, he would enter his bedroom and stand there, red-faced and swaying, and stare at him until his liquor-soaked brain could come up with some complaint to make of him. The day he died, half of England celebrated, including Nathaniel.

That late evening, Nathaniel had been roused from bed by his father's valet, who insisted Nathaniel attend to his own father. With no one else available, Nathaniel headed out alone to fetch his father home. When he'd arrived, Lord Berkley, considered one of the most powerful men in England at the time, had taken him aside and told him in no uncertain terms that his father was no longer welcome as a member of the society. Indeed, he was not welcome in the same room as Lord Berkley in the future. It was, perhaps, one of the most humiliating moments in Nathaniel's life. Of course, when he'd arrived, his father could hardly focus on him and had what Nathaniel had come to call the "hundred-mile stare." He'd become exceedingly belligerent when Nathaniel suggested the pair of them return home, and it was only when two footmen appeared to bodily remove him from the society that he agreed to leave, perfectly affable and sloppily acquiescent.

That had been eleven years ago, when Nathaniel was still only fourteen and home on holiday shortly before his father died, but the humiliation of that moment still burned in his chest. Seeing Clara on the new earl's arm burned nearly as much.

It was at that moment when he most regretted his plan, when he wondered if he could have used the Andersons' love of the aristocracy to his advantage and perhaps enlisted their help in finding the diamond. Now, he realized, that might have been a better plan. A woman with an eligible daughter who wanted nothing more than for her daughter to marry a title would have been easy to manipulate. They might have hired workers to assist them, thinking that if he found the diamond, they would also have found a husband for their daughter.

How easy it would have been if he'd known then what he knew now.

But he hadn't, and now here he was, two months into his search, with winter bearing down on Lion's Gate and tenants who were facing another grueling season with less than adequate housing, still searching for the damned diamond. If his grandfather hadn't been so sure, so precise with his story, Nathaniel would have quit long ago. The diamond had not been found, so it was still here, still in St. Ives, still buried in the Andersons' garden. Somewhere. A thousand times, he had closed his eyes and tried to imagine his grandfather as a young man, walking up the hill to see this property. It would have looked much the same as when he, himself, had stepped onto the land. If he were a young man who wanted to hide something, where would he have hidden it?

"It's in a box made of black locust, so it wouldn't have rotted, with metal straps. It's still there...It's..." His voice, hardly a whisper, barely audible, words said slowly and with extreme effort. "It's..."

He'd waited, holding his grandfather's hand. "It's all right, Grandpapa, we'll talk again when you've rested."

The old man had opened his eyes, his lips had moved...and then he was gone. Nathaniel had watched as the life flickered out, as his face went slack, and he'd dropped his head to his grandfather's still chest and wept. It wasn't until weeks later that he even cared to recall the diamond. By then, it had become imperative that he find it.

His plan, ill-conceived and driven by desperation, had seemed like a good one at the time. Find the property, dig about for a while, and leave a richer man.

Now all he had for his labors was a pretty little garden and a girl who was making her way into his heart.

And he couldn't tell her.

How had he allowed this to happen? Yes, he could very well imagine the conversation he would have with her eventually. "I've something to tell you, darling. All this time when you've thought I was nothing but a gardener? I'm a baron. Just what you were looking for all along. Why was I pretending, do you ask? I was simply attempting to steal something from your property. Ends justifying the means and all that."

And what if he never found the diamond? She was an heiress and he was a man in desperate need of an heiress, one of those men her mother had been hoping to find for years. Here he was! A desperate peer in search of a bride. And what a coincidence! They already were quite fond of one another, if only she could find it in her heart to forgive him for lying and lying and lying. What possible explanation could he give for impersonating a gardener?

No matter the damage to his heart, he needed to simply walk away, whether he found the diamond or not. And that meant never touching her again, never kissing her. Never doing any of the things he longed to. Another thought entered his practical mind, pushing his heart firmly out of the way: He knew Clara did not come with the sort of fortune he would need to do what he needed to do for his estate and certainly nothing that could come close to the value of the diamond. He would not be the first man in history to forgo love for the sake of his legacy and he would not be the last.

It was a depressing thought. Just the thought of leaving, even with the diamond in hand, made his chest hurt. He would miss her.

During the few social events he'd attended while at university, he had not conversed at length with a member of the opposite sex. It was a dance, this looking for a mate business. Few women knew him, knew what made him smile or laugh or made him angry. Clara knew, though. Those long afternoons while they toiled in the garden were spent discussing far more than the health of her rose bushes. He knew, for example, that she loathed the aristocracy, that she was beginning to resent being molded into the kind of person she detested. It was like pressing a bit of once pliable clay, now hardening, into another shape. He admired her resistance while at the same time recognizing the deep irony of his position.

Only she knew he missed his home, never knew his mother, and mourned the death of his beloved grandfather. Only she knew he was fond of gooseberries but didn't care for strawberries. Only she knew the sound he made when he wanted a woman so badly, he shook with it.

All of this had been imparted through those long days that were now growing shorter with the approach of winter. A snap in the air, the changing leaves, all pointed to the cooler days to come. At Lion's Gate, they would soon see their first snowfall. He'd thought he would be home by now, supervising the changes that were needed to bring his estate back to life. The old home was the last on his list, but by God, he wanted to bring her back as well.

This, Clara did not know. She knew only that he was alone in the world.

Chapter 8

"You are in a fine mood today," Clara said, noting her sister's high color and general bon vivant spirit.

"I am having luncheon with my friends," she said, gazing in the mirror and adjusting the ribbon beneath her chin. Harriet, who had not seemed to mind what she looked like, had of late been taking a bit more care with her appearance. Perhaps her friends were having a positive influence. "Would you like to come with me? The girls miss you, you know."

"The girls" were Harriet's group of friends—Alice, Rebecca, and Eliza. Clara often had accompanied Harriet to her outings with them, but had never felt part of their group. Today was a gloriously sunny day and she already heard the sound of Mr. Emory's hoe in the soil. Despite their awkward meeting the previous day when she'd been on Lord Berkley's arm, Clara was determined to spend time in her garden.

She looked outside pointedly, and said, "What do you think?"

"I think you would much rather be outside in your garden than cooped up in a room with four gossipy women. You are such a strange bird, Clara."

Clara grinned, liking that description of her. She plopped on her gardening hat, pushing it down for good measure. "I adore being strange."

"I'm off then," Harriet said with a laugh.

Clara sighed after Harriet had disappeared, and wondered what her sister would think if she knew Clara had been kissing their gardener. No doubt, she would be horrified and concerned. Likely just as horrified and concerned as Clara was. While she refused to call the kiss a mistake, it certainly was something she had no intention of repeating. Her curiosity had been assuaged. No more kissing their gardener. No more flirting. No more staring at him like some spoony girl who'd never had a beau.

And then, all those thoughts flew from her mind the moment she stepped outside and saw him and her heart picked up and her insides gave an odd clench. She smiled and swallowed and allowed her eyes to dip to his mouth, upturned in a smile, which hardened into a straight line as she watched.

"Good morning, Miss Anderson," he said gruffly.

"Good morning, Mr. Emory."

They stared at one another for a moment too long, breathing in unison, bodies taut. Clara was about to turn and run back into the house, afraid of the feelings that swept through her, her inability to calm her heart and tame her desire, when he said, "I'll be right back. I need something in my room."

He dropped his hoe and spun about before heading directly to the shed, leaving Clara standing there uncertain about what had just happened. Before he disappeared into the darkness of the shed, he stopped, just for a moment, then continued on and closed the door behind him.

"Oh," she whispered, and pressed her fists against her stomach. She didn't think, didn't dare allow herself to, before walking toward the shed, hands clenched tightly in her skirts, heart beating madly in her chest. As she reached the end of the shed, the part where his small room was, a hand shot out, wrapped around her neck, and pulled her out of sight of the house, causing her hat to slip from her head and land at her feet behind her.

Before she knew what was happening, Clara was pushed against the rough shingles, a hard, male body warm against her, lips capturing hers in a head-spinning kiss that nearly made her swoon. He dropped his hand from her neck, and soon both were around her waist, then sweeping down and back to cup her bottom so he could pull her even closer. He let out a low sound as he pressed the hard length of his arousal against her center.

"You are driving me mad," he said, pulling away just far enough for him to speak. "Do you realize that?" He pushed his hips toward her so she could feel him, and he let out another groan. "God, I'm sorry. I shouldn't be doing this." He said these words, but tightened his embrace and kissed her long, and deep, and in such a carnal way, Clara was lost. In some dim part of her mind, she knew she was acting immorally, like a common hussy, but his body against hers, his mouth teasing hers, his tongue drugging her with his skillful caress, all served to turn that practical part of her brain off. The feel of him, his scent, the sounds that came from his throat, everything combined to send Clara into a state she had no name for. Rapture? Abandon? Never could she have imagined a kiss—no, this was more than a kiss—could take control of every bit of her.

He stopped suddenly and rested his forehead against hers, breathing heavily. "I'm so sorry," he said again, but this time he seemed to be filled with deep regret, the sort that meant this would never happen again.

Mr. Emory stepped back and Clara noticed that his hat had fallen from his head to rest near hers. His hair was mussed, and she recalled dragging her hands through his thick, wavy locks, pulling him closer to her. His expression was harsh, his jaw clenched, his eyes dark and piercing. Angry. "You're no different from any other woman," he said, his words stunning her as much as a slap would have.

"I'm not?"

"No, you are not. Why, then, can I not control myself around you? Why do you do this to me?" he asked, crudely indicating the long length of him that showed clearly through his trousers. "You are making this impossible, Miss Anderson. I don't know if I can continue here." He shook his head as if searching for an answer.

"I'm sorry," she said in a small voice, because it seemed to her that he was blaming her for the passion that flared between them. Indeed, she'd been taught most of her life that it was up to a woman to tame a man's baser side.

He let out a sigh and his expression softened. "No, no, you are not to blame. I apologize if that is what you thought I was saying. I'm no good at this sort of thing. The blame, all of it, is on me. I just don't understand why I cannot keep my hands to myself around you." He smiled. "You haven't bewitched me with some strange Cornish curse, have you?"

Clara let out a giggle. "If I had that ability, I daresay Lord Berkley would have proposed by now."

He scowled at that, which only made Clara feel better. "This," he said, waving a hand between them, "cannot happen again. It cannot, Miss Anderson. It will only lead to one thing and it is something you will regret for the rest of your life. You understand what I am saying."

Clara nodded. "Fornication."

"Yes. I am a man who is not typically ruled by the physical, but I find it nearly impossible to resist you. It would be easy for us to forget the dire consequences of allowing ourselves to be caught up in whatever it is that is happening between us. I cannot allow that to happen." He closed his eyes briefly. "You deserve better than to be treated like some common trollop. I cannot marry you, Miss Anderson. You do know that, do you not?"

Her cheeks burned as she nodded. "I never contemplated such a union." That was a patent lie, for she had allowed herself to imagine they might marry, that she could convince her parents that love was more important than social status. Perhaps she could convince her father, but Hedra was about as stubborn as a person could be and it was highly doubtful Clara would be able to sway her away from her plans to elevate the family socially. She'd even imagined herself and Mr. Emory hightailing it to Scotland with her father hard on their heels. So, yes, telling Mr. Emory she hadn't thought about a match when it had begun to consume her was a rather large fib, and it stung a bit that he was so obviously opposed to the notion. "I suppose I didn't do much contemplating at all."

He chuckled at that. "Nor did I. But we must. *I* must. I do realize that matrimony is a consuming topic to young ladies and their mothers, but I am in no position to marry any woman."

Raising one eyebrow, Clara said, "Certainly. So it is not me in particular that you are so opposed to, but matrimony itself. And I am not so terrible?" Silly, but it meant something to know that he held her in a bit of esteem.

"You are an angel and I am not at all the man you believe me to be. I am not kind. I am not charming. I am single-minded and determined. My greatest fear is that one day you will see me for the scoundrel I am."

Clara smiled at that. "I know you, Mr. Emory. You are a man of honor." When he made to protest, she held up a hand. "How many men would have stepped back just now? With a willing girl in his arms?" Bending down, she picked up both their hats, then placed hers back upon her head and handed his over to him. "But you are correct. We have been crossing a line that should never be crossed between an employer and an employee. This cannot happen again." Saying that aloud was far more unpleasant than she'd anticipated.

"I am glad we are in agreement."

"And if it should happen again—"

"It will not." He stepped back to prove his point.

"Mr. Emory, please hear me out. Yes, you were here waiting for me. But I was the one who came to you. You are not to blame, not entirely, at any rate. I suppose the only thing you are guilty of is making me want to come back here. Should this happen again, I will know full well what I am doing. I want you to know this."

She watched his Adam's apple dip as he swallowed.

"I shall push you away," he said.

His words were cold but his eyes flared with heat. "I believe you shall, Mr. Emory." She smoothed down her skirts. "I am going to return to the garden and putter about for a while. I am confident we will be able to act properly."

"Perhaps you should just go inside, Miss Anderson."

She glared at him a long moment. "Perhaps. But I shan't."

After she'd gone, Nathaniel leaned against the shed and lifted his head to the sky, filled with remorse and, worse, the feeling that he might die if he didn't have her. His grandfather would have been so disappointed in his behavior, and he was glad the old man was not around to witness his shame. Clara was a sweet, innocent girl. Not so innocent anymore. No girl could be completely innocent who'd had a man pull her against his raging erection. He let out a humorless laugh.

It would take some time before he was presentable if he continued to revisit what had just occurred. He looked at the pond, contemplating a quick swim fully clothed, anything to douse the desire that ran hot in his veins. Instead, he settled on dunking his head beneath the spigot and letting the icy water run down his back. When he had stopped throbbing and his friend had stopped its insistent call for love-making, Nathaniel headed back to the garden and tried not to look her way. It took little for him to become aroused when she was nearby: the sound of her sigh, the way her dress tightened across her breasts when she reached over to nip a bud, the sight of her full lips tilting up in a smile. My God, he felt like a young boy experiencing the first thrill of getting hard.

The sound of a wagon pulled his attention away from her and toward a team of horses pulling a large load of building materials. Work on the hothouse was about to begin, apparently, and Nathaniel breathed a sigh of relief. With all the workers about, he would have absolutely no opportunity to drag Miss Anderson behind the shed. The fact that he had, that he had been so weak and allowed himself to maul her, filled him with no small amount of shame. He knew he was in the wrong, and yet he'd continued to kiss her, caress her, allowing his passion to rule his head. Even though he'd resolved never to touch her again, he could not stop his mind from wondering what it would be like to sink into the wet heat of her, to hear her cries of passion, feel her legs wrap around his torso...

"Mr. Emory," Mr. Billings called as he began unloading the wagon. "If you wouldn't mind giving a bit of direction."

Nathaniel snapped out of his lustful fog. "Of course." He jogged over to the wagon, laden with a large pile of boards that would be used to create the frame for the hothouse. Nathaniel had thought the idea of the hothouse was a stroke of brilliance. It had allowed him to dig up a large expanse of the garden all at once. But his shovel had never struck a box or anything other than loose and worthless stones. A large mound of earth was proof of his fruitless labors. He'd thought, when discussing the possible location of the hothouse, that this area, near the edge of the property and away from the house, might have been the ideal place for his grandfather to have buried the diamond. It had been another failed endeavor. There were times when he looked out over the garden that he found it impossible to believe the diamond could still be here. With every shovelful of earth he moved, there was less earth still left to search.

Where the bloody hell could it be?

As he helped Mr. Billings remove the boards from the wagon, he looked over the garden and for the hundredth time tried to imagine where his grandfather had hidden the—

And then he looked at the pond, and he felt the blood drain from his head. No, his grandfather would never have put a wooden box in a body of water, not even locust wood, known for its ability to resist water. As he stared at the small pond, his mind whirled. Had the pond always been on the property?

"Mr. Emory," Mr. Billings said, gaining his attention. He'd been standing there holding his end of the four planks they carried for too long.

"Gathering dust," he said as an apology, then placed his end of the load and returned to the wagon again. "What do you think of a gazebo near the pond, Mr. Billings?"

The older man squinted his eyes. "Not until spring. And I'm afraid this hothouse is going to have to wait as well. Every man in this county who knows how to hold a hammer is working at Costille House. The new earl is renovating it. Lady Greenwich made some changes to the old place he didn't care for." He smiled as if he was glad of the earl's disapproval. "Thought it was nice, though, but the earl, he wants it back the way it was. I'm only here today to deliver the wood. Thought maybe you could get started without me. It's a simple enough project if you know anything about building."

Nathaniel grimaced. "Unfortunately, I do not," he said. "But I will relay the news to the Andersons that the hothouse will likely be delayed. When do you think you'll be able to begin?"

"Not until right before Christmas," Mr. Billings said, pulling a large tarp from the bottom of the wagon. Nathaniel quickly moved to help the man and the two of them draped the tarp over the wood. After they'd finished, Mr. Billings moved closer, as if to impart some important bit of information. "With all this digging you're doing, you find anything…unusual?"

After pretending to think for a moment, Nathaniel said, "Now that you mention it, I did find an unusual rock, a fancy bit of blue quartz."

Mr. Billings's eyes widened and Nathaniel couldn't help but chuckle, causing the older man to scowl heavily. "Aye, you're a right funny fellow, you are."

Shrugging, Nathaniel smiled. "If I find the diamond, you'll know quick enough because the Andersons will be posting for another gardener."

"Bah," Mr. Billings said, apparently not appreciating his sense of humor. "I'm starting to think that fancy fellow from London is having a grand time pulling our legs."

"You could be right about that, Mr. Billings. You could be right."

The fine folks of St. Ives had reacted very much as Roger had predicted. Every lane he walked down he saw evidence of someone digging holes or poking the earth. Rumors about the diamond were flowing fast and free, but as time went on, he was beginning to sense a bit of hostility. The villagers were beginning to think he was disingenuous in his claims. It was too bad, really. St. Ives was a pretty little town and he found the brilliant blue-green of the sea soothing to his soul. His wife would have loved it here. On his third day in St. Ives, he'd walked along the beach, empty but for a few plovers skittering along the edge of the foamy tide, wondering if the current Baron Alford had disappeared for a reason. Perhaps he had already found the diamond and had disappeared somewhere to sell it. America?

The old baron had died, and it didn't take too much imagination to think he might have told his grandson where the diamond was hidden. Nathaniel Emory was as much a mystery as the diamond itself. Few people knew him or could even say they'd ever met him. Apparently, the young man had been somewhat shunned by the aristocracy thanks to his drunken father, who had made more enemies than a man should in one brief lifetime. The Emory family seemed to be rife with scoundrels, and Roger had no doubt Nathaniel Emory was the same as all the rest.

"Where are you, Alford?" Roger said, gazing out to the sea. A man could not simply vanish from the face of the Earth, certainly not a peer. Speaking with the family attorney had gotten him no closer to finding the baron, though Roger was certain the man knew more than what he was saying. Roger would bet the three hundred pounds Mr. Belmont had given him that the attorney knew where the baron was.

Roger had found himself in this picturesque little village by following the old baron's trail. When he was a young man, not much older than the current baron, he'd been set upon by thieves and left for dead—on the road coming from St. Ives. What would a man of his station be doing on an isolated road, far from both London and his country seat? What business could have brought him to St. Ives, not a few months after returning to England? As it was fifty years prior, Roger could find little information. The current constable kindly went back through his records and had found a small mention of the incident, but it was woefully empty of details. Alford had been unconscious when he'd been found and it wasn't until later that his name was added to the report. The incident had been blamed on smugglers who at that time used St. Ives' isolation and safe harbor as a place to store their goods.

He was loath to leave, but there was nothing in St. Ives to keep him much longer. If someone did indeed find the diamond, which he doubted would happen, he or Mr. Belmont would most certainly hear of it. Just thinking about Mr. Belmont made him uneasy. The man had given him a fortune to find the diamond or, at the very least, find Baron Alford, and he had failed to do either. He dreaded returning to London with so little to show for the time spent away. St. Ives, it seemed, was another dead end.

Chapter 9

Clara watched with a large dose of dread as Jeanine hurried to pack the last of her gowns for their trip to London. She had so many reasons for not wanting to go, first and foremost the knowledge that though her mother was convinced Baron Longley had agreed to sponsor her, they'd heard nothing from him to indicate he would. Still, armed with the baron's London address, Hedra convinced herself this was a chance worth taking. They had rented a townhouse in a reasonably fashionable area of London—at least that's what Mrs. Pittsfield had told her mother. Clara couldn't help but think Mrs. Pittsfield, whose career as a lady's maid had ended fifty years earlier, likely knew little of the current state of things. Still, she certainly knew far more than the Andersons.

"Are you excited about going to London?" Clara asked her maid.

"I am," Jeanine said, but there was a clear "but" after that sentence. "I do wish it wasn't for so long. I don't like missing Christmas at home. My mother was counting on me to make my saffron buns."

"I adore your saffron buns," Clara said. "Perhaps I can convince you to make some in London."

"Oh, I doubt the kitchen staff there would want me moving about their kitchen," Jeanine said. She seemed uncommonly puckish, so Clara turned and gave Jeanine her full attention.

"You don't want to go at all, do you?"

Jeanine shook her head and forced a smile. "It's not only about the saffron buns."

"I didn't think it was."

Her maid closed a small case filled with Clara's unmentionables. "I think Charlie was going to propose this Christmas. He hinted as much."

"Oh, Jeanine, I am so sorry. But certainly he can propose any time."

Jeanine gave a quick little nod and her eyes got a bit misty. "It's just that his family has a tradition, and if he can't propose this Christmas, I'll have to wait a whole year. I'm already nearly thirty and I'm getting too old to have children."

Clara laughed lightly. "You are not anywhere near too old for that." Jeanine kept her back toward her and Clara feared her maid might be weeping. Clara was about to go to her and give her a comforting arm when Harriet burst into the room, bringing with her the fresh scent of the outdoors. Her younger sister had the glow of health lately, likely due to all her invigorating walks. While Harriet didn't seem upset to be left behind, Clara felt nothing but guilt, which Harriet waved off as she usually did.

It would be so much more amusing to have Harriet with her than to have to face the aristocracy on her own. At least they could giggle together when people turned up their noses at her.

"I fear Mother will only be disappointed. Again." Clara lowered her voice so that Hedra would not overhear. "When will she end this?"

"When a duke begs to marry you."

Clara laughed. "You and I both know that is not going to happen. Dressing a pig in a gown does not make the pig less of a pig."

"You are not a pig, Clara. You are a lovely girl whom any man would be lucky to call his bride."

Clara waved a hand at her. "You know very well what I mean. It doesn't matter how many times you or I try to explain to her that no member of the peerage will marry the daughter of a tin miner—"

"Tin mine owner," Harriet pointed out, as Mother so often did.

Clara stuck out her tongue and wrinkled her nose. "I just go along," she said on a sigh. "Eventually, she'll let me come home and just live, won't she?"

"You do want to marry, don't you?"

Did she? No one had ever bothered to ask that question. Marriage seemed such an odd concept, one with vague images of her with some faceless man living in some cold mausoleum of a house. Lately, though, she allowed herself to picture an entirely different scenario, one in which she lived in a cozy little cottage with a strapping young husband who liked to garden.

Clara let out a light laugh. "I have thought many times that I would switch places with you. You are so lucky to stay home. I'll muddle through it–I always do."

"Who knows? Perhaps Mother's persistence will pay off and some prince or duke will take one look at you and fall at your feet and beg you to marry him."

She wrinkled her nose. "Fall to his feet because he's too old and doddering to remain upright. Can I tell you something?"

"Of course."

"You remember Mother talking about Baron Longley? I know she fostered hopes that he would offer for me and I cannot tell you how relieved I am that he has not. But, Harriet, what if he did? He is supposed to be in London to introduce me. What if he makes an offer for my hand? What would I do?"

"I don't know," Harriet said miserably.

"But after all this, the expense, the traveling, everything. How could I say no?" It was something that had weighed on Clara's mind heavily since their last meeting. Even though the Gardeners had invited her to their home simply to test her for a companion position, Baron Longley had seemed interested in her. Clara hadn't missed the long, assessing looks he'd given her.

After telling Harriet about Baron Longley, her sister confessed to having an unfortunate infatuation with Lord Berkley, a rather shocking confession, for Clara knew how Harriet disdained the idea of marrying so far above their station. Harriet thought their mother a bit touched in the head for continuing her quest to find Clara a titled husband.

When Hedra appeared at the door, Clara felt a small flush of guilt that she'd been thinking ill of her. Mother only wanted what was best for her and Harriet, of that Clara had no doubt.

"We leave in the morning, Clara." Then, looking at Harriet, she said, "I wish we had ordered dresses for you, Harriet. Now that we are ready to depart, I am doubting my decision to have you remain here. Unchaperoned."

The two argued for a bit, and Clara watched with amusement, knowing that nothing would change: Clara would still go to London and Harriet would stay here in St. Ives. Lucky girl.

Chapter 10

Nathaniel watched the Anderson carriage leave with mixed emotions, relief being topmost. He was deeply ashamed of his behavior, for allowing his baser needs to overrule what had always been a pragmatic mind. Worse was that he suspected Clara had begun to dream of a marriage between them, of a time when she would be able to convince her parents that a marriage to their gardener was acceptable. Hell, he'd even allowed his mind to drift there, to imagine the two of them, married and settled with children running about. The nights alone in his tiny room were long and lonely, so who could blame a man for dreaming things that could never be? The painful truth was, if she found out he was a baron, that he'd been lying to her for months, she would never forgive him. Nor would he blame her. He could not even forgive himself.

By all accounts, he would have more than a month to do as he pleased in the garden, to search without anyone about. Surely he could complete the task now that Clara was not hovering about. It had been exceedingly difficult to continue on with his search when she was following her plan, which included working on areas of the garden where he'd already searched. With his hoe in hand, Nathaniel began, plunging the tool again and again into the earth, digging only when he thought he'd struck something. He'd grown rather good at determining what it was he'd found simply by the sound the hoe made when he struck an object. Still, he looked no matter what the sound, for fear of overlooking the diamond. What if the box had disintegrated? What if that sound of the hoe hitting stone was really the hoe hitting the diamond? It was tedious and back-breaking work, but Nathaniel felt more positive about his chances than ever before.

Work was progressing remarkably quickly, and Nathaniel realized a week after the Andersons had departed that his search would be completed long before the family returned. If his gut ached at the thought of leaving St. Ives without seeing Clara again, without touching or kissing or hearing her sighs, then so be it. It was far less disturbing than what would happen if she returned, smiling and happy and glad to see him, only to watch him walk away without a word. If she cared for him, she would get over it. They had done nothing irrevocable. He had not taken her innocence or declared his love for her. Nothing had happened that time would not erase. But it would be damned hard to leave her, to sneak away in the middle of the night, if she were home. That thought made him redouble his efforts, until sweat soaked through his clothing, until his arms ached and his hands burned despite the sturdy work gloves.

"Mr. Emory, a word if you please." Mr. Barkley, the under butler, stood at the edge of the garden.

"How can I help you, Mr. Barkley?" The under butler had taken over butler duties as Mr. Standard had gone with the Andersons to London.

"You've received a letter from London, sir, and Mr. Standard directed me to tell you immediately should you receive correspondence." Mr. Barkley held out his hand containing the letter, and Nathaniel dropped his hoe to retrieve it. Though he could tell the under butler was curious about the letter, he said not a word, simply handed it over, then returned to the house. No doubt the letter would be fodder for gossip around the table that night until he arrived for supper. With most of the staff gone, it would be a far smaller group to chat about their mysterious gardener.

> *Dear sir,*
> *I believe it is imperative that you return to London immedi-*
> *ately. Certain events have occurred that are best not discussed*
> *via the post. I await your arrival.*
> *Samuel Gordon esq.*

Well, hell. If he returned to London, he would have to return as Baron Alford, not ordinary Nathaniel Emory, gardener to a St. Ives country home. Clara was there with her family, and though he had little concern he would run into them, it was a worry. The thought of running into Clara while he was dressed as a gentleman, with people "my lording" him, was abhorrent. He could imagine such a meeting going very badly for all.

Still, his solicitor would not have written such an urgent and cryptic letter if it had not been absolutely necessary, so Nathaniel resigned himself to returning to London. He'd simply have to keep an eye out for an overly decorated carriage. He tried to recall the details of Clara's trip to London, but he confessed he could not recall much other than the family was renting a townhouse for a full month, much to Mr. Anderson's objections. For the life of him, he could not remember where the blasted townhouse was, and he only prayed it was not nearby the Brown's Hotel where he always stayed, mainly because of its private dining room. He was fairly certain the Andersons would have picked the most fashionable address possible and as luck would have it, the Brown's Hotel was located in Mayfair, an area that had been more popular fifty years before. Surely, the Andersons would not be there.

Samuel Gordon's offices were located on Bond Street, not far from Nathaniel's hotel. It was a dreary day, with low-hanging clouds that threatened to let loose rain at any moment, but he managed to make the short trip without a drop falling on him. When he entered, Gordon's assistant shot to his feet, but couldn't hide the look of dismay on his face when he realized who he was. His ill-fitting clothes, tanned face, and shaggy hair combined to give him the look of a laborer.

"Lord Alford, Mr. Gordon is expecting you. Please, go right in."

Nathaniel nodded, ignoring the long, questioning look the man gave him, and entered Gordon's office after a quick knock. His solicitor stood, and if he noticed Nathaniel's less-than-polished appearance, he gave no indication.

"I am glad you were able to make the trip, my lord," Gordon said, indicating a leather chair set up in front of his desk. "May I offer you refreshment? Brandy, perhaps?"

"No, thank you, Mr. Gordon. I'd rather just get this business over with, if you please."

"Of course. I do apologize for pulling you away from…" His voice faded before he gave Nathaniel a grim smile. "…your endeavors. Just last week, I had not one but two visitors inquiring about your whereabouts. Of course, I claimed not to know where you were. This Mr. Belmont was quite adamant, seemed inordinately angry, to the point that I came close to calling the constable."

Gordon was a diminutive fellow with a voice that matched—reedy thin and not all that pleasant to listen to. He was, however, a damned good solicitor and one of the most discreet men Nathaniel had ever met. "Did he become violent?" Nathaniel asked, concerned. It was unconscionable that anyone threaten someone who was merely protecting him.

"Only to my desk," Gordon said with a self-effacing smile. "But it was not only the visits that concerned me; it was the story he told, a story in complete opposition to your grandfather's. I got the distinct feeling that Mr. Belmont is not only interested in the diamond and the funds it would bring, but also in retribution for what he believes were ills done to his father. He is, shall I say, quite impassioned."

Mr. Gordon related the tale he'd been told by Mr. Belmont, leaving Nathaniel stunned by how much it varied from his grandfather's tale. He had no doubt at all that his grandfather's story held more truth than Mr. Belmont's.

"Did he seem unreasonable?" Nathaniel asked.

Mr. Gordon gave him a look of concern. "He seemed quite angry, sir. That is why I felt it urgent to speak with you in person. His obsession seems to have turned to you."

Knowing how close the investigator had been to him provoked more than a little disquiet in Nathaniel. Mr. Belmont's father had nearly killed his grandfather and he couldn't help but wonder if the man searching for him would resort to similar violence. His grandfather had made the most of what life had dealt him, but he'd suffered terribly, physically and emotionally. "You believe I'm in danger."

"I do, my lord. Very grave danger."

After leaving his solicitor, Nathaniel felt the need for a brandy, but given the early hour, opted for a bracing cup of tea instead. Down a side street in an area not usually frequented by the aristocracy, or anyone else who wanted to be seen, was a small, nondescript tea shop where he thought he might have some privacy while he mulled over what Mr. Gordon had told him. London was a large city, teeming with people, but he had no wish to frequent any spot where he might be seen by the Andersons. No doubt, the Andersons would be at Gunter's Tea Shop, if they were out at all on this dreary November day.

He was just about to take his first sip of tea when he heard, "Alford? Is that you?"

He looked about until he saw a well-fed man with thinning blond hair and a big smile. "Bennington." John Bennington, second son of Viscount Kingsley and a former classmate at Oxford, strode toward him, tugging a pleasant-looking young woman along with him. The woman, with a headful of artfully arranged curls beneath a dashing feathered hat, reminded Nathaniel of the expensive dolls the rich bought for their pampered daughters. She was the epitome of a young English lady, dressed impeccably and fashionably, and with an air of privilege that was nearly impossible to ignore. Nathaniel immediately stood and greeted his old friend.

"I haven't seen you in years. You're looking well," Bennington said, his voice trailing off as he truly looked at his old friend. Nathaniel was not looking well, at least not as a young baron should look.

"I've been traveling," Nathaniel said as a way of explaining his tanned skin. He could not explain, however, why he was wearing such an ill-fitting suit nor why his hair was unfashionably long. "The valet at Brown's nearly fainted when he saw me, but I'll soon be put to rights, I assure you."

The two laughed, accepting Nathaniel's explanation. When Nathaniel had tried to don the suit of clothes that had fit him perfectly not two months earlier, he'd nearly laughed. Two months of hard labor had drastically changed his body. His waist was smaller, his arms and chest larger. He'd looked in the mirror and at first laughed at the sharp tan line around his neck and on his arms where his gloves had ended and his often rolled up sleeves had started. It looked a bit like he was wearing bracelets. It had been months since he'd gotten a good look at himself as he had only a small handheld mirror that was barely adequate for shaving. What he found when he stared into the full-length mirror in his room was a fine specimen of manhood, if he did say so himself. But for those ridiculous and sharply delineated lines between proper pale skin and a laborer's tan, he was happy with the changes. Unfortunately, his new body did not fit well into his old clothes. He looked very much like a man whose clothing had shrunk, but for his pants waist, which hung about him as if he were wearing his father's trousers.

At the horrified urging of the hotel's valet, Nathaniel's first bit of business had been a visit to his tailor, who expressed as much dismay as the valet over Nathaniel's present suit of clothes. Though his funds were limited, Nathaniel knew it was imperative to keep up appearances should he be required to resume his own identity. News that an obsessed madman was looking for him made it far less appealing to go back to being Baron Alford, and he would likely return to St. Ives even more quickly than he'd originally planned. As Nathaniel had been out of society for some good time, he hadn't thought he would run into anyone he knew, but here, standing in front of him, was the biggest gossip in London. Nathaniel wondered if he were cursed.

"Looks like you've been traveling someplace with a bit more sun than we get in London," Bennington said cheerfully, looking out at the mist-covered street. "Allow me to introduce my bride, Alicia Bennington. My dear, this is Lord Alford. We attended Oxford together and he was the finest cricket player we had."

Mrs. Bennington dipped a curtsy and extended her hand. "A pleasure, my lord."

"Congratulations on your nuptials. Are you still newlyweds?" Nathaniel asked, indicating that the couple should join him at his table.

"Indeed we are," Bennington said, smiling over at his wife and patting her hand, which remained in the crook of his arm even as they sat. "Just five months now. Happiest five months of my life."

Mrs. Bennington blushed prettily. "Where have you been traveling, sir?"

"Oh, around and about. I'm only in London a short time to take care of some pressing business."

"Ah, yes, I heard about your grandfather. My condolences." Bennington turned to his wife. "Baron Alford passed away just this year."

"Condolences," she said softly, but then a small glint appeared in her eyes. "Are you here with your wife?"

"I have not had that pleasure," Nathaniel said blandly.

"A pity you will not be in London long. There are a great many things to do in town at the moment."

Bennington laughed, but Nathaniel hadn't a clue why. The couple exchanged a look he could not interpret. "Now that my wife has found such matrimonial bliss, she is making it her mission to find husbands for each of her friends. And younger sister."

Nathaniel's feelings on that must have been apparent, for Bennington laughed and clapped him on the back, almost painfully. "No need to panic, my friend."

"Surely you will be in town long enough for some entertainments. One ball, perhaps?"

"Yes, one ball. We shall insist you accompany us." Bennington was seemingly aware of Nathaniel's reticence and was apparently delighted by it. Nothing was worse, in Nathaniel's opinion, than a happily married man. It seemed they wanted all of mankind to share in their matrimonial bliss.

"I regretfully must decline."

Mrs. Bennington blinked; clearly she was unused to being thwarted. "The Grosvenor Gallery exhibit then. Mr. Bennington and I were planning to go tomorrow. I hear it is quite impressive."

"A grand idea, Mrs. Bennington," her husband said, lifting his wife's hand up for him to kiss. "Such a clever idea."

Nathaniel could hardly say no to an exhibit, though he dearly wanted to. It would be disastrous if he ran into the Andersons while he was here in London, worse if Mr. Belmont caught wind of his visit. Then again, what were the chances that the Andersons would not only attend the same exhibit, but at the same day and hour? The Andersons were far more likely, if they were going to a gallery at all, to tour the Royal Academy rather than the Grosvenor, which was considered rather avant garde and daring.

"Of course, and I thank you for the invitation." He saw the couple exchange another look, this one of triumph. "Oh, no, do not tell me you are planning to invite your sister and all of your friends. I must warn you now that my family name has been quite muddied. They would hardly thank you for an introduction."

Bennington waved his concerns away. "Your reputation, sir, is impeccable. Whatever sins your father committed are not visited on his son, I can assure you." When Nathaniel raised a brow, Bennington harrumphed in discomfort. "Then they should not be. It's not as if your father was a murderer."

Mrs. Bennington looked on with interest, and Nathaniel thought he sensed a bit of dismay in her features. Likely the lady was wishing she had not issued the invitation after all.

"You may withdraw your invitation, Mrs. Bennington. I can assure you, my feelings will not be hurt."

"I'll not hear of it, Alford," Bennington blustered, then turned to his wife. "It's water under the bridge and ancient news. No one under the age of fifty would be able to recount a single unfortunate episode."

"May I ask…oh, no, it is presumptuous of me. But…"

"My father had a habit of going into public places and acting in, let us say, an inappropriate manner. He became a bit of a laughingstock and there are those who have not and will not forgive such actions. The family has been banned from Whites. Among other clubs and organizations."

Mrs. Bennington raised her gloved hands to her throat as if that were the most terrible sentence to bestow upon any man. "Have *you* ever gone into a public place and acted inappropriately?" she asked, her clear eyes steady on him.

"I make it a habit not to go into public at all, which may explain why Mr. Bennington hasn't seen me since university. I am excruciatingly boring and dull."

"Perfect," Mrs. Bennington said, and Nathaniel laughed. "Besides, you would be surprised by what is forgiven and forgotten when a gentleman has 'lord' in front of his name."

Nathaniel grinned, reassessing his first impression of the lady. She might look like a vacant doll, but Mrs. Bennington was a canny lady. His friend had done well.

The next day, wearing his newly tailored suit and feeling rather spiffy, Nathaniel headed to New Bond Street and the Grosvenor Gallery. To his thinking, even should he run into Mr. or Mrs. Anderson, they would hardly recognize him without his loose-fitting trousers and shirt and his ever-present cap. Freshly shaven and sporting a neat haircut, he was every inch the London gentleman. His high collar and cravat hid the sharp tan line, and his new suit of clothes was tailored to perfection, showing off his athletic form. In all, Nathaniel was pleased. It was, frankly, startling how a good shave, a haircut, and a fine suit of clothes could make such a difference in not only how he felt, but how others perceived him. Doormen snapped to attention, fine ladies and gentlemen nodded politely, and if he were honest, it felt damned good. He was, after all, a baron. His grandfather had schooled him well in deportment and responsibility, and Nathaniel often wondered how he had failed so miserably with his own son.

Grosvenor Gallery had been open just one year and had already garnered much interest among the ton—and the patrons of the arts. One either loathed the art within or loved it, and it seemed the common view was that this gallery founded by Sir Lindsay and Lady Fitzroy was a rousing success. It welcomed artists rejected by the Royal Academy, those who liked to focus their talents on subjects other than the accepted themes of religion and battle.

Nathaniel had yet to tour the gallery, but he was quite familiar with the Royal Academy, having visited several times when his grandfather was alive. When he stepped down from his hired hack and looked at the building's façade, Nathaniel found himself already impressed. The gallery was housed in a large building designed in the renaissance style and featured a main door taken from a 16th century Venetian church. The Benningtons hoped to tour the gallery and then had invited Nathaniel for tea in their home, something he found himself, much to his surprise, looking forward to. How long had it been since he'd enjoyed a formal tea?

As he was about to step up, Bennington called out to him. The two, who apparently lived not far from the gallery, were heading his way. Bennington was sporting a top hat and Mrs. Bennington wearing her own version of a top hat—hers with a small garden of flowers atop it—as they hurried to where he was waiting. They seemed, he thought, to be a happy couple, well suited, a pair who enjoyed one another's company and he was glad, suddenly, that he had accepted their invitation. He couldn't remember the last time he had allowed himself a leisurely afternoon immersed in the arts, surrounded by his own ilk. It was, he thought, a bit like coming home after a long absence. St. Ives was lovely, but it was not home.

"We shall have to view Whistler's painting, *Nocturne in Black and Gold*," Mrs. Bennington said, lowering her voice. "It caused quite a stir. You were out of town, so you may not know. A reviewer said such horrid things about it, Mr. Whistler sued him for libel. Can you imagine?" Mrs. Bennington seemed delighted by this. "The reviewer gave Mr. Whistler a set-down for throwing paint at people," she said.

"For 'flinging a pot of paint in the public's faces,' is what I believe it said," Mr. Bennington corrected, making Mrs. Bennington frown.

"Mr. Whistler sued for defamation," Mrs. Bennington said with a nod. "Oh, I do hope the painting is still on display."

The three entered the gallery and Mrs. Bennington made a great show of surprise to find two of her "dearest friends" just inside. Bennington gave Nathaniel a wink and a shrug as Mrs. Bennington made hasty introductions, and Nathaniel had to admit they were a lovely twosome, dressed sedately and fashionably for a day at a gallery. Thus far, he'd been able to avoid such matchmaking gestures, mostly because he'd avoided social situations and he'd only just come into his inheritance. He wondered how enthusiastic these two would be if they knew he was a pauper.

Then again…perhaps one was an heiress who could save him from his life of drudgery as a gardener. One was the daughter of an earl and one the granddaughter of a viscount. They were the sorts of girls he was supposed to end up with, those who had been bred to be ladies, to run grand households, those who would never, under any circumstances, end up behind a shed in a passionate embrace with a gardener.

They both bored him silly and seemed to be trying far too hard to impress him with their wit—as was the case with the redhead—and their pedigree, as was the case with the brunette.

The gallery, Nathaniel had to admit, was an impressive place, which displayed the art in an unusual way he'd never before seen. Rather than cram as many paintings as possible on a wall, as did the Royal Academy, each painting was given its own wall, its own alcove, which served, to his mind, to elevate the importance of the work. He quite liked it.

The small group was about to enter the west gallery and its soaring, glass-filled ceiling, when the two ladies who were in front of him stopped suddenly, one clutching the other's arm. "Oh, there she is. The one I told you about. They were in Rotten Row two days ago in the most hideous carriage I've ever seen. It was all anyone could talk about, such a gaudy show," the brunette said with a sniff.

Nathaniel got an immediate and terrible sinking feeling in the pit of his stomach. Gaudy show could apply to any number of people, but he feared in this case it described one particular family—the Andersons.

"Look what she's wearing," the redhead said and began to giggle behind her kid glove.

Nathaniel still could not see whom they were speaking of, and carefully made his way forward, his gaze seeking out, and finding, the Andersons. *Oh, good God.*

"Really, you two. You mustn't be unkind. She obviously doesn't know." This from Mrs. Bennington, who despite her words, was trying not to smile.

And the reason for that smile was immediately clear. Clara stood looking spectacularly overdressed in a gown more suited for a ballroom than a stroll through a gallery in daytime. His heart ached for her, because he suspected Clara knew what she was wearing was inappropriate, and likely knew she was an object of ridicule. At that moment, he wanted to throttle her parents, who were so clearly oblivious to their daughter's suffering. Worse, he could do nothing to protect her.

"Some people think a bit of money will elevate them to a higher class. They'll learn soon enough, I expect," Mr. Bennington said, not unkindly.

"Yes, we all know marriage is the only thing that can do that," Nathaniel said with deep irony.

Bennington chuckled. "I'm in wholehearted agreement. I was nothing until I married Mrs. Bennington." That won him a smile from his wife.

"Are you saying that even *those people* could elevate themselves by marrying up? I daresay, she would never be welcomed into polite society," the brunette said. "I've seen the type, the social climbers who believe a fine dress makes them a fine lady. It's my understanding he's a pig farmer or some such. Can you imagine? A pig farmer!"

Nathaniel saw Clara stiffen and he knew she must have heard the comment. Her cheeks flushed and she raised her chin a notch. God, he wanted to take her away from these prying eyes and vicious comments, but he was hardly in the position to do so. He wondered how she could endure such humiliation. And how dare her parents put her in a position to be ridiculed. "Despite her origins," he said softly, "she is lovely, isn't she?"

The brunette gave Clara an assessing look. "She's one of the most beautiful girls I've ever seen," she said, surprising Nathaniel. "In a way, I feel sorry for her."

"Everyone feels sorry for her," the redhead said. "But they also think she is ridiculous."

"I believe Whistler's painting is in the other gallery," Nathaniel put in, leading the small group away from Clara. Just as they turned away, from the corner of his eye he saw Clara look in their direction and he jerked his face aside so she would see nothing but the back of his head. It was imperative that she not know he was in London, that he was a baron, that he was part of the group who had just been cruel to her. It had nothing to do with the diamond and everything to do with how he felt at that moment. Whatever was between them, it could not end this way, and certainly not so soon. When she returned from London, he would tell her the truth about who he was.

And pray she could forgive him.

"I just don't understand it," Hedra said. "We've done everything correctly. We've gone to 'yde Park, the galleries, even the opera. I know you are causing a stir. I see the eyes following you."

The Andersons had been in London for more than two weeks, days spent attending public amusements that Hedra was convinced would bring attention to Clara. For her part, Clara did her best to keep her mother happy, though it was getting more and more difficult. Worse, the family was spending an ungodly amount of money. Her father went along silently, and while Clara knew he was just as determined as Hedra to find her a good match, the cost of the hunt weighed heavily on his mind.

Clara watched her mother pacing back and forth, wringing her hands, and her heart ached. Hedra had been certain this trip would be the success the other trips to London had not been. Armed with what she'd thought was the proper knowledge to garner invitations, Hedra had been certain this time would be different.

"We are not one of them, Mother. It is as simple as that. Perhaps we should set our sights…"

Hedra's eyes flashed with anger. "Do not say it, Clara. Nothing good will come from lowering our expectations." She slumped down onto a seat, then glared at it, for the furniture in their rented house was exceedingly uncomfortable. "If only Baron Longley had responded to my letter letting him know we are in town. He seemed so affable when we met him at the Gardeners'." She stood suddenly, her face brightening. "Do you think perhaps he never received my correspondence? Why, that would explain his silence. He was so taken with you."

"I think more that he was taken with his brandy," Clara said, producing another scowl from her mother.

"We shall have to visit the baron in person."

"No, Mother." Good Lord, the thought of showing up uninvited on a baron's doorstep was horrifying.

"Why ever not? He practically issued an invitation at the Gardeners'. I remember precisely what he said: 'You should spend some time in London, Miss Anderson. I would be more than happy to make the introductions.' If that is not an invitation, I do not know what is."

"Yes, I know what he said, Mother. But I don't think he thought we would take his invitation seriously."

"Why would we not?" Hedra said, throwing her hands in the air. She was getting agitated and Clara knew it wouldn't be long before her face grew flushed and she became flustered. Even after all this time, Clara hadn't gotten the courage to tell her mother the true reason the Gardeners had invited them to their home.

"We should visit his lordship tomorrow," Clara said in an effort to appease her mother. "Do you think we should send a note first?"

Hedra calmed immediately. "No. Let's just visit. He did invite us, after all."

The next day, the Andersons piled into their carriage and drove to Baron Longley's home in St. John's Square. When they pulled up in front of the large, Greek-inspired home with its soaring pillars, Clara swallowed heavily—at the same time her mother let out a small sound of awe. "I had no idea the baron was so wealthy," she said, then grinned at Clara. "Oh, can't you just imagine being mistress of such a fine home?"

Clara gazed up at the monument to wealth and power that was the baron's home, and felt slightly sick. Nothing good would come of this visit, she was sure of it. But perhaps this was just what her mother needed to finally accept that her dreams of marrying Clara to a titled gentleman could never be realized. Once the step was lowered, the Andersons descended from the carriage and milled in front of the house.

"You're sure of this, Mrs. Anderson?" her father asked, and Clara realized her father was nearly as nervous as she was.

"Yes," Hedra said with a firm nod. But when she rolled her lips together, Clara realized her mother was a bundle of nerves as well. Hedra looked Clara over, hastily adjusted her hat, then started up the steps to the massive entrance.

Her father lifted the large knocker, a boar's head, its mouth holding a brass ring with a hammer, and let it fall. The three jerked at the overly loud sound the knocker made, and Clara had to stifle a bit of hysterical laughter. A door opened revealing an excruciatingly proper butler, who looked them over, quickly determining they were no one of consequence despite their fine clothes and expensive carriage.

"How may I help you?" he said, addressing Clara's father.

"His lordship issued an invitation that we visit him when we were in London. We're the Andersons. Of St. Ives. Here to see Baron Longley." Clara's heart ached for her father, who seemed to be getting more and more flustered the longer he spoke. He was completely out of his element. They were *all* completely out of their element, and Clara wished she'd had the courage to insist to her mother that this visit was a mistake.

"Your card, sir." The butler held out the small, gleaming silver platter held in his pristine white-gloved hand and waited patiently while her father fished about in his pockets, finally producing a card. The butler looked at the card and hesitated before stepping back and allowing them entry, and Clara let out a breath of relief. She'd been terrified that the butler would leave them standing on the stoop. Nearly as bad, but not quite, the family was left in the foyer and Clara wondered if her parents were aware of the slight. Based on her mother's beaming face, she thought not. Clara was only aware because of her training at finishing school and the stories the other girls had told.

To Clara's surprise, the butler returned momentarily with Baron Longley not far behind. Perhaps she had been mistaken; perhaps the baron did remember the invitation. Clara dipped a curtsy, her heart hammering in her chest. The baron looked just as he had at the Gardeners', except now, the man was frowning at them.

"Mr. Burke informed me that I had issued an invitation to you. I do apologize, but I do not recall doing so."

Hedra's smile faltered a bit, but she gamely responded. "When we were at the Gardeners'. You recall, Clara was there and she sang with Miss Gardener."

The baron looked at Clara as if he'd never seen her before in his life and his eyes swept over her form in a most insulting manner. Then his expression cleared and he laughed. "I recall now. You're the companion."

Clara's cheeks flushed red.

"I'm sure you are mistaken, Lord Longley. We were invited guests of the Gardeners," Hedra said calmly enough, though Clara sensed her mother was taken aback by their reception.

The baron's gaze became icy as he turned toward Hedra. "You are the upstarts who made fools of yourselves trying to pretend you are something you are not."

"Now, now," her father said, taking a step forward. "Who do you think you are talking to?"

The baron turned to Clara's father, seemingly amused by his bluster. "You, sir, are the tin miner, are you not? While I do appreciate your... fortitude...I must ask you all to leave my home. Did you really believe I had issued an invitation to visit me in my home?"

"You did, my lord," Clara said, feeling her anger grow. "I recall precisely what you said. Then again, I was not inebriated, as you were."

The skin around the baron's thin mouth turned white. "You may leave. Now."

Clara's father made to take another step toward the baron, but Clara laid a hand on his arm. "Let us go, Father. I never did enjoy the scent of false superiority." She glared at the baron for good measure, then turned her back and headed for the door, praying her parents would follow her. With cheeks burning and eyes blurred with tears of anger and humiliation, Clara hardly was aware of the footman who opened the door for her.

Two days later, she sat with her parents in their carriage, headed south. Her mother was weepy, her father stoic, and Clara, despite her guilt, was elated. Her only regret was that her mother was clearly suffering from all that had happened in London.

"All that money, wasted," her father would mumble at least once per hour. That would bring on more tears, and Clara would comfort her mother.

"I just don't understand it," Hedra said for the hundredth time.

Clara looked at her mother sympathetically, but inside she was baffled at how consciously blind Hedra had been. No one had ever opened their arms to the Anderson family. If they were accepted at all, it was only because there was some ulterior motive. But Clara had gone along, simply to make her mother happy, to fall into the fantasy that she might be Lady Clara one day.

"No more," she said softly. At least she'd meant to say it softly. Her mother's head snapped in her direction and she began a fresh bout of tears.

"For God's sake, Mrs. Anderson, the girl is right. Enough is enough. She'll marry a good Cornish man from a good family and that will have to satisfy you."

Hedra was silent—stunned—for about thirty seconds before she began wailing, and Clara watched, frozen in place, as her father's face grew redder and redder. She wondered if she were about to witness her father strike her mother for the first time. Instead, he stared stonily out the window, and eventually Hedra's tears subsided and she fell asleep, falling against her husband, who put a gentle arm around her. Clara looked at her father and gave him a small smile. From his expression, a mixture of regret and understanding, she knew with certainty that her father had been doing for years the same thing she had—trying to make his wife's dreams come true no matter the cost.

Soon enough, the motion of the carriage and the blessed silence inside it served to lull her father to sleep, leaving Clara wide awake and alone with her thoughts. Despite her mother's misery, Clara could not stop the surge of joy that bubbled up inside. Finally, she was free. Even if she never married, at least it would be her choice. She and Harriet could live together as old spinsters in that cottage Harriet dreamed up when she'd been a girl. Or...

She could marry a handsome gardener and live on a large estate. Perhaps Lord Berkley could hire Mr. Emory and they could live out their days in St. Ives, happy together, having a family. That was all she'd ever truly wanted from life and now it seemed it might be in her grasp.

All she had to do was convince Mr. Emory that she would not be settling by marrying a gardener. At that moment, buoyed up by her joy, she thought it only a matter of time before she could convince him they could be happy together. Surely he felt the same way. A man didn't kiss a girl the way he kissed her if he were not in love. She could hardly wait to get home to see him, to convince him she had absolutely no interest in the aristocracy. If she never saw another lord or lady again it would be too soon. Other than Lord Berkley, of course, who would be their employer, and he was very nearly pleasant. For a peer.

Clara leaned her head against the well-padded carriage and gazed out the window, a dreamy smile on her face as she watched a pretty little village pass by. She'd be in St. Ives tomorrow, home, and she would never have to leave again.

When Nathaniel looked up and saw the Andersons' carriage, he had to stop himself from running toward it to make certain Clara was within. The family wasn't to have returned to St. Ives for several weeks, and he wondered what had precipitated their early return. London in the winter, with its choking fog and disease, was the last place on Earth he'd want someone he loved... He stopped that thought abruptly, shocked that it had formed in his mind so quickly, as if loving Clara was something he'd long since accepted. As the carriage went out of sight, he tried to come up with a reason to go to the front of the house but could not.

After a time, he wandered into the kitchen to see if he could get word about why the family had returned. What he found was a group of servants, some happy to be back and some bitterly disappointed to have missed Christmas in London, gathered around the large dining table for tea. They looked up as one, for he had never shared tea with the staff, instead relying on Mrs. Ellesbury to have a bit of tea delivered to him.

"Suppose you're as curious as the rest of us about why they've returned early," the cook said, her cheeks rosy from rushing around the kitchen to prepare tea for the staff.

Nathaniel took his seat and shrugged. "I am."

"That baron fellow decided not to introduce our Clara after all," she said, ignoring the butler's frown. It was his strict policy to not gossip about the family below stairs, though the staff often managed to do so. "It's a crying shame, it is. Not a lovelier girl in all of England than our Clara. Her heart must be broken."

Nathaniel had a feeling that Clara would not be at all broken-hearted, given what she'd said about the baron. Indeed, she was likely as relieved as...he was. Nathaniel frowned fiercely, which the others took as an expression of affront at what had happened to the Andersons.

"That's what 'appens when you pretend you're better than you are," Sara said, and even though she received a few glares, Nathaniel sensed everyone was in general agreement.

"Be that as it may," Mr. Standard said, "it is our role to make certain the family is well settled and glad to be home."

The remainder of the tea was taken up with listening to the adventures of the members of the staff who had been fortunate enough to travel to London. While Nathaniel found it enlightening to hear their opinion of a town he'd spent a great deal of time in, he grew bored with all the chatter and excused himself to return to the garden. Part of him regretted the Andersons' early arrival, for he would not be able to search quite as vigorously with Clara about, but the far larger part of him was glad she was back. He'd missed her, and knowing he'd missed her meant his heart was far more engaged than he wanted it to be.

This could not go on any longer. He was going to have to tell her who he was, why he was in St. Ives, and beg her to remain silent until he found the diamond. She would be angry, of course, but he prayed she would not be so angry that she gave him up to her parents. Just the thought of facing Mr. Anderson's wrath was enough to make even the bravest of men quake. The man looked like he could bend iron with his bare hands and Nathaniel had a feeling the older man wouldn't take kindly to be made a fool of.

As he made his way back to the garden, Nathaniel rehearsed in his head what he would say to her. He would apologize, of course, kiss her until she forgave him. Now that made the lies well worth it, he thought. It was well on dusk, so he resigned himself to another lonely night in his room. At least it would give him enough time to go over what he planned to say to Clara to lessen the blow. Flinging himself down onto his small bed, he allowed himself to imagine that more than kisses were required to convince her to forgive him. And from there, it didn't take much for him to imagine her naked, warm, and willing beneath him.

He reached into his trousers and let out a low groan as he wrapped his hand around his cock. He was hard and hurting and there was only one thing that could ease the ache at this particular moment, given he was alone and would likely remain so for the foreseeable future. God, what he wouldn't give to have her hand touching him, giving him the release he desperately needed. Her mouth there, her breasts before him, her tongue tasting him...

"Mr. Emory?"

Nathaniel withdrew his hand as if he were holding a live snake, not his rock-hard cock, and stifled a harsh curse. Swallowing, trying to draw air into his lungs, he sat up, then yanked his shirt from his pants in an effort to cover his obvious physical state.

"Mr. Emory?" This time her soft call was accompanied by a knock on his back door.

"One minute, Miss Anderson," he called, fumbling for a match so he could light a lamp. While he'd been lost in his delicious fantasy, it had grown nearly completely dark. What the hell was she doing outside his room?

His frustration must have shown on his face when he opened the door, for she stepped back, suddenly looking wary. She gave him a small smile. "We're back."

"I can see," he said, which made her giggle.

"How..." She looked toward the house as if reconsidering her visit. Clearing her throat, she asked, "How is the garden?"

"You are not here to talk about the garden."

Another woman might have dipped her head in embarrassment at being so transparent, but Clara laughed. "No," she said, still smiling. "I am not. I am here to see you."

Should this happen again, I will know full well what I am doing. I want you to know this.

His erection, which had only slightly subsided, once again pressed hard against his trousers. It was Nathaniel's greatest wish at that moment that he was not a man of honor. If he had no honor, he would drag Clara into his arms and make love to her without a single regret. Alas, he was not brought up to deflower innocents nor to baldly lie to those he cared for.

"Miss Anderson," he said, aware that his voice sounded strained. "We should not."

Her brow instantly furrowed, and then the sudden realization of what he was saying hit her. Her mouth flew open, quickly followed by her hand, which made an audible sound when it covered her mouth. "Oh, goodness," she said, her words muffled.

"I misunderstood, it seems," Nathaniel said, ignoring a sharp stab of disappointment, which he masked with a low chuckle, aimed more at himself than at her.

Her eyes turned to half moons above her hand and she started to laugh. "I can certainly understand why you came to that conclusion," she managed to say when she withdrew her hand after finally getting control of herself.

"Why are you here, Miss Anderson?" Nathaniel asked, grinning. "If not to torture me and give me false hope?"

"You are a cad," she said lightly, then tilted her head in thought. "I wanted to see you, I suppose. To let you know the family has returned."

"Yes, I know."

"But do you know the reason why we returned?" He shook his head and she continued. "As tragic as this trip was to my mother, it was wonderful for me. I am finally free, Mr. Emory. My mother no longer has delusions that I will marry a titled man."

"What happened?" Nathaniel asked gruffly, remembering how the Andersons had been mocked at the art gallery. By God, if anyone had hurt her, they would pay.

"May we walk?"

Nathaniel put out the lantern he held and placed it back on its hook before following Clara out into the garden. Indeed, it was completely dark outside, without even a moon to light their way, and it took a few moments before Nathaniel could see well enough to follow her. Though it was nearly Christmas, the air was brisk, rather than cold, and the sky above them was clear. "Tell me your tale of woe," he said when he reached her side.

She told him about a baron, some rude sod who'd leered at her and likely wanted her in his bed but certainly not in a church as his bride. Nathaniel could feel his blood burning as she related the humiliating scene, just one of several humiliations the family had faced in the short time they'd been away. He wasn't certain whether he wanted to throttle the baron or her parents more. What in God's name had they been thinking, dragging poor Clara around London like some pet pony?

"I hate them all," she said fiercely. "Every last one of them and I think that, finally, my mother feels the same." She turned to him, and he could see the fury on her face even in the darkness. "How dare they believe they are better, that somehow my blood would taint theirs? They have done nothing to deserve the position to which they were born, and most of them, even with their power and money, do nothing but squander their lives on frivolity. Yes, some of them give to the poor, but it's only to assuage their own guilt. None of them would know what it means to have nothing, to work hard and save and make yourself into something respectable. Like my father. He's ten times the man the baron is, and yet he was made to feel less. I will never forget that feeling, the way my poor father was humiliated and scorned by a man who isn't fit to walk the same path."

She was so angry, she nearly lost her breath on the last word and Nathaniel was momentarily horrified that she might faint.

"Surely, not all members of the aristocracy are bad," he said, seeing his hopes of her understanding his lies slip away. *Not all barons are bad, Clara, I am a baron and I'm a good fellow. Except for lying to you for months and pretending I am someone I am not for the purpose of removing something from your property.* Yes, that would be lovely.

"I've yet to meet one I would like to spend more than a single hour with. Pompous fools. They waste what they've been given and marry heiresses simply to go on with their wasteful lives."

Nathaniel could feel his cheeks blush, for her description very nearly matched his own situation. "I know there are good men in the peerage who take their responsibilities seriously, who would sacrifice their own comfort to help those who depend upon them. Yes, there are those who become impoverished thanks to their own actions or the actions of their forefathers, but you must not cast them all in the same light."

"Mustn't I?" she asked, and marched away from him, clearly upset with his response. "You sound like one of them." This was muttered, under her breath, and for one long moment, he debated telling her the truth. *I am one of them.*

But he couldn't. If he did, he would lose her forever and it was vitally important that he not. What the future would bring, he couldn't know, but he wasn't ready to have her hate him. Not yet. It would happen, of this he was certain, but for now, he wanted things to remain as they were.

"What of Lord Berkley?" he asked, just the smallest amount of desperation in his voice. "You've said good things about him."

She stopped and whirled about. "Do you believe for one instant that the earl would offer for me? Do you? I'm pretty. I speak like a lady and comport myself like a lady. Most of the time. Be honest, Mr. Emory, would he?"

Nathaniel looked down at the dew-covered grass before looking at her. She was so damned beautiful, so strong and fierce and any man would be lucky to call her his wife. Yet he knew with a certainty that the earl would never offer for her. "No, he would not."

"Why? Because of my low birth? What does that even mean?" She flung her arms akimbo in pure frustration. "And if he was desperate enough to marry a nobody, he would always think in the back of his mind that I was not worthy of him. It would be there, this stupid rule society invented to keep the classes apart. I tell you I am glad my mother has finally understood what I have known all along. Now I can marry whom I please, Mr. Emory. That is what I came out to tell you this evening."

Those words hung there between them until they grew thick and heavy and fell away. If he were a gardener, he might have gotten down on one knee in that instant and asked her to marry him. But he was not a gardener. He was a baron, a member of the aristocracy, a part of society Clara loathed with all her being. So he said nothing and tried to ignore the momentary pain that flickered on her lovely face.

"We've been invited to the earl's ball," Hedra gushed. It was the day after her parents' return from London and they'd been eating breakfast in silence. Her mother was still acting as if someone in the family had died, and her father's silence seemed even heavier, making Clara feel terribly guilty about feeling such vast relief over what had transpired. Until her mother said those words.

"Mr. Anderson, do you hear? The earl's ball! The very same ball that we would never have been invited to if not for our luncheon. I *knew* he was interested in our Clara. I just knew it." Hedra read the invitation again and with every word, Clara's stomach clenched tighter and tighter. It would never end. Never.

"Mother," Clara said, trying with all her strength not to scream. But Hedra was so excited, she either ignored or didn't hear her daughter's tone. While Clara was glad to see her mother smiling once again, she couldn't help but wonder why the earl had bothered to invite them. It made no sense that he'd done so, given the list of peers rumored to have been invited to the ball. No secret had been made of the fact the ball was being held for one reason and one reason only: for the earl to find a bride. And now, her family had been invited and her mother's hopes were raised again.

With a sickening feeling of dread, she knew this could not go well. Clara wasn't certain she could take another humiliation, especially after what had happened between her and Mr. Emory the night before.

Of all the humiliations that London had wrought—and there had been many—nothing had been quite as humiliating as the silence that followed her declaration that she could marry whom she pleased. What had she thought? That he would fall on bended knee and beg her to be his wife?

That actually was precisely what she had imagined might happen. She could understand his not acting immediately, but she could not understand him saying nothing. Finally, she'd let out a nervous laugh and said, "It's a good thing because the baker's son has been sweet on me for years. I can marry him now. Or anyone."

"I am glad for you."

I am glad for you. Ugh!

She'd thought she and he wanted the same thing, that the only thing separating them was her parents' wish that she marry above herself. Their night had not ended with a kiss, as she had secretly hoped, but with a polite nod. As if as soon as she mentioned marriage, something inside him had switched off.

Perhaps kisses had been the only thing he'd ever wanted. God, she was such a fool.

Her mother was prattling on about dresses and the ball and things Clara didn't care a fig for. She wanted to scream for everyone to stop talking, for everyone to just leave her be. She wanted to scream and scream and scream.

Instead, she smiled and pretended to be excited by the news. Even Harriet, who disliked such social events, seemed excited by the possibility of going to the ball. Then again, Harriet had grown a bit spoony about Lord Berkley. The earl had been inordinately kind to her younger sister during their luncheon together, had even commented on Harriet's pretty eyes. She prayed the earl would continue to be kind. Wasn't the invitation proof of his kindness?

Once breakfast was finished, her mother disappeared to decide what she would wear to the ball and Harriet disappeared, an odd dreamy look on her face that Clara had never seen before. She prayed Harriet was not putting too much stock on the invitation. Her father put aside his newspaper and made a poor attempt at stifling a belch, which made Clara smile. While Silas might dress like a gentleman and follow his wife's plans, Clara had a feeling his participation was not nearly as whole-hearted as he pretended.

"You don't want to go to the ball, do you, Clara?"

"I hate to see Mother disappointed again."

He sighed. "You used to call her Mama and me Papa." He frowned briefly, as if wishing he hadn't said that thought aloud.

"I remember. And I remember our little room under the rafters. I love this house, I do, but sometimes I miss the way it used to be."

He grunted out something that Clara took for agreement, then said, "Your mother, she'll be fine."

When her father left, Clara sat for a long moment alone, staring at her uneaten breakfast and feeling slightly ill. The man she loved clearly did not love her and her mother still harbored hopes she would marry the earl.

On any other morning that was sunny and bright, as that morning was, Clara would have immediately grabbed her straw hat, apron, and gloves, and headed out to the garden. Today, though, it seemed as if she shouldn't. Mr. Emory would be there, of course, and the thought of speaking to him after the prior evening's humiliation was just too much. Why, it was almost as if the man hadn't a clue what she'd been hinting at.

It was then, just as she was heading to her room to read or mope about aimlessly, that she stopped suddenly. Was it possible that Mr. Emory hadn't understood what she'd been hinting at? How many times had she heard her mother or her maid complain about how thick-headed some men were when it came to women? Charlie hadn't even known why Jeanine had started to sob when they'd learned they would miss Christmas in St. Ives.

"How could he not know?" she'd wailed. "He must know I'm expecting a proposal this year. He must!"

But he hadn't. Charlie was a good fellow who adored Jeanine, and yet he hadn't realized why she was upset until, upon their return, Jeanine finally broke down and told him why. He'd been flummoxed, then thoughtful. And then told Jeanine she had nothing to worry over. That she was just a silly goose. Since then, Jeanine had been floating on a cloud, dreaming of setting up house and having babies. Truly, she was impossible to speak to for her mind continued to drift away.

Was it possible that Mr. Emory hadn't realized that she'd been telling him she could marry anyone—including him? That the only reason she would bring up such a subject was so he would ask her? Of course that was it! She thought back to their talks, their passionate kisses, the words he'd said to her before she'd left for London, how he thought he wasn't good enough for her. But he was so wrong!

You deserve better than to be treated like some common trollop. I cannot marry you, Miss Anderson. You do know that, do you not?

She would simply have to let him know that he *could* marry her, that her father would have no objection—at least she didn't think he would have an objection. Oh, it didn't matter if she were an heiress and he was a gardener, not if they loved one another... Was it possible he didn't love her? She couldn't go up to him and ask, could she?

Clara headed to her room, hoping to quiz Jeanine about the moment she realized Charlie was in love with her. She found Jeanine going through the wardrobe and pulling out all Clara's ball gowns, which only made Clara wince. She did not want to think about the ball, not at a time like this when it seemed her entire life hung in the balance.

"Jeanine, come away from there. I don't want to even think about the ball tomorrow night. Perhaps we could just sit and talk."

Her maid immediately stopped what she was doing. "It looks like you've got something buzzing about that head of yours," Jeanine said.

"I do." Clara took a seat at her tufted vanity chair and faced her maid. "How long have you known you loved Charlie?"

Jeanine's cheeks instantly pinkened. "Oh, three years now."

"Truly? You only began mentioning him to me last year."

Jeanine shrugged. "It wasn't something I wanted to discuss. Not until I knew he returned my feelings."

"And how did you know that?"

"He brought my mother my saffron buns. I couldn't go home that year; you'd been invited to that house party in Coventry. Remember? I was a bit upset, and he said, 'I'll bring 'em to your ma, Miss Parker.' And that's when I knew."

Clara frowned. "Oh."

"You see, my mother lives a good twenty miles from here and there is no easy way to go. No rail line or direct road. It took him two days, there and back, just to bring my mother saffron buns. That's when I knew."

Silly tears threatened Clara's eyes. "Yes, that would do it, wouldn't it?" She paused, worrying her lower lip a bit. "Has he ever said the words?"

"That he loves me? Nah," Jeanine said, laughing. "I don't need words to know."

"But wouldn't it be nice if he did say them?"

"I suppose it would be nice. He's said other things, though. He once said the only thing he liked better than a day fishing was a day spent with me." She giggled, sounding like a young girl. "If that's not love, I don't know what is. You know how much he loves to fish."

Clara laughed, glad that Jeanine had found someone she understood— and who obviously understood her.

"I think I'll go out and work a bit in the garden. It will keep my mind off of the ball."

Jeanine laughed. She was one of the few people who understood how much Clara dreaded such events.

Though the sun was shining, it was a cold, blustery day and her garden looked rather sad. While she had been in London, Mr. Emory had prepared the garden for the winter, pruning back her roses and gathering seeds from plants that lived only one season in anticipation of the spring. Though the temperature rarely dipped below freezing in St. Ives, gardens lost their luster, the only brilliant color coming from the fire bushes that lined one walkway. If they had a hothouse, Clara would have plenty to work on, but as it was, there was little for her to do in the garden and no real reason to be out there at all.

When she reached the plot, she found herself alone and feeling a bit foolish for coming out at all. Walking along the gravel path, now littered with dead leaves, Clara felt uncommonly melancholy, as if the glory and joy of her garden would never again be realized. Strangely, Mr. Emory had continued to work land that wasn't part of the garden plan, and Clara wondered what he was devising. Small disturbances stretched from the edge of the cultivated land outward, as if he'd driven a spade into the land again and again. Curious, Clara followed the path of the marks, noting the sharp slices in the earth, each about six inches apart, long rows that ended abruptly about twenty yards from their small pond.

Since Mr. Emory was not working, Clara continued walking toward the pond, imagining a small fountain in the middle. Wrapping her coat more tightly around her, she sat down on a small bench Mr. Emory had placed there, and could feel the cold iron even through her thick layers of clothing. The citizens of St. Ives were luckier than most residents of England, many of whom were likely experiencing the snow and ice of the winter season. Still, Clara found herself longing for those long, warm days of summer.

"Your mother wants a folly."

Clara smiled upon hearing Mr. Emory's warm baritone behind her. It was so breezy, she hadn't heard his approach. She turned and looked up, screwing up her features and holding her hand over her eyes to block the bright sun. He stood there in silhouette, all brawn and strength, a shovel resting on his shoulder.

"A small folly might be charming," she said, trying to steady the mad beating of her heart. "Perhaps we can build one after the hothouse is completed."

He came around to the front of the bench and propped one foot on it, looking down at her with an unreadable expression. A sudden gust of wind nearly blew the hat from his head and he smiled crookedly as he wrestled it back on. "Seems cold, but where I grew up, this is what summer feels like."

"Where did you grow up?"

"Cumbria, not far from the Scottish border. We'd get snow starting in November. Likely snow on the ground even now."

"I've never seen snow. I was hoping to in London. What's it like? I imagine it's lovely."

"It's cold, that's for certain, and yes, it's pretty. It'll take your breath away, seeing the sun shining down after a storm, everything covered in white, the air so cold you can hardly breathe. St. Ives seems tropical compared to that."

Clara drew her knees up and wrapped her arms around her legs; it was hardly the most ladylike pose, but she cared not. "You must miss your family."

"I have none," he said matter-of-factly. "My father died when I was fifteen and my mother the day I was born."

"What is your birthday? Have we missed it?"

"Just. October twenty-eighth I turned twenty-six."

"As old as all that?" Clara asked, teasing him. She would have guessed him older, for he had a small amount of gray by his temples. "No one remembered, did they?"

"No one has in a very long time," he said without the smallest bit of self-pity. Still, it made Clara's heart break to know he was so alone. "Women tend to remember such things, and I have had no women in my life for many years. I vaguely remember my grandmother, a stern woman who smelled like peppermint."

"And do you come from a long line of gardeners?"

He looked suddenly uncomfortable, and Clara wondered if he were ashamed of his profession. "I am the first," he said with a small bow, as if he were introducing himself.

Clara wanted to ask him more about himself, but she sensed her questions would not be welcomed. Still, she did wonder how a man whose diction was nearly as fine as Lord Berkley's ended up laboring in a garden. Clearly, he'd received some sort of education. Many families fell on hard times and lost everything, so perhaps Mr. Emory's story was similar.

"Someday I hope to hear more, sir, but for now I'll let you be."

"And what of you? What are you doing out here alone, staring gloomily at the pond?"

She wrinkled her nose. "I am a bit out of sorts, if you must know. Lord Berkley issued a last-minute invitation to his ball. It's well known he's throwing the ball to find a bride. My mother is beside herself with joy."

He let out a deep chuckle. "And you, less so, I take it."

"I very much fear she will again begin her quest when all I really want—" She snapped her mouth shut, unwilling to go down that particular humiliating path again.

He let out a long sigh and sat down beside her, and Clara briefly squeezed her eyes shut. That sigh seemed to hold more meaning than many long speeches, and it suddenly became important that he not say whatever it was he was preparing to say.

"Mr. Emory, you do not have to make your speech. I have a tendency to see things, believe things, that can never be. In that way, I am more like my mother than I would like to admit. It is true, I did think more of our friendship than I should have—" He laid a finger on her lips and she gave him a hesitant look.

"Stop talking, Miss Anderson. Please." When she raised her brows in question, he dropped his finger. "What were you supposed to think when nearly every time we were together, I molested you." When she made to protest his characterization of their relationship, he smiled and showed her his index finger as a teasing warning, and she snapped her mouth shut. Another sigh, this one a sharp puff of air. "I need to say something to you, and that is I adore you, Miss Anderson. I think about you more than I should. I think about what it would be like if my life wasn't what it is, if I were free to do what I wished. You cannot know, not now, what the reasons are for my silence. I pray someday I will be in a position to tell you. Only then will you understand why it is impossible for us to plan a future together. I have no future to offer to you."

Clara did understand his words—she was not a dolt—but what she actually heard was that he wanted to marry her, but that something was holding him back, something that someday might be resolved. And that meant that someday they would be able to be together. She could hardly keep her heart from leaping out of her chest. "If you are in trouble, I may be able to help you," she said.

Her words seemed to make him miserable. "God, you are too good, Miss Anderson." He stared down at his fists, clenched together between his knees. "You may hate me someday."

"I could never—"

His head snapped up and he appeared nearly angry. "You may. You likely will."

Raising one eyebrow, she said, "You cannot make me hate you, Mr. Emory. No matter your deep, dark secret." She was silent for a time, her thoughts buzzing about her head. "It isn't murder, is it?"

"No."

Another, worse, thought came to her. "Are you married?"

He let out a low chuckle. "No."

Relief nearly made her weak. "Then I daresay there is nothing so horrible that I could not forgive you."

He shook his head, a worrying gesture, for Clara couldn't imagine what he was hiding that would cause her to cast aside her feelings for him. "Of all the women I have ever met, Miss Anderson, you deserve to be a lady. You are more worthy than any other."

"That is where you are wrong. I will die before I marry one of those pompous prigs."

He chuckled lightly as he looked away. "That is a rather dire prediction and one I pray does not come true."

"It won't, as I have no intention of marrying a title. It's a mister for me or nothing."

Chapter 11

If Clara hadn't seemed quite so miserable about the prospect of going to a ball filled with the hated aristocracy, Nathaniel would have found it difficult to remain at the Anderson home while she was likely being ogled by titled gentlemen. His mistake was wandering to the front of the house that night, like some lovestruck fool, hoping he might catch a glimpse of her in her finery. Hiding about in bushes wasn't the most dignified thing he had ever done, but he found he could not help himself. This... thing...that had happened to him was rather terrifying. He could not stop his heartbeat from speeding up when he saw her; nor could he stop the state of near-painful arousal whenever he allowed his mind to go where it shouldn't. Worse, his heart ached for her nearly as much as his cock.

He loved her. He loved her and he was going to lose her. But at least he could enjoy her company a bit more before he was forced to tell her who he was. When he found the diamond, he would tell her everything and pray she could forgive him. His conscience bothered him more than he wished, but he'd be damned if he walked away now, not after all this time. The bloody diamond had to be in that small section of land he hadn't yet had a chance to investigate.

A sharp rectangle of light showed on the front lawn from the well-lit parlor. Inside, he could see the younger daughter looking particularly pretty in a gown that looked like it cost a small fortune. Mr. Anderson turned his back to his daughter and snuck a drink of something, and Nathaniel smiled. The old dog was likely dreading this evening as much as his daughter. And then, the old man turned and smiled, and Nathaniel had a feeling Clara had just walked into the room, for there were very few people in the world who could resist smiling at her.

Nathaniel breathed in sharply, stunned by how beautiful she looked. Day after day he'd spent with her in the garden. He'd thought her beautiful in her plain clothes and that silly straw hat, but seeing her dressed in a rich burgundy ball gown that showed off her lovely curves, her hair in an intricate coiffure, he could hardly take his eyes from her. Suddenly, the thought that other men would be talking with her, dancing with her, touching her seemed unacceptable. My God, she would look lovely as mistress of Lion's Gate. They would hold a ball, a celebration of the restoration of his estates and his tenants' livings. Perhaps in a year or two, when things were looking better, when the farmers had a chance to increase their earnings, he would invite the entire region to meet his baroness.

In that moment, staring at her, he realized he wanted her there, by his side, until the day he died. And he also realized that his lies might have doomed his love before it even had a chance to show itself. He wished suddenly, fiercely, that his grandfather had never told him about the diamond. Perhaps he would have met Clara at an event, seen her at the opera, perhaps even attended the very ball she was now attending. Surely, he would have recognized her for the beauty she was. He had no relatives to object to their marriage, no one who would disown him if he married a commoner, and not only a commoner but one who came from such a family.

"I'll make you understand," he whispered as he watched her father lay a cloak across her shoulders. He closed his eyes and imagined himself there, in that room, bending his head to kiss her smooth shoulder, moving to her neck, bringing his hand around to her front and pulling her against him. Well, of course not with her parents in the room. He chuckled at that unsavory image.

For several long hours, Nathaniel lay awake, knowing he was waiting for the sound of the family's carriage coming back. His lamp was still lit and he'd been trying to read, to no avail. It would be hours before they returned, perhaps not even until the sun was beginning to rise. All the balls he'd attended had ended in the wee hours of the morning, the eastern sky turning pink. He was leaning over to turn down his lamp when he heard the unmistakable sound of a carriage moving up the drive. It couldn't be the Andersons returning; the ball would have just been getting under way.

Curious, he sat up and pulled on his boots before quickly donning his coat and heading outside to see who it was arriving at the Andersons' at such an unseemly hour.

"'arriot, you're our lash 'ope," he heard a woman wail before a door closed firmly.

The Andersons' garish carriage sat in front of the house with the driver and footman lingering, heads together as they talked. They looked up when he approached. "Home early," Nathaniel said.

"Smoke?" the driver offered. Nathaniel took the cigar with thanks and bit off the end before holding it to the flame the driver held out. "They got thrown out on their tails."

"Thrown out?" Nathaniel said, trying to stem his concern.

"I don't like telling tales, but the mister and missus were as drunk as an 'and cart, they were. I think that's why they tossed 'em out like so much garbage," the footman said, then leaned forward and whispered, "From the look on Miss Clara's face, I think she might 'ave done something. She looked like a cat that just ate a mouse. Now, Miss 'arriet, she seemed right upset. No tears, mind you, but none too 'appy."

Knowing Clara's dislike of the aristocracy, Nathaniel thought it wouldn't be too far a stretch of the imagination to think she might have gotten upset at some slight then let her opinion be known. "You don't know what happened, then?"

The driver spit. "Nah. But, like I said, the two of 'em were drunk."

"Yes," Nathaniel said. "As a hand cart." He chatted with the two men for a while before wishing them a good night and heading back to his room, only to see a shadow flitting toward his room that looked suspiciously like it was wearing a ball gown.

Walking stealthily behind her, he followed Clara as she went around the back of the shed. He watched, amused, as she tiptoed to his door and tapped lightly. "Mr. Emory?" she whispered harshly.

"Yes?"

Claire would have let out a scream, but a large hand covered her mouth before even the smallest of sounds could escape. She could feel, more than hear, him laughing at her, the scoundrel, but she was soon joining him. When he dropped his hand, he replaced it with his mouth, a soft, lingering kiss that managed to clear her mind of everything but him.

"Hello," he said, drawing back. "To what do I owe the pleasure?"

"Tonight was an unmitigated disaster," she said happily.

"So I heard. What happened?"

Clara leaned against the shed and he joined her there, his arm against her shoulder, warm and comforting and just slightly improper. They stared at the moon, a silver sliver in the sky, as she related the story of the ball, how her mother had gotten drunk and caused a scene, how her father had only made matters worse.

"So you see? It is finally over."

"What is finally over?"

"My mother has given up the aristocracy! She hates them as much as I do. Isn't it wonderful?"

"Not particularly," he muttered, then kissed her when she was about to protest. His kisses had a way of making her go instantly quiet. A low rumble of pure male satisfaction vibrated through him as he deepened the kiss and she became a rag doll in his arms. That was another thing that happened when he kissed her—she lost all feeling in her limbs, and all other feeling coalesced in her breasts and between her legs in a rather delightful way.

"I've wanted to do this all night," he said, then dropped a kiss on her bare shoulder. His beard was rough against her skin, but it was a wonderful sensation that made her feel almost delicate. One by one, he dropped slow, soft kisses on her shoulder, her neck, her jaw, her throat, then moved down until he kissed the top of one breast peeking above her gown. Running her hands through his hair, she let him do as he wished, reveling in the sensations he was producing. All thoughts of what was proper and improper were gone, replaced only by another, more urgent thought: Don't stop.

Clara had spent summers at her grandparents' farm and she knew the basics of what making love was, though she wasn't quite sure how a man and woman went about it. When he dipped his hand beneath her gown and brushed her nipple, she knew if he asked, she would gladly lose her innocence to him. She would allow him to make love to her and she would welcome it. Celebrate it. Perhaps that made her wanton or as common as everyone thought her, but with him touching her as he was, she couldn't bring herself to care.

The cool night air struck her breast as he tugged her gown down to expose her left breast, pale in the moonlight. For a moment, he stared at her, then smiled. "Look what I've done."

"Nothing that cannot be undone," she said, sounding breathless.

He frowned at that. "Nothing that happens this evening cannot be undone. I am not such a cad as that. Clara."

"Clara. Yes." She knew what he meant, that he would not take her virginity this night, and as much as she desired him, at that moment, she was relieved.

He dipped his head and flicked his tongue against her turgid nipple, then drew the peak into his mouth, sucking lightly, and Clara thought she just might dissolve into a million pieces. The flood of desire that hit her at that moment was nearly more than she could take without crying out, but she pressed her lips together and let out a small whimper. He immediately stopped.

"No," she managed to say.

"Very well, I am—" He began to pull away, but Clara hung on tightly.

Clara shook her head and tried to find the right words in her muddled head. "I meant, no, do not stop." She smiled at his relief. "It's quite lovely." Then he grinned and kissed her, thrusting his clever tongue against hers, teaching her how to kiss a man. She could feel his arousal against her stomach, long and hard, and so foreign. Men were such odd creatures, so the opposite of women, and at that moment, Clara was glad of it.

Again, his kisses left a trail from her mouth to the tip of her exposed breast, the breeze cooling her heated skin. With one deft movement, both breasts were revealed, and Clara let out a short laugh when he said, "Look what I've done now."

"You are very clever," Clara said, winning a smile. He took one breast in each hand and moved his thumbs over her stiff nipples, and Clara couldn't help but let her head drop back against the rough shingles of his shed. This was divine, she thought, then gasped when he again suckled her, first one breast, then the other. His manhood pressed against her, between her legs, producing the most exquisite feeling she'd ever had and making her nearly frantic for more, though she didn't know how or what to ask.

"Shh, darling. Let me ease you. Let me."

Clara was gasping for breath, unaware of what he meant, until he began lifting her skirts and she knew where his hand was headed. She stiffened instinctively.

"No?" he asked, pausing.

"I…I don't know. I don't know what I want." She took a long, shaky breath. "Is it very wicked if I say yes?"

"Very," he said. "But I rather like it when you are wicked." He kissed her, a quick buss. "But if you want to stop, I will. I will always do as you say."

"Always?"

"In these matters, yes."

She bit her lip. "Will it hurt?"

"No. I am not taking your maidenhead, that is for your husband on your wedding night. This will feel like you've gone to heaven and back."

"Go on with you," she said, in a clear Cornish accent, which produced another laugh from him.

"Have you…" He kissed her breast. "…never touched yourself? Down there?"

"No." Though lately, she'd wanted to, had squeezed her legs together simply to produce that lovely feeling that came when she thought of him kissing her. If she had touched herself, she very much doubted she would have admitted such a mortifying thing.

"Then let me show you. Will you?"

Clara hesitated only a breath before she nodded.

"Just that. I promise." He kissed her again, one of those long, drugging kisses that made her want to squeeze her legs again. But he was raising up her skirts and she could feel his hot hand high on her thigh with only the thinnest silk drawers between his palm and her flesh, and she found she could hardly breathe with anticipation of what he would do next. All the while, he kissed her, dipping now and then to suckle one nipple, drawing it into his mouth, flicking it with his tongue. She felt herself melting again, felt herself grow embarrassingly wet. When his fingers touched the apex of her legs, felt how wet she was, he let out a growl. "Ah," he said low against her ear. "Here you are."

Clara inhaled sharply. Yes, there she was, that was the place where all sensation seemed to center, that spot. That very spot that he was touching, her beloved Nathaniel. She squeezed her eyes shut, trying to keep all the feeling in, keep everything in, lest it go flying away.

"Oh, God," she said when she didn't think she could take much more. It was so good, so different from anything she'd ever felt before in her life. She wanted him to touch her forever and wanted it to stop, for how could one body feel such pleasure without bursting? Without thought, she rocked her hips as he moved his hand against her, his breath, harsh and warm, against her ear. Her own breath quickened and his movements increased, a subtle pressure. And then, she did burst; colors and light and incredible sensation flooded her body, made her cry out, made her hips move uncontrollably. He'd brought her to heaven just as he'd promised, and she leaned against him, drained, as her body continued to pulse.

For a long moment, they were silent, their breaths mingling as he held her tightly. "Heaven?" he asked.

"Heaven," she whispered. He pressed himself against her, and Clara realized he was still hard. He groaned, then drew back, his hands on her naked shoulders before he gently returned her dress to its proper place.

"Do you realize how much I want you?"

"A great deal?"

He let out a short laugh. "Quite a bit more than that. You are so lovely and I…"

"Yes?" *I love you. I love you. I love you.*

"Mr. Emory. Hello?" It was Mr. Standard, and he was just on the other side of the wall.

With quick movements, Nathaniel pulled Clara into the shadows and entered his room to find his future butler standing at the threshold, a dark silhouette. "Ah, Mr. Standard," he said loudly. "Just enjoying this lovely night. Have a seat, will you?" He prayed Clara understood that she should make her escape back to the house.

Nathaniel quickly relit his lamp, then dragged his only chair and swung it about until it faced his bed. "Have a seat, will you? You must be weary from the trip to London and back."

"Indeed I am, sir," he said. The butler had conditioned himself to not call Nathaniel "my lord" but he still found it difficult to call him mister. "I would not have interrupted your evening, but this came moments ago and seemed urgent." He handed over a telegram and Nathaniel took it, foreboding filling him. His solicitor had been instructed to contact him via telegram only in an emergency.

Lion's Gate fire. Stop.

Nathaniel's heart plummeted so quickly, he felt ill. He stared at the telegram, hoping he'd misread the words and silently cursing his solicitor for his brevity, no doubt precipitated by the man's unwillingness to part with money. Did he mean Nathaniel's beloved home was in ruins? Letting out a low curse, he crumpled the missive.

"I hope it's not bad news, sir." Then Mr. Standard blushed, aware of his transparency. "I couldn't help but read it. Lion's Gate is your country seat in Cumbria, is it not?"

"Yes, Mr. Standard, and it's the only home I have left other than a small estate near Lancaster that is in total ruins. And this humble abode," he said, looking around his mean little room. "It appears I need to request a leave, sir. It's actually good timing, as I have little to do here until the hothouse is built."

Mr. Standard leaned forward. "Shall I continue your search? If you could tell me what it is you are looking for, I'm certain I could be of help."

Nathaniel considered the offer briefly before shaking his head. "I believe that would only arouse suspicion. I know you are eager to begin your new post, and I promise you it will come to you one day, but it can wait. What cannot wait is my leaving for Lion's Gate immediately. I would appreciate it if you could inform Mr. Anderson of my departure and assure him I will return before spring."

Nathaniel stood and the butler followed suit. "Do you happen to know when the first train to London is?"

"Nine o'clock to St. Erth, then on to London. Wish we had taken the train. Would have cut our travel in half."

Nathaniel slapped the butler on his back and led him out. "When we leave here, you can be assured we will take the train."

Once the butler had gone, Nathaniel packed a bag and set it aside for the morning. Staring at the small trunk, he wondered how he could get a message to Clara without arousing the suspicion of the staff or her family. He certainly couldn't give a note to Mr. Standard and ask that he hand it to Clara. Leaving now, after what they'd shared, seemed wrong but he wasn't sure what alternative he had. If Lion's Gate had been destroyed, he would at the very least have to assess the damage and devise a plan, a depressing thought. His funds were woefully low and his debts mounted by the day.

Weeks he'd be gone, weeks lost in which the diamond would continue to sit in the earth. Perhaps the worst thought to cross his mind was knowing that he if married Clara, he could at least begin to make some of the changes he needed to. If she were his wife, his search for the diamond would no longer have to be done in secret. But for her to marry him, he would have to tell her the truth, that he had lied and betrayed her, had listened, amused, to her rant about the aristocracy.

Still...

She was an heiress. He loved her. And the diamond was still here, still hidden. Marrying Clara, which had seemed such an unlikely thing not long ago, now seemed to be the perfect solution to his problems. Nathaniel sat on his bed and banged his head gently against the wall, and then not so gently. "Damned if you do and damned if you don't," he said softly. No matter what happened, neither he nor Clara could be happy. That fairy tale had ended the minute he'd taken her in his arms.

"He's what?"

"Gone, miss, for at least a month, perhaps more. A family emergency."

"But he has no family." Even as Clara said the words, her mouth snapped shut. Could this day get any worse? Harriet's heart had been broken—even now she was up in her room quietly crying. Lord Berkley had come this morning to see Harriet, and Clara had been convinced he was here to ask her sister for her hand in marriage. But he'd left without proposing, and Harriet had immediately gone to her room, her soft sobs filtering through the wall that separated their rooms. Now, the man Clara loved had left without saying a word. "Very well. Thank you, Mr. Standard."

Jane Goodger

"He did extend his apologies for not being able to organize the garden shed before leaving."

Clara had begun walking away when Mr. Standard said those words, which caused her to pause briefly. The shed had been meticulously organized the last time she'd been inside. "Thank you, Mr. Standard."

Clara immediately stepped outside and walked directly to the garden shed. It seemed strange that Mr. Emory—Nathaniel—was gone and she half expected to see him in the garden, toiling beneath the sun. She opened the shed door, allowing the day's bright sunshine into the large room, her eyes immediately going to a jumbled pile of small garden tools left in one corner of the room. Never before had an untidy pile delighted Clara more, although part of her wondered at the obvious nature of it. Obvious to her, at any rate.

Without a care for her dress, she knelt on the hard floor and began sifting through the small tools, smiling when she spied a bit of paper at the bottom, folded neatly. She pulled it out gently, and opened it, as if it were something delicate.

His writing was bold and lovely, the penmanship of a well-educated man.

> *Dearest Miss Anderson:*
> *I have been called away on an emergency. It is with a heavy heart that I leave, this day of all days. Please know that you will be in my thoughts and that I promise I will return to you. I adore you, Miss Anderson. Never forget that.*
> *Yrs,*
> *Nathaniel Emory*

Tears pricked at her eyes as she re-read the words. *I adore you.* That was very close to a declaration of love. And he promised, not to return to St. Ives, but to return to her. She would most certainly wait. She would happily wait forever for him to return.

Chapter 12

It was bloody cold in Cumbria, Roger thought as he stared at the weak December sun trying to filter through a thin layer of clouds that portended even more snow. He was staying at a small inn on the outskirts of Keswick, not far from Derwent Water. Indeed, he could see the lake from his window. It was a lovely view, snow-covered trees, cozy homes with trails of smoke pouring from chimneys. But he was in no mood for anything pretty at the moment.

Christmas was just a day away and he was lonelier than he had ever been in his life. It was good, he thought, that he was not home, where memories lived in every item he looked at. But those memories could be comforting; at least he knew at one point in his life, he had been loved, he had been happy. The last Christmas his wife and daughters had been alive had been a festive time. Mary had decorated their small home with holly and ribboned wreaths, and the sharp smell of cider and cinnamon had filled the air. They were not rich, by any means, but they were happy in their little flat. The Kings were better off than most, with a large goose ready and dressed for their dinner and the girls playing with their new blocks, sent from their grandparents all the way from Kent.

Roger closed his eyes, trying to picture himself there with his family, trying, trying to see their faces, to breathe in and smell that goose cooking, to hear their laughter, those little giggles he remembered adoring. They'd been gone for seven years now, and no matter how hard he tried, he simply could not see them clearly anymore. The only comfort he had was that they were spitting images of his wife, and he at least had her wedding portrait and could dream of how they looked before that terrible day. If he thought about Christmas, he could drive those other images away, the ones filled with blood and horror.

Roger pushed himself away from the window and gathered up his notes. He pored over them each day, hoping to see something he had missed before. Three mothers of twins, dead. Four children slaughtered from one end of England to the other and yet he could find nothing that tied these murders to any one monster. Once he'd discovered the third murder, he'd written a letter to Scotland Yard. The evidence had been summarily dismissed and he'd been cautioned him against spreading "virulent rumors that will frighten the population." He'd crumpled up that letter and tossed it in the fire, feeling his hope of ever finding his family's murderer slipping away. Up until most recently, he hadn't had the time nor the funds to devote all his time to the search. But once he had solved the mystery of the missing diamond—and the missing baron—he would have enough stashed away to search for months.

Mr. Belmont, it turned out, was far more patient and understanding than Roger would have thought. While he was no longer paying Roger ten pounds per day, he was continuing to pay him ten pounds per week, plus expenses. Roger could search for his family's murderer for a year and still not worry about money. His gratitude to Mr. Belmont was immeasurable, and he'd be damned if this case would be drawn out longer than it needed to be.

Which was why he'd set Lion's Gate on fire.

This was not the work of a demented man, but rather the work of a man who was in a hurry to flush out his prey. Find the baron, find the diamond. And since no one seemed to know where the baron was, Roger was left with little choice. If Baron Alford was in England, he would come to assess the damage. He was certain the baron's solicitor was aware of his whereabouts, and just as certain that he would inform the baron of the fire. Given the condition of his estate—the family was known to be in financial straits—the baron should come at least to see how great a loss he'd sustained.

It was just a middling fire; most of the structure still stood and only the east wing had sustained any real damage. And he'd made damn sure no one was in the building before setting the blaze. It was a case of the ends justifying the means. Any day now, the baron would arrive in Keswick and he would be able to solve this case. And then he'd be able to do what he'd wanted to do for years: devote every waking minute to finding a madman.

Nathaniel stamped his feet in the snow and looked at the damage wrought by the fire, relieved that most of the structure remained standing. Around him, snow swirled, lightly falling and leaving a fresh layer of white on the landscape. Lion's Gate looked abandoned and was in dire need of repair, but at least it was still standing, despite the charred remains of the east wing.

Behind him, the hack driver, the same man who'd brought him nearly a year ago to say good-bye to his grandfather, waited, his collar turned up, his arms folded across his chest as plumes of vapor streamed from the noses of his team. "My cousin can set you right, m'lord," the driver said. "But he can't be doing any construction until the weather breaks."

"In June, then," Nathaniel joked, and the driver laughed in appreciation.

The driver looked up to the gray sky and grimaced. "We'll be getting more snow tonight, I'll wager," he said. "But as soon as the sun is shining, Tommy will be ready to get to work." He studied the house. "May take a while and he doesn't have a crew."

"He'll have me," Nathaniel said, and ignored it when the driver raised his eyebrows in surprise. He couldn't very well leave until the most necessary repairs were completed, and if that meant helping out, he would do it. After laboring in a garden for months, Nathaniel wasn't afraid of a little hard work, especially if it meant returning to St. Ives—and Clara—sooner. He needed only to do enough repairs to keep out the weather and prevent any more damage to the already sad estate. Even now, snow was accumulating in what had been the home's music room. Though there were no instruments at risk—his father had sold anything of value years ago—Nathaniel did not want any more damage done to the old home. If everything went as planned, he would be living here by summer. With his new bride.

"Lord Alford? Ho there."

Nathaniel looked behind the carriage to see a man approaching on horse, his figure obscured by the snow. "Do you recognize this fellow?" Nathaniel asked the driver, who twisted around so he could get a look at the approaching man.

"No, sir. Never seen him before in my life."

"Do you have a firearm?" he asked, and the driver looked suddenly alarmed.

"Surely a robber wouldn't call you by name." Sensible fellow.

"Of course." A knot of worry filled his stomach. No one knew he was in Cumbria but his solicitor, and this man was not his solicitor.

Nathaniel studied the visitor as he dismounted. He was young, with dark blond hair and sparse muttonchops that did little to make his youthful features more mature. Tall, thin, and pale, with deep circles beneath his striking green eyes, the fellow appeared to be ill.

"You are Baron Alford?" he asked.

Nathaniel schooled his features, careful not to show any surprise. He noticed two things about the man: The stranger was completely focused on Nathaniel's person, even though they both stood outside a fire-damaged building. And the other man was quite certain, despite his question, of who he was. "I am. And you are?"

"Roger King. I am looking for a blue diamond."

Though his gut clenched, Nathaniel raised one eyebrow and made a casual show of looking about at the snow-covered ground. "Good luck," he said.

Mr. King smiled blandly. "I am here on behalf of Mr. Jonathon Belmont. The diamond belongs to him."

Nathaniel quickly debated whether to let on that he knew what Mr. King was talking about, and decided to prevaricate. "I do apologize, Mr. King. But you have me at a disadvantage, as you seem to know what you are talking about and I do not. What is this about a blue diamond?"

Mr. King moved closer, obviously aware of the driver behind them listening to every word. "Your grandfather stole the diamond from my client's father. It is worth a fortune."

Nathaniel started to laugh, then looked behind him. "This is the country seat of the Alford barony. Does it look to you as if we have a fortune? I daresay I would appreciate having a fortune so that I might begin making the necessary repairs and taking care of my tenants. My needs are great and my funds are nonexistent. So, please, Mr. King, do tell. Where is this mythical diamond that can save my estate from ruin?"

Frowning, Mr. King looked uncertain for the first time. "Do you know of any papers your grandfather might have left behind that I could examine? They may offer information as to where the diamond is."

"After my grandfather died, I spent two months going through his papers and learning the extent of the estate's debts. If there is a paper I missed, I wouldn't know where to look for it. Sadly, I saw no mention of any hidden treasure." This was true. Despite his instinct not to reveal his knowledge of the diamond's existence, he did not feel entirely comfortable blatantly lying to this gentleman, who seemed so earnest in his inquiry. "If you have time, I would like to discuss this with you in a warmer, drier place. Perhaps I have information that could help you in your search."

The younger man seemed taken aback, very nearly disappointed, with his cooperation. "I believe that would be beneficial to both of us."

"Certainly." Nathaniel chuckled. "I am staying at the George Hotel. I will be here for a time, but I can meet you…" He pulled out his pocket watch. "…at four o'clock." He smiled. "Perfect. Tea time."

Mr. King smiled uncertainly, as if confused by the way the meeting had gone. It was almost as if he'd expected resistance, and Nathaniel congratulated himself on his decision to pretend ignorance. Now he would find out Mr. Belmont's motivation and whether he was as obsessed about the diamond as his father had been. If his life was in danger, he would like to know about it.

Just before four, Nathaniel returned to the hotel and found Mr. King already seated at a corner table in the hotel's small dining room. Only one other table was occupied, for the hotel rarely drew visitors during the winter months, remaining open mostly to serve drinks and meals to the locals. The Lake Region drew many visitors in the warmer months, but was quite desolate once winter had set in.

"So, Mr. King, tell me the tale of the blue diamond," Nathaniel said, once they had been served a pot of tea.

Mr. King folded and re-folded his napkin, clearly deep in thought. "Some of what I have to tell you does not shine a particularly flattering light upon your grandfather," he said hesitantly.

Nathaniel tensed inwardly, but smiled blandly. "My grandfather and I were hardly close, so I can assure you, you needn't feel as if you must tread lightly on his memory. He squandered my inheritance, leaving me with no staff, an estate in shambles, and a mountain of debt. Do go on." *Forgive me, Grandpapa.*

The story Mr. King related was so far from what his grandfather had told him, it was difficult to believe it was the same tale. Outwardly, Nathaniel seemed horrified by what his grandfather had done, but inwardly, he grew more and more enraged. He had no doubt that his grandfather had told him the truth, that he'd had every intention of sharing the proceeds of the sale of the intact diamond. In all his life, he'd never met a man of greater honor than his grandfather, who, despite his infirmity, had managed to protect Nathaniel from his father and make his childhood, if not carefree, then at least happy.

"I knew nothing of this tale," Nathaniel said, secretly delighted that he was able again to tell the truth. This story was not the story he knew. "You believe my grandfather hid the diamond in St. Ives?"

"I do," Mr. King said. "Or somewhere nearby. Mr. Belmont's father could think of no other reason for your grandfather to have been in St. Ives. Perhaps you did not know this, but your grandfather enjoyed anagrams."

Nathaniel was very much aware of his grandfather's love of word games. They had spent many hours challenging one another. "Really? And how do you know this?"

"The letters he wrote to my client's father before they had a falling out. He always included an anagram. In his last letter, after he'd returned to England from Brazil, your grandfather wrote one last letter containing only two words: gravesite dens. Of course, it made no sense to Mr. Belmont, not having read the other letters. Do you know what the solution is?"

Nathaniel thought for a moment before he realized what his grandfather had written. Gravesite dens had all the same letters as St. Ives garden. Nathaniel's lips twitched in admiration for the old gent and his inability to completely keep a secret. "St. Ives garden," he said. "Clever, I suppose, but what makes you believe that is where the diamond is hidden?"

Mr. King shrugged. "I cannot know for certain. But was not your grandfather accosted just outside of that village? Proof that he was there. A strong coincidence."

"Indeed." How he wanted to tell Mr. King the truth of what had happened. How his client's father was not the victim in this tragic tale, but the villain. It would do no good to tell him, not yet at any rate. Not until he found the blasted diamond. "Shall we hie off to St. Ives together?"

Mr. King shook his head. "I've been there. It's a bit like looking for a needle in a haystack, isn't it? I got the locals interested for a time, but I think they've already grown weary of the search and are probably doubting the tale I told them. I was hoping you could shed some light on this mystery. I fear I'll have to return to Mr. Belmont empty-handed. In truth, I don't know what else I can do." He took a bite of scone and chewed thoughtfully. "Would you object to my poring over those papers? Perhaps I can spot something of interest that you missed."

Nathaniel smiled, knowing there was nothing in the papers that would be helpful. "Of course. They are all in London with my solicitor. Stacks and stacks of them. I hate to see you waste your time, Mr. King. I can assure you there is nothing there of interest."

"Perhaps, but I'll feel better having a look myself." Mr. King stood and held out his hand to shake. "It has been a pleasure meeting you, my lord."

"I'd wish you good luck with your search, but I highly doubt Mr. Belmont would be willing to share the proceeds from the diamond."

Mr. King allowed himself a small smile. "That is the one thing about this case I am fairly certain of."

Chapter 13

"Lord Berkley has just arrived. With Harriet!" Hedra had rushed into Clara's room, her cheeks flushed, her face beaming. They both ran across the hall to her mother's sitting room so they could look below. "Oh, good Lord, he kissed her!"

Indeed, Lord Berkley, who had broken her sister's heart so coldly, was now kissing Harriet rather passionately beside a smart little gig. Or rather, they were kissing each other rather passionately. Clara had no idea what had precipitated this change, but she was thrilled for Harriet, who had been so melancholy of late. Even more melancholy than Clara herself.

It was March and weeks and weeks had passed since Nathaniel had been seen or heard from. She couldn't expect a letter from him; that would be seen as highly improper. When she had finally gotten the courage to ask Mr. Standard if he'd heard from him, he said he had not. Just last night, looking out over their new hothouse, Clara had come to the realization that Nathaniel would not return, despite what he'd written in his letter. Perhaps when he wrote those words, he'd meant them. But it was clear now that if he had once intended to return, he no longer did. Either that or something terrible had happened to him, and Clara refused to dwell on that possibility.

Next to her, Hedra did a happy little dance and squealed, sounding like a young girl. "Oh, it's happening, Clara. It's truly, truly happening." She ran to her mirror and fluffed up her hair before turning around and waving at Clara to follow her. "Where is your father? Oh, at work, of course. Of course! Have Joseph fetch him, will you, Clara? I'm nearly certain Lord Berkley has come to ask permission for Harriet's hand." She snapped her mouth shut, and suddenly looked doubtful. "You do think that is why he is here, don't you? He'd better be, hadn't he, after that kiss."

"I can think of no other reason for him to behave with Harriet in the manner in which they did unless he was here for that very reason," Clara said, praying she was right.

Hedra spun around and headed for the door, then stopped again, her face alight. "Do you know what this means, Clara? With a sister who is a countess—a countess!—you will have so many more opportunities. This is a miracle. A miracle! Now go fetch Joseph and have him make haste."

Laughing, Clara promised to make Joseph ride as quickly as possible to find her father. She chose to ignore her mother's other statement, for she had no wish to travel down that particular road ever again. How could she even begin to contemplate marrying anyone when she was still in love with Nathaniel? As foolish as that was, she could not keep her heart from longing for him.

As Hedra made her way down to the parlor, where the couple could be heard talking, Clara found their footman and directed him to fetch her father immediately.

"Shall I give him a reason? Mr. Anderson does not like being pulled away," Joseph said.

"Tell him Lord Berkley is here with Harriet and that they seemed supremely happy," Clara said with a huge smile. Joseph returned her smile, clearly pleased with this news. "But please don't say a word to any of the staff just yet. It's not quite a fait accompli."

"Yes, miss. And I'll make haste, do not worry!"

Clara hugged herself, hardly able to contain her happiness for Harriet. Indeed, she'd been so worried about her little sister, who had been listless and uninterested in anything of late. She'd even abandoned talk of her little cottage, that imaginary place where the two of them would live together into their dotage. And now she would be a countess! Lord Berkley had best not break Harriet's heart again or his life and limb would likely be in danger.

When she reached the parlor, Hedra was weeping and Harriet seemed to be consoling her, and her heart broke…until she spotted Lord Berkley looking at the pair with a chagrined and rather helpless look on his face.

"Happy tears?" Clara asked him, trying not to laugh aloud.

"I believe so," Lord Berkley said solemnly.

"Of course they're 'appy tears," Hedra said, slipping into her Cornish accent. "Our 'arriet is to be married, Clara. Married to an earl!"

"Mother, sit down before you faint," Harriet said, leading Hedra to the nearest chair.

"I'm not going to faint," Hedra said irritably, then beamed another smile. "Oh, dear. Where is Mr. Anderson?"

"I've just sent Joseph for him and they should be here momentarily." Clara caught Harriet's attention and gave her a look that tried to convey to her sister how very happy she was.

The four sat in tense silence for a time as they waited for her father to arrive, until Clara said, "If you don't mind my asking, how did this all come about?"

"I came to my senses," the earl said, giving Harriet such a look of adoration, Clara was rather taken aback.

"Clara, wait 'til you see. He built me my cottage." Harriet's eyes glistened with unshed tears. "It's rather grander than I pictured in my imagination, but it's perfect. It's almost as if he reached into my mind and found the paintings I had created of the place."

"Oh my."

"I needed to prove to Harriet that I was serious about my attentions. I'm afraid I bungled things considerably," Lord Berkley said.

The way they were looking at one another, with such obvious affection, made Clara momentarily jealous. Clara wasn't sure of the details of how the earl had come to love Harriet, but it was obvious that he did—and just as obvious that Harriet loved him. Hedra started crying again, abruptly stopping when her husband strode through the door.

"What's this all about?" he said angrily, seeing only that his wife was crying and that Lord Berkley was standing in his parlor, uninvited.

Clara rushed to his side and laid a placating hand on his arm, instantly calming him. "Lord Berkley is here to see you about Harriet," Clara said, unable to stop the smile that spread over her face. Her father's eyebrows at first snapped together, but as he realized what those words meant, his expression cleared.

"In my library, my lord?"

Lord Berkley nodded. "Of course, Mr. Anderson."

The two men disappeared, leaving behind three women who could hardly contain their excitement, particularly Hedra. "He came around," she gushed. "I knew he would."

Clara and Harriet exchange a look, for that was such a blatant lie it was very nearly laughable. Everyone in the family, including Harriet, had long given up hope that Lord Berkley would return—and certainly not to ask for Harriet's hand.

"He loves you," Clara said softly, and Harriet nodded.

"He does." She shrugged. "I really can't fathom why but I'm glad he does. You should see the house, Clara. It's perfect. He even made a room for you, overlooking the garden."

Clara smiled, but those words hurt far more than she let on. At the moment, just thinking about the garden was more painful than she could bear. It was wonderful that Harriet had found her love, but it only drove home the reality that Clara had not—and might never find love. Perhaps when Harriet and Lord Berkley were traveling on the continent, doing things that earls and countesses did, she could live in that little cottage, the spinster sister. And she would look out at the garden and wonder what it might have been like if Nathaniel hadn't disappeared, if he had stayed and they had married.

"Mother is ecstatic, thinking you can now help me find a titled husband." Clara sighed. "I fear this will only make her redouble her efforts on that front."

Harriet winced. "I am sorry, Clara. I cannot help it that Augustus is an earl. I do wish he wasn't, but he is and I must adjust to the idea."

Clara laughed. "Listen to us. Most girls would give anything to be in such a position, and here we are making do. Perhaps Mother had it right all along; we should just be happy and appreciate what fate has dealt us. In truth, your marriage will make me more attractive to the ton."

Harriet wrinkled her nose. "I do hope we aren't forced to socialize too much in England. You know how I am in crowds."

"It doesn't matter, now that you're a countess."

The sisters' laughter came to an abrupt stop when Lord Berkley entered the room, a solemn expression on his handsome face. "It took some convincing, but your father agreed."

Harriet stood. "You had to convince him to allow you to marry me?"

"That part was easy. The difficult part of the negotiations came when I insisted we marry posthaste. Wednesday."

Harriet's eyes widened. "*This* Wednesday?"

The earl looked a bit sheepish. "I have a chapel at Costille House, as you know. I took the initiative to have the banns read. Three times. And I obtained a license." He gave Harriet a quick grin. "I was rather hoping you would say yes."

Harriet narrowed her eyes and looked as if she might chastise him for his confidence before relenting and smiling. Smitten, indeed. "And Father agreed?"

"After some argument. And given our…celebration…" Harriet's cheeks burned red and a small strangling sound came from her throat. "…I thought it prudent. So, Wednesday?"

"Mother will faint," Harriet said. But Clara knew her sister would not argue the point. She turned to Clara, looking so happy, Clara felt her throat close. "You will be my maid of honor, and the girls shall be my bridesmaids. Except perhaps for Alice. It's a bit too soon after the birth." She put her hands on either side of her cheeks. "Oh, there is so much to think about."

"Mother has been planning a wedding in her head for years now. I'm certain she can get it all together, even if it is less than a week," Clara said on a laugh.

Clara was in her garden, a vast, beautiful place with wandering paths and fluttering butterflies and fat bumblebees lazily flying between impossibly enormous red roses. Dreams like these were her favorite, dreams from which she would slowly awaken, a smile on her face, until she remembered Nathaniel was gone. This dream was better than most, for she could see him there, his white shirt taut against his back, his thick brown hair peeking beneath his hat. He was digging, as he so often had, a soft rhythm, shh, shh, shh. For some reason, her garden had a bubbling brook going through it, and there was a boy fishing there, oblivious to his audience. Then, the boy was gone, the brook along with him, leaving Clara alone with Nathaniel in her garden, bathed in sunshine, a soft breeze making her flowers dance. Shh. Shh.

Clara opened her eyes, willing herself back into that perfect dream, and let out a sigh. And then she tensed. Shh. Shh. It wasn't a dream, it was a real sound she heard, coming from below her window.

She flung off the covers and ran to the window, her heart pounding madly in her chest, hope making her feet fly across the thick carpet. But when she reached the window, still obscured by her curtains, she closed her eyes, afraid that what she was hearing was something else. Or someone else. Perhaps her mother had hired another gardener and had not told her. After all, she'd hired Nathaniel without saying a word.

With one quick movement, Clara pushed the curtains aside and opened her eyes, and let out a small sound.

He was back.

"Jeanine, I'm up!" she called out cheerfully, then pulled the cord that would let her maid know she was needed. "Calm down, you ninny," she said to herself. "You don't want Jeanine to know why you're suddenly so happy." Then again, Jeanine was still floating about on a cloud herself, planning her June wedding to her long-time beau. It seemed everyone she knew was either already married—Harriet was in Paris on her wedding trip—or getting married. And now, Nathaniel was back, just as he'd promised.

Clara ran to her wardrobe and pulled out one of the dresses she wore when she was planning to spend time in the garden, wrinkling her nose. Though she longed to put on something a bit prettier, it wouldn't do to call attention to herself. She took the dress and flung it on the bed, then ran to her vanity and pulled out her brush. By the time Jeanine made it to her room, Clara was sedately brushing her hair as if nothing monumental had happened.

"Good morning, Jeanine," Clara said, keeping her voice neutral.

"And good morning to you, miss. Guess what the cat dragged in last night? Our very own Casanova."

Clara turned as if she hadn't any idea what her maid could mean. "Who?"

"The gardener. Turned up last night as if he'd never left and Mr. Standard welcoming him back without even a question asked. Those two are thick as thieves," Jeanine said with a sharp nod to her head. "Arrived just in time for supper, wouldn't you know. You might think he was Cook's long-lost son, coming home from war, the way she was carrying on. And the girls." Jeanine let out a sound of disgust. "They were all over themselves trying to get his attention, asking him all sorts of questions about where he'd been and how long he was staying."

Clara laughed. "I really do not understand your animosity for the poor man."

Jeanine stopped what she was doing, a quizzical look on her face. "Wouldn't you know it? I really don't understand it either." The two women laughed. Jeanine came up behind Clara and gently pushed her hands out of the way. Clara had been struggling to braid her hair but was making a muck of it. In no time, Jeanine had braided her hair and pinned it at the nape of her neck. "I imagine you'll be going out to the garden today?"

"I need to instruct Mr. Emory on the changes I would like to make. I have quite a long list."

"Hmph."

Clara had no idea what that "hmph" meant, but she had a feeling Jeanine had a bit of an idea that her mistress rather liked their gardener. Perhaps too much.

Nathaniel glanced at her window for perhaps the hundredth time, wondering where she was, whether she still thought of him, whether someone else had swooped in and stolen her away. It would serve him right if someone had. He didn't deserve her, but that didn't stop him from wanting her.

All these weeks apart, every night, every morning, every time he saw a blasted woman with blond hair, he would think of her. A laugh, a soft feminine curve, a full bottom lip—he could not escape her no matter how he tried. He couldn't even think of lying with another woman, not when he only wanted her. Last night, the staff was in such a tizzy about the younger daughter's marriage to Lord Berkley, they hardly spared Clara a mention. It would have seemed strange for him to ask after her, so he'd remained silent and prayed she was still at home and not off somewhere. Returning to his role of gardener after being Baron Alford for weeks seemed even more disingenuous than before. These people knew him, liked him, and he felt strangely as if he were betraying their trust. Through all of this, he'd never considered their reaction when they discovered he was a baron—and they would discover it. How would Cook react when she realized she'd been serving a lord at the kitchen table all these months?

Nathaniel had always believed the ends of his deception justified the means, but as the days passed, he was becoming more and more uncertain.

A movement above him attracted his eyes and he looked up at the house—had the curtain fluttered? No, she was not there, looking down at him, smiling as she had so often done. He went back to the tedious job of looking for the diamond. After all this time, very little of the garden had not been searched, just a small patch near the edge of the property by the pond. He had little excuse to be digging so far from where the main garden was, but he would have to do so anyway.

"Have you seen the hothouse?"

He smiled and pressed down the surge of joy he felt just from hearing her voice. "I have," he said, turning slowly around, bracing himself, trying not to make a fool of himself when he first saw her. But there she was, wearing her silly straw hat and an ugly brown dress, grinning at him, her cheeks blooming with good health, her eyes merry. He'd never seen anything more beautiful in his life.

She pressed her lips together, and they stood there awkwardly, staring at one another for a long moment, too many feet apart. "I have to...go to my room to fetch...something," he said, then stalked off, praying she followed him to the back of the shed.

He entered the cool, shadowed interior, feeling like a young boy about to experience his first kiss. He had missed her. Seeing her made him realize just how much, and he vowed they would never be apart again. He could hardly bear the thought of it.

Nathaniel half-ran through the shed, to his room, and out the back door, where the sun beat hard against the back of the building. Lifting his face to the warm rays, he smiled when he heard the rustle of skirts. When she turned the corner, he thrust out his hand and encircled her upper arm, then dragged her into his arms.

"Am I being presumptuous, Miss Anderson?"

"Not at all, Mr. Emory."

And then he kissed her as he'd longed to since the night he'd left. Though it had been weeks and weeks since he'd held her in his arms, she melted against him, pressing her pretty body and her warm mouth against him, letting out those sounds that he'd tried to recall on his lonely nights in Keswick.

"God, I missed you," he said, not caring that he sounded like a man besotted. He *was* a man besotted and at the moment, he didn't care. She felt so damn good in his arms, as if she belonged there. Forever. It was there, at the tip of his tongue, to ask her to marry him, but he found a small bit of sense before he did. He would not ask her to marry him until she knew exactly who he was, until she understood why he had lied, until she told him she loved him and none of his lies mattered. Ah, such a fantasy he was building in his head, but Nathaniel didn't care. He loved her enough to make her understand. If it took days or weeks or years, he would convince her that he loved her.

It never occurred to him, until that very moment, that she might not feel quite the same. He wasn't fool enough to believe he could make her love him…

"I love you," he said, pulling back so he could see her expression. It was, he could see clearly, one of complete surprise, and a sick feeling tugged slightly at his gut. "I can see you were not expecting such a declaration."

"No, I wasn't. It is a lovely declaration." She bit her lip, and damn if his groin didn't tighten even more. When she stepped back, it felt a bit like she was stepping on his heart.

"It is not one I make lightly," he said, and he knew he sounded more like a baron than a gardener. At that moment, he could hardly care.

"My sister has married an earl."

"Yes, it was all the staff could talk about."

"Now my mother is more convinced than ever that I should marry a title."

He scowled. "One marries a man, not a title. Good God, Clara, you are not the same girl—"

He stopped abruptly when he realized she was trying not to laugh. "Of course I love you, you silly man."

He pulled her in for a searing kiss, a punishment, a brand, that would show her she was his. Leave it to Clara to brand him right back with her own searing kiss, little vixen. "I haven't asked you to marry me, you know," he said, nibbling on her throat.

"It hardly matters, now that you've returned."

"I'm not yet in a position to ask, but…" He kissed her jaw, her cheek, her lips. "…I will soon. I promise you. And your parents will approve."

"No, they will not, but I don't care. I don't. You know I loathe the aristocracy. I'll go with you to Gretna Green or wherever we need to go to be together. They'll come around if we're married. We can leave tonight and be married in just a few days. Oh, let's do it, Nathaniel. Let's go tonight."

He pushed her gently away. "We can't. We must do things properly. I must ask your father for permission—"

"He'll never give it, especially not now with Harriet being a countess. I do not believe they would care for having an earl for one son-in-law and a gardener for the other. Please, Nathaniel, let's go tonight."

Nathaniel dropped his hands and stepped back. "No, Clara. I cannot. I just returned."

A crease formed between her eyes. "Returned? For what? To labor away in this garden? To be a servant? I want us to have a life together, to raise children."

She looked at him, confusion clear in her gaze, and Nathaniel nearly blurted out the truth. *Not yet, you fool.* "Yes. I do want that. Just…not quite yet. Please be patient, my love."

"Why can you not tell me, Nathaniel?"

He didn't pretend not to understand that she was asking for his secrets. "I will. I promise."

"Soon?"

He thought of that small patch where the diamond must be. It must. "Soon."

Chapter 14

"I simply cannot wait until next year," Hedra said, coming into Clara's room and clutching a thick volume against her chest. Since Harriet's wedding, she had been incessantly happy and Clara knew that a great part of that happiness came from the realization that her sister's advantageous marriage had opened the door for Clara to marry in kind. Despite her weariness of the subject, Clara smiled as Hedra entered, glad to see her mother content. Hedra had inserted one finger into the book as a place holder.

"This is where your sister's name will appear." She opened Debrett's with a flourish and pointed to the listing under Earl of Berkley. "Can you imagine?"

Clara smiled, enjoying her mother's giddiness, but feeling a bit melancholy. She missed Harriet, and the thought they would never gossip together late at night, would never laugh at their mother's eccentricities, was disheartening. It had only been a week since Harriet had left and already Clara missed her sister terribly. She glanced at the odd paperweight her sister had given her just before the wedding, wishing she could see Harriet instead.

"I'll leave this with you, shall I? Perhaps you'll be inspired." Hedra gave her an odd, hopeful smile, and Clara gave an internal sigh. How could she ever tell her mother she was in love with a lowly gardener? That it was only a matter of time before Nathaniel asked for her hand?

"I'll memorize every page," Clara said, crossing her heart.

"The good Lord tallies our lies, you know," Hedra said, smiling.

Clara made a show of opening the book to study its pages and her mother let her be. Sighing, Clara closed the book and set it aside. She walked to the window, looked out and stared for a long moment at the soft light coming from Nathaniel's quarters. Would they ever be together as they hoped? Proclamations of love were all well and good, but she wanted to begin their life together. Still, she understood Nathaniel's reticence; he could hardly create a life for them on his meager gardener's salary. He needed to find another position, for it would be untenable for the two of them to live here, in the main house with her parents, and just as untenable for her to move into his tiny quarters.

It was late and she should probably be sleeping, not dwelling on her troubles. Reading Debrett's was one sure way to put her to sleep, she thought, pulling back the covers and taking up the book. She began flipping through the pages, recognizing some names from reading the *Tattler*. To think Harriet would one day be listed in this book was remarkable. She'd reached the section on barons and wrinkled her nose, remembering the one baron she'd ever met: Lord Longley. What a horrible man he was. She fully believed that Harriet had married the last handsome, noble member of the peerage. All the rest were vacant, dull creatures with pasty faces and soft limbs. So unlike her handsome, strong gardener. Clara giggled aloud. How delicious it was just thinking about touching the hard planes of his stomach, the strength of him as he held her. No nobleman's physique could ever match Nathaniel's.

First on the list of baronies was Baron Alford, Daniel Emory, one she'd never heard of. It was the surname, of course, that caught her eye and made her smile. She would have to joke with Nathaniel that he might be a descendant of a baron. They would have a good laugh about that. Perhaps she could call him Lord Alford and give him a curtsy. She giggled aloud and was about to set the book aside, when another name stopped her: Nathaniel.

Her gaze flew back to the beginning of the listing: George Emory, 5th Baron Alford, M.P. Cumbria, m. 7 June, 1821 (d. 4 Jan. 1877), Lady Mary Capel (d. 12 Nov. 1839), yst. dau. of Hon. Thomas Capel, and had issue: 1. Ann (d. 15 Feb. 1822) 2. Charles (d. 24 Nov. 1866), m. Laura Peterson (d. 28 Oct. 1851) who had issue, one son:

Nathaniel, 6th Baron.

She stared at the entry, brows furrowed, for several long minutes, going through her mind the things that Nathaniel had told her, small pieces she'd learned about his past. He was from Cumbria. He was twenty-six years old. His father, Charles, had been a wastrel. His mother, Laura, had died in childbirth. Nathaniel's birthday was October twenty-eighth. Laura Peterson died October twenty-eighth.

Jane Goodger

"It can't be," she whispered, shaking her head and smiling. She laughed aloud. Nathaniel, a baron? Yes, of course, barons always worked as gardeners on a lark. A lark that lasted months. She could picture it: "Yes, old chap, I daresay I feel like rusticating in St. Ives. On holiday? Goodness no! I've decided to become a gardener." She giggled again and nearly put the book aside.

Still…

She glanced at the entry again and a feeling she didn't like filled her slowly, like some black, thick poison that made her stomach wrench. All the details, all these facts, seemed to agree with what Nathaniel had told her about his life. His very birthday, his father's name, his mother's. The fact of her death the day he was born. "It can't be," she repeated, but this time those words sounded like lies.

Suddenly, it felt as though a heavy weight were pressing against her chest and she found it difficult to breathe. She knew he had a secret, a terrible one he could not tell her… "It cannot be."

It was all silliness; it had to be. Certainly, one way to find out was simply to ask. He would laugh when she suggested he might be a baron, and they would laugh together that she had come to such a conclusion. Throwing on a wrap, she walked with determined steps down the stairs, through the long hall that led to the back of the house and the garden. She hesitated only a second before opening the door and walking outdoors, barefoot, onto the cold, dew-covered grass. His light was still on.

"It cannot be. It cannot be," she whispered, over and over.

She opened the door loudly and stood in the opening of the shed. And waited. His door opened, revealing him holding a lantern that bathed him in its golden light. He was wearing only trousers and a hastily donned shirt, unbuttoned, revealing his muscled torso. It occurred to Clara as she stood there, trying not to fall apart, that on any other occasion she would have admired his beautiful form.

He smiled to see her standing there, then his expression slowly turned to one of concern. "Clara, what is it? What is wrong?" He took a step toward her, but when she stepped back, he halted, his entire demeanor changing. It looked to Clara as if he were bracing himself for something. He put the lamp down slowly, carefully, on a shelf, and when he looked back at her, she tried with all her strength to stop her heart from aching for him. *It cannot be. Please God.*

"Who are you?"

There, instantly, she could see it in her face, and it seemed before her eyes he became someone else, someone she didn't know at all. Still, her heart rejected what she knew to be true. *Please, tell me anything but the truth.*

"Clara." Those two syllables held the truth, and she wanted to crumple to the ground and scream.

She drew in a shaky breath, trying to find the strength to ask him outright. "You are Baron Alford." Her tone held no question.

He hesitated for only the space of a breath. "Yes."

Even though she knew it was true, she flung her hand to her mouth to stop from crying out and panted harshly through nostrils that flared with each breath. *Swallow. Breathe. Oh, God, I cannot breathe.* And he stood there, his eyes filled with agony, his bearing unmistakably that of a peer, and she could hardly bring herself to care.

She flung her hand away, drawing her fisted hands to her stomach. "You liar," she cried. "You dirty, horrible *liar.*" *Breathe. Breathe.* "How could you? Oh, my God. How could you pretend to be someone you were not all this time? When I think of the things I said to you... My God, how you must have laughed."

"No, Clara, no." His voice cracked and he took another step toward her but she back away and he stopped, stricken.

Shaking her head, she said, "Why would you do such a thing? Was it a lark? A game? Go to the country and seduce some stupid, ignorant girl? Did you go to London and laugh at me with all your chums? 'You should try it. Those country girls will believe anything you tell them.'"

"God, no. It's not like that at all. I love you." In the lamplight, she could see his eyes were glittering with unshed tears, but Clara could spare no sympathy.

"Love! You do not lie to someone you love. You do not pretend to be someone you are not. All this time, you know I *suffered.*" She let out a bitter laugh that bordered on hysterical. "I thought we could not marry because of the difference in our stations."

"I never said that."

She looked at him incredulously. "Well, hurray for you, sir." Her voice shook with anger and despair. "That's one lie you did not tell. But you *knew* I believed we could not marry because you were a servant and I the daughter of the family. You knew and you said nothing." She let out a bitter laugh. "But, now that I think on it, it is true. We cannot marry because you are a baron and I am a nobody. I just don't understand why. *Why*, Nathaniel?" She looked down, idly noting that, like her, he wore nothing on his feet. "It doesn't make sense. It's been months. And why a gardener?"

And then it came to her, and if she felt foolish before, now she was completely humiliated. She pressed her fists harder against her stomach, feeling as though she might be ill. And he stood there, looking as if his world was ending, and she just wanted to slap him.

"You were looking for something," she said softly. "All this time. Something buried on this property."

He shook his head but said a barely audible, "Yes."

Tears that had hovered in her eyes, making for a blurry world, spilled over. "What? What were you looking for?"

He stretched his neck and looked at the lamp for a long moment as if debating whether to tell her the truth. "A diamond."

"A diamond?"

"A very rare and exceedingly valuable blue diamond. It's worth a fortune." He looked at her beseechingly. "My estate is in shambles, my tenants living in near squalor, what tenants I have at any rate. My father sold everything of value, every bit of unentailed property. The debt is catastrophic. The diamond is my only hope to save what's left of the Alford legacy. My grandfather nearly died trying to protect it. You must believe that I never meant to lie to you. I thought I would be here and gone. I never intended for any of this to happen."

A strange calm came over Clara when he said this last. Her tears stopped and the pain that had been wracking her dissipated. "I want you gone by tomorrow morning."

"Clara, please." Again, his eyes filled with tears, but Clara was fairly certain it was because of the diamond he would never find and not because he was losing her. "I did try to tell you. The longer I waited, the more impossible it became. Please. Clara."

"Good-bye, my lord," Clara said, before dipping down in a perfect curtsy.

Spinning around, she left him standing there, mourning the loss of his bloody blue diamond. Her footsteps slowed. Blue diamond... *Blue.*

Lifting her skirts, she ran into her house and flew up the stairs and directly to her room. After hastily lighting her lamp, she said, bitterly, "Hello." Her paperweight, the one Harriet had found all those years ago and had jokingly given to her the day of her wedding. Sitting on her desk on top of her stationery, was Nathaniel's blue diamond.

Nathaniel watched her walk away and dropped to his knees, his hands on the rough brick in front of him. He knew he had just destroyed the only good thing in his life. He stayed that way for several long minutes, not caring that he had lost any dignity he'd ever had. "Stupid fool," he whispered harshly, pulling his fingers into a fist, relishing the pain he felt when his fingers scraped the brick.

He'd *known* this would happen. All this time, the more important she became to him, the worse the black guilt became. He'd known, and yet, coward that he was, he'd wanted to delay the inevitable. Even though he'd known it would end, he hadn't anticipated the pain he would feel when it did. His grandfather's death, while devastating, was nothing compared to the agony he now felt knowing he'd just lost the only woman he would ever love.

"I'll get her back," he whispered, straightening and wiping his face with his shirt. "She'll come 'round."

Those words had just left his lips when he heard her hurried steps on the gravel outside. She'd stopped to don shoes, he realized, and hope bloomed in his chest. Standing quickly, trying to pull himself together, he stood and wiped his hands on his pants. And waited.

When she walked into the shed, the pounding in his chest physically hurt, so he pressed his right hand over his heart and kneaded the ache. Ah, there she was, his beautiful girl, her face oddly devoid of emotion, her hair looking mussed, as he imagined it would after love-making. He stood, silent, waiting for her to speak. It seemed at first she didn't see him standing there, and then she did, and the most terrible expression marred her features.

"Here is your bloody diamond," she said. Then, before he could guess what she was doing, she flung something at him and he didn't even have the presence of mind to duck. Something hit him hard, just above his left brow, with enough force to fling his head back, to make him momentarily lose his balance so that he nearly fell.

"What in hell?" he muttered, bringing his hand up to touch his face. His hand came away covered with blood. He heard her gasp and he snapped his head up to see her startled expression. She looked momentarily concerned before her expression hardened once more, and then, without uttering another word, she turned and left him there, blood streaming down his face.

Obviously, she wasn't going to come 'round this night, he thought with chagrin.

Blinking away the blood in his eye, he remained there staring where Clara had stood just moments before. Then, to his great shame, he picked up the lantern and held it high, searching for whatever it was she'd thrown at him, his curiosity winning out over his conscience. Even though he suspected whatever had struck him could not possibly be the diamond, he looked. It took long enough to find the object for his gut to start churning with disappointment. *It wasn't the diamond, you idiot.*

Still, he couldn't bring himself to give up, not after all this time. Getting down on his hands and knees, he placed the lantern on the floor and looked beneath a shelf, his head pounding from the movement, blood dripping onto the bricks. And then he saw it, under one of the shelves that held several old clay pots. Reaching underneath, he grabbed the object and pulled it into the light.

"Thank God," he said softly, for he knew he held the diamond his grandfather had hidden more than fifty years ago. It was extraordinarily ordinary, just a large blue-ish stone that resembled a bit of quartz, and he had the terrible thought that perhaps his grandfather had been wrong about the stone. What if it wasn't a diamond? What if whomever had told him it was worth a fortune was playing a cruel joke on a young Englishman?

What if hurting Clara, using her all this time, was for nothing?

At that moment, Nathaniel was filled with such self-loathing, he began retching. It felt as if his stomach were being squeezed painfully by an unrelenting fist. And he knew Clara would never forgive him. How could she? What he had done to her was so completely unforgiveable. Worse, he'd known what he was doing was wrong, but he'd convinced himself that the ends justified the means.

Holding that diamond in his hand gave him little satisfaction, but he was a man with responsibilities, with duties.

He would do what he'd promised his grandfather he would do: He would save Lion's Gate and the Emory name and, by God, Clara would be by his side.

"I need to speak with Mr. Anderson immediately."

Mr. Standard, who was in the process of inspecting the home's massive and ornate collection of silver, turned to Nathaniel with surprise. The butler's eyes darted to the cut on his head, but he said nothing. He must have sensed something of import had happened, for his demeanor changed. "You've found what you've been looking for, then, my lord?"

Nathaniel smiled grimly. "I have, Mr. Standard."

"He is in his study." Nathaniel could tell Mr. Standard was curious as to why it was necessary to speak to Mr. Anderson, but he would find out soon enough. The butler led him down a hall lined with portraits and hunting scenes, past tables laden with vases and statues and all manner of breakable objects. The home looked rather like a shop for decorative items, for it seemed every available space had been stuffed with...things.

"One moment, Mr. Emory," Mr. Standard said with a wink; he was still uncomfortable addressing him so informally. The butler knocked softly and waited for Mr. Anderson to call him in. "Mr. Emory would like a word, sir."

"Who the hell is Mr. Emory?"

Nathaniel smiled to himself.

"The gardener, sir."

"Gardener? Then he wants Mrs. Anderson."

The butler hesitated a moment but forged ahead. "He asked specifically to speak with you, sir."

Nathaniel heard the man's huff of impatience. "Very well."

Mr. Standard stepped back outside and spared him another wink before heading back to continue working on the silver. Nathaniel entered the room, a large, wood-paneled space that was sparsely furnished and hadn't a single flower, vase, or statue in sight, but for a bronze figure of a spaniel sitting on the man's large mahogany desk. The desk was an impressive bit of furniture with fierce-looking talons clutching balls at each corner. His grandfather had once had a similar desk—his had lion's paws—but it had long since been sold to pay for his father's schemes.

Mr. Anderson gave him a hard look, his gaze stopping briefly at the wound on his forehead caused by his daughter, mild curiosity in his gaze. "Mr...."

"Emory. And not mister, I'm afraid."

The man's brows snapped together.

"I am Nathaniel Emory, Baron Alford, and I am here to ask for your daughter's hand in marriage."

To his credit, the older man hardly blinked. He set aside some paperwork he'd been reviewing and folded his great hands in front of him. "Have a seat, my lord, I imagine this is going to take some time to explain."

With a rather large dose of relief over the man's calm demeanor, Nathaniel sat and began relating his story—his grandfather's deathbed confession, his massive debt, his search for the blue diamond, and finally, his love of Clara. Throughout the tale, Mr. Anderson was silent, his intelligent eyes studying Nathaniel with unrelenting steadiness. Finally, when the tale was done, Mr. Anderson leaned back in his chair.

"Does Clara know who you are?"

"She does now. She discovered it last night. This," he said, pointing to the cut and bruise on his forehead, "was her reaction. It was caused by the diamond being thrown quite accurately at my head."

One side of Silas's mouth curved up in a smile. "I take it she was not pleased with this discovery, yet you are here asking to marry her. It seems to me, sir, she is not interested."

Nathaniel swallowed. He had hoped that when he revealed his status, Mr. Anderson would have immediately become deferential and leapt at the chance to have another of his daughters married off to a titled man. Such was not going to be the case, obviously.

"She is angry and likely hurt, something I would have avoided if I could have. I fully planned to disclose my identity, I swear to you."

Mr. Anderson narrowed his eyes. "After you found the diamond."

"Yes. If I told her before, then…"

"You would have been thrown from the property. And rightly so. I have enjoyed your tale, my lord, but the diamond was found on my property. Therefore, it is mine."

"He's what?"

"In speaking with your father," Jeanine said as she placed another pin in Clara's hair. When she'd come in that morning, she'd noted Clara's puffy eyes, which Clara attributed to a bout of silly tears over missing her sister. It was a believable enough story, and Jeanine didn't question it. The truth of it was, though, Clara could hardly bring herself to get out of bed. Her heart hurt, far more than it ever had in her life. The ache was stunning, in fact, and she very nearly wondered if she should see a physician. Surely this sort of physical pain should not accompany emotional pain, but apparently it did.

That pain, caused by heartbreak, was quickly replaced by outrage that the scoundrel was still here and had requested an audience with her father. She had a good feeling what Baron Alford was in speaking to her father about, and she was going to have none of it. "That cad."

"Who?"

"Mr. Emory," Clara growled out. She spun about in her chair. "You'll find out soon enough, I'm sure, and you are not to tell another soul—not even Charlie—until everything is resolved and Mr. Emory is back in London or wherever he comes from."

"Cumbria," Jeanine said, looking astonished by Clara's reaction. It was a clear, feminine growl.

"Yes, I know where he is from. And I know who he is." Clara raised one brow.

"I knew it," her maid said triumphantly. "Some sort of criminal? An *actor*?"

"No. Worse. He's a baron."

Clara left Jeanine behind, staring open-mouthed and shocked speechless by this revelation. With determined steps, Clara headed directly to her father's study, only to stop short when she heard shouting within. It seemed her father wasn't any happier with Baron Alford than she was. Ha!

Without knocking, Clara flung open the door, which served to act as a gag on the two men, who immediately ceased their yelling and turned toward her.

"This does not concern you, daughter," her father said sternly.

"Doesn't it? He's here asking to marry me, is he not?" When neither man responded, a flood of humiliating doubt rushed in. "Isn't he?" she asked in a small voice.

"Yes, I am," Nathaniel said, and began to walk toward her, only to be stopped short by a sound only a father can emit when his child is in mortal danger. "Sir, if I could have a moment with your daughter."

"Over my dead body."

"Never," Clara said at the same time her father spoke. She met her father's eyes and the two shared a silent understanding. *We're in this together.*

For the first time since entering the room, Clara realized that her gardener no longer looked like a gardener. He looked like the baron he was. His suit was impeccable, his hair neatly combed, his jaw cleanly shaven. Clara's blood fairly boiled. Not even the sight of the wound she had given him could stem her anger.

"How dare you think we would ever agree to such a match!" Clara said. "You are nothing but a lying scoundrel."

"And a thief," her father said. Nathaniel's expression grew hard, but he remained silent.

Clara's initial and unwanted reaction was to defend Nathaniel. He had not officially stolen anything, but rather she had given him the diamond rather violently. Still, he had intended to steal it and who knew what he would have done if he had found it before being discovered? No doubt he would have absconded with it and left her behind, wondering what had happened to their "gardener." Just thinking about it made her furious.

"I am not a thief," Nathaniel said, his tone clipped and proper. The offended peer. Clara clenched her fists and resisted the urge to walk across the room and smack him. "The diamond belongs to my family. I will admit that I went about this all wrong. Entirely wrong. But desperate men sometimes do act desperately, and that is what I did. I wholly intend to compensate you a fair amount, sir." Her father let out a scoffing sound. "The point we are now arguing is my marriage to your daughter."

Clara knew how wonderful those words would have sounded just one day ago. Now, though, they were the words of a man who had been discovered, who found himself forced to do the honorable thing. The lordly thing. She looked about for something to throw at him but nothing was within reach except the bronze dog and that would likely kill him. She didn't want him dead; she simply wanted him gone.

"I will never marry you," she said through gritted teeth.

"You must. I love you."

"I don't love you." Her words struck home; she could tell they wounded him, and Clara fought back the remorse she instantly felt. It was a lie, of course. She *did* love him, would probably love him forever. But at the moment, she was far too angry and hurt to admit such a thing.

Nathaniel gave her a long, hard look. "That is of no consequence," he said in a tone she had never heard from him before. Then he turned to her father. "I have compromised her."

Clara immediately placed herself in front of him, fists planted firmly on her hips. "You did not."

"I did, sir," Nathaniel said, looking over her shoulder at her father. "I will not go into details, but suffice it to say, your daughter is no longer innocent."

Clara spun around to face her father. "That's not true. We didn't... Not entirely..."

"But we nearly did. In my world, you were more than compromised. I, of course, take full responsibility."

"Father, please do not listen to him," Clara said when she saw her father's expression go from livid anger to thoughtful. "I hate him and if you force me to marry him, I will never forgive you."

Nathaniel made a small sound behind her and she pushed down the pain of that sound.

"Now, now, Clara, do not become hysterical," her father said, using the tone he always used with Hedra when she became overwrought.

"Do not patronize me, Father." She took a calming breath, one that caught in her throat when her mother came into the study, looking from Nathaniel to her to her father.

"What is this all about?"

Nathaniel stepped forward and gave her mother a small bow. "Let me introduce myself, Mrs. Anderson. My name is Nathaniel Emory, Baron Alford, and I've come here today to ask for your daughter's hand in marriage."

"No!" Clara shouted, but it was already too late. Her mother's face bloomed into a smile, and she looked over to her husband to verify that this was the case. Silas nodded, and Clara suddenly felt so deflated, she found it difficult to stand. Until Nathaniel took a step toward her, apparently having noticed she was reaching the end of her endurance.

Silas quickly explained the situation to her mother, and the longer he spoke, the larger Hedra's smile got. In the end, she said, "Why, this is wonderful, isn't it? Of course, you may marry my daughter."

"Mother, I don't want to marry him."

"Of course you do. He's a baron and he loves you. You'll come 'round, I know you will."

"Did you not hear how he lied to us, how he planned to steal from us?"

Hedra tilted her head. "Not really stealing if it's his own diamond, now is it?"

"Mother, you cannot seriously be considering this."

"What if news got out that you've been compromised? No man would want to offer for you then."

Clara threw out her hands in exasperation. "And who would tell? The only people who know are in this room."

"People have a way of finding out things, Clara. Things slip out." In that moment, even though she knew her mother's threat was idle, she accepted defeat.

Clara sagged, then slowly walked to a large leather chair and slumped into it. "I cannot believe this is happening," she said, dragging a hand across her forehead. "I wanted to marry a gardener. I wanted a simple life in St. Ives, and now you're forcing me to be part of a society I hold in disdain and loathing. You want me to be miserable with a man I can never trust again. Is that what you want, Mother? Father?"

"That's about right," Silas said, and Hedra nodded in agreement.

"Oh, you'll see," Hedra said. "Things will work out, Clara. They always do. Just look at Harriet!"

Clara gave her mother a look of complete disbelief before closing her eyes. Maybe if she wished hard enough, when she opened them, everyone would be gone and none of this would have ever happened. Instead, she opened her eyes when she felt her mother's hand on her arm.

"He's a baron, Clara. And he loves you."

"Which is more important, Mother?" Clara asked wearily.

Hedra's soft smile wavered. "In the world we live in, I think you know the answer."

Clara leaned over so she could meet Nathaniel's eyes. "I will not make you happy," she said.

"I suppose I deserve that. I swear to you that I will make you happy. Or at least I will try."

Clara sat up, back straight, chin high and turned her gaze to the wall. "Very well."

She wasn't certain, and perhaps it was just her imagination, but she thought she heard him whisper, "Thank God."

Chapter 15

"Mr. King, thank you for meeting with me."

Nathaniel and his solicitor sat across from Mr. King, who appeared even paler and thinner than he had two months prior. The man had a haunted look in his intelligent green eyes, perhaps a consequence of constantly dealing with the shady side of life. He had a feeling the man's solemn eyes missed very little.

"I want to tell you the truth about the diamond. I'm afraid the tale you told me when we first met was the fabrication of a demented soul."

Mr. King's eyes narrowed slightly, but other than that small change in his expression, he did not react to Nathaniel's words. In a measured tone, Nathaniel relayed the truth of what had happened on that fateful trip to Brazil, and its aftermath. He told of growing up with a man confined to a wheelchair, who bore the scar of the bullet that was meant to kill him. As he spoke, the detective remained silent, waiting until he was finished before speaking.

"What do you intend to do with the diamond?"

"I intend to bring it to the finest jeweler in the kingdom and have it cut. And then I plan to sell it to the highest bidder. Not a penny goes to the Belmonts, not after what Zachariah Belmont did to my grandfather. I am not naïve enough to believe the man will accept my story or my decision about what to do with the diamond and the fortune it will bring. My grandfather more than paid the price of the diamond."

Mr. King pressed his lips together and finally shook his head. "Mr. Belmont may have a different opinion. However, he is far more reasonable than his father, and I have no doubt he will at least listen to your side of things and may even conclude that his father was in the wrong. As his son, he must have had some sort of inkling that his father was deranged. I think finding the journal the late Mr. Belmont wrote explained his father's madness to a son who was looking for answers. Would you consider meeting with him?"

Nathaniel glanced at his solicitor, who gave him a subtle nod, though his eyes were troubled. "I would. You can arrange the meeting?"

For the first time, Mr. King's face relaxed, as if a large weight had been lifted from his shoulders. It seemed odd to Nathaniel that he cared so much for the outcome of this particular case, but perhaps Mr. King was exceedingly dedicated to his job. "I can, of course. How long will you be in London?"

"A fortnight only. I'm getting married in three weeks." That statement did not bring the joy he had thought it would. No matter how often he vowed that he would bring Clara to love him again, he was not at all sure he could. This marriage could be disastrous for both of them, and he hadn't any idea what to do to earn Clara's forgiveness.

"Congratulations."

The way he said the word, with little expression, made Nathaniel wonder if this astute man had picked up on his reticence. "You don't care for the idea of matrimony?" Nathaniel asked, pretending to be amused by the man's grim countenance.

"I care for it very much," he said. "My wife died several years ago."

Nathaniel was taken aback, for the man look far too young to be married, never mind a widower of several years. "I am sorry."

"Thank you. She was murdered and I have been searching for the culprit for seven years." He smiled. "The resolution of this case will allow me to devote more time to that search."

"Then I am glad for you and wish you well." Nathaniel stood, prompting the other men to rise to their feet. "Send a note 'round to my solicitor here when I can have my meeting with Mr. Belmont."

Three days later, Nathaniel sat in an opulent parlor in a St. James Square house that covered nearly a city block. It was clear the Belmont family was in far better funds than he was. The tapestries alone in this room would go far toward building a steelworks to provide income for the families living around his estate.

When an older man entered, Nathaniel stood. "Mr. Belmont?"

"Indeed I am, my lord. Please have a seat." Mr. Belmont sat across from him and brought one booted foot up to rest on his knee, a casual stance that put Nathaniel at ease. "I've been informed that you have found the diamond and that your understanding of what happened is far different from what I was told."

"That is true. My grandfather and your father were good friends, but sometime during their trip to Brazil, things changed." After Nathaniel relayed his grandfather's side of the tale, Mr. Belmont steepled his hands under his chin, and Nathaniel felt the urge to squirm beneath the older man's steady stare.

"My father was a desperate man and he was jealous of your grandfather in a way that is difficult to comprehend. This story, I've discovered, had little to do with the diamond and almost everything to do with a woman. Your grandmother."

Now this was a complete surprise, and Nathaniel didn't even pretend to hide his astonishment. "Your father…"

"…loved your grandmother. I don't believe your grandfather knew. You see, my father was a third son with little chance of inheriting a title. But he felt superior to your father, as the son of a viscount. It's all in his journal. My father died when I was a young man but our relationship was not close. He was a difficult man to understand. Odd. Distant. Exceedingly melancholy. He committed suicide when I was but twenty-one and I've been seeking answers ever since. When I found his journal, I thought I'd discovered the reason for his tragic end."

"I am sorry for that," Nathaniel said, relieved that the man seemed so reasonable when many other men would have sought retribution. "I can understand why your father harbored such animosity toward my grandfather given what happened to him on that ship."

"It broke him. That experience, added to the knowledge that your grandfather was living with the woman he loved, damaged him beyond repair. I cannot excuse his actions against your grandfather. It was all such a stupid, silly disagreement and they were very young. Two children fighting over a toy. The real tragedy is that my father knew he would one day come into a large inheritance, but he didn't care to wait for my grandfather to die. He was poor, yes, but it was only a temporary condition, as you can see," he said, waving his hand to indicate the opulence that surrounded them.

"About the diamond…"

Mr. Belmont smiled, a quick movement of his lips. "When I first read about the diamond in my father's journal, I became incensed. I felt it was one more thing that had been stolen from him, that his very life had been stolen. And I believed my father had been taken from me as well. That is why I commissioned Mr. King to find it for me. My initial intention was simply to make certain that no one in your family ever benefited from it."

"What has changed?"

"I went back and read all of my father's journals and it helped to give me a much clearer picture of the man he was and the demons that tormented him. Hearing what happened to your grandfather simply confirmed what I had already concluded; that my father was a man who was ill and who had little understanding of reality. All because of a woman and a rock."

"But a lovely woman and a spectacular rock," Nathaniel said. "It's amazing, actually, what a man will do for such treasures."

Roger King sat in a pub that looked like a hundred other pubs he'd been in over the years, looking for the monster who had murdered his family. As yet, he'd found no other murders that matched the ones he'd discovered and was beginning to doubt that the same man had committed them. Strange coincidences were rare, but they did happen.

This particular pub was in a town not far from St. Ives, that little haven of sea and warmth he'd discovered the previous year. Often, when he'd lain alone at night on yet another uncomfortable bed in a hot and cramped room, he would think of that small village and remember how it had affected him. It seemed people there were more content, happier, than any place he had ever been. Just the thought of being content was enough to make him want to weep. Perhaps when this was over, he would return to St. Ives and find himself a small cottage where he could live out the rest of his days.

The Fisherman's Inn was a small pub tucked behind the main thoroughfare, which stank of bait fish and brine. Inside were the usual folk, the locals with hardened eyes and work-worn hands, the kind that felt like a brick when you shook them. Unlike other pubs, however, this one clearly held the touch of a woman. Bright yellow and white checked cloths covered the table, and the floor was meticulously clean. And on each table was a small white vase containing a daisy.

He'd almost become ill when he walked in; he'd almost left. Instead, he'd sat down, taken the pretty vase that sat in the very center of the table, and placed it on the table behind him. One of the locals chuckled when he did.

"Can't say I like 'em either." The man's voice was gruff, his profile hard and slightly crooked, the kind of profile a boxer might have.

Roger turned to the man, ready for some meaningless conversation. But over the years, he'd learned that innocuous conversations could sometimes lead to information, so he forged ahead with his story as he had so many times before. "I have a good reason for not liking that particular flower," he said, his eyes studying the man, who relentlessly tapped the top of his mug with one index finger. Tap tap tap. "You see, my wife and children were murdered, and the person who killed them left behind a daisy." The tapping ceased, suddenly, as if someone had grabbed the man's hand, stilling it.

Slowly, he turned toward Roger, revealing a face damaged by a blade, old scars that re-shaped what would have been a handsome visage. "What did you say?"

Roger's heart began to beat hard and fast in his chest as he realized he just might be sitting next to his wife's murderer. He'd dreamed of this moment, planned for it, but was not prepared for the calm that stole over him after the initial excitement. "The man who murdered my wife and two daughters left a daisy on her chest," he said, gauging the man's reaction, searching his eyes for guilt or panic or madness. "And they were not the only ones. Mothers and twins, murdered, with a daisy left behind. Three times."

"My God." The man stared at his mug, then took a quick drink before placing it back down on the table with exquisite gentleness.

Roger swallowed hard, knowing after all these years, he had found him. "You."

The stranger shook his head. "No, sir. No." He closed his eyes briefly. "But I think I know who it was. I think I do." His voice grew quiet as he spoke. "My brother."

Roger found he could hardly take a breath into his lungs. "Who is your brother? What is his name?"

"Clarence Teller. And I am Carl. He was my twin; he died two years ago." Carl let those words settle around Roger before turning toward him, and Roger tensed, fearing he was about to be accosted. The man's injuries were nearly as unsettling as the look in his eyes.

"My daughters were twins."

Carl gave him a crooked smile. "Of course they were." He shook his head and closed his eyes briefly. "What do you think would be worse? Having this done to your face"—he jabbed a thumb toward his scars—"or watching it done to someone you love?"

"My God."

"We were seven and my mother was mad. She thought we were spawned by the devil. She hated us and feared us. We were identical in every way— the way we looked, talked, laughed. Everything. We were inseparable; it's a bond that is difficult to understand even now. We even had our own language and she thought it was Satan speaking through us." His mouth lifted in a small crooked smile. "We sometimes liked getting her goat, like any boys, I suppose. We were afraid of her but we never thought…"

"She did that to you?"

He nodded. "And Clarence had to watch. She tied me to a chair and made him watch as she cut into me, to make me different, to cleanse me of the devil. I'll never forget the way he screamed and begged her to stop, as if he were feeling the knife, not I. She did this, too, later." He held up one hand, which was missing its pinky. "Clarence changed after that. He began to think Mama was right—we were evil, we were spawned by the devil. All twins were. By the time he was seventeen, our mother was dead and he was just as mad as she was. I joined the Navy to get away from it all."

"I am sorry for your story, but how do you *know* it is your brother I seek?"

Carl let out a humorless chuckle. "It was him, alright. Our mother's name was Daisy."

Just like that, Roger felt that thick darkness he had carried with him for so long shift, open, become weightless. It was over. Finally.

Chapter 16

Clara stood before her mirror, a beaming Jeanine next to her, and stared at herself in her wedding gown. It seemed as if everyone were excited about the wedding but her. Once the staff had discovered Nathaniel was a baron, they immediately celebrated the match and forgave the lord for his eccentricities. Imagine, pretending he was a gardener! To think they'd been sitting down at the same table with him, flirting with him, and he'd never given them a clue. And how very romantic that he'd fallen in love with their Clara. They just *knew* there was something special about him. They were thrilled at the prospect of having such lofty visitors to the house in the future, and celebrated their newfound status as staff for a countess and a baroness—even if neither would be living in the Anderson home.

Clara could hardly credit it, how quickly everyone seemed to accept the fact that their gardener was actually a member of the peerage. It was maddening.

For his part, once he'd gotten her parents' blessing (she was still seething about how easily they'd given in) Nathaniel had immediately hied himself off to London to take care of the business of cashing in on his treasure; there had even a story in *The Times* about its discovery and an artist's rendering of the gem. All these years, Harriet had used it as a paperweight, and Clara had made fun of her for keeping the ugly thing in her room. If not for the fact that Harriet had married a sinfully wealthy earl, Clara might have felt guilty for giving the diamond away. But no one mentioned it. No one cared about anything, it seemed, but for the baron's declaration of love and his proposal.

In the last three weeks, the banns had been read and the license procured, and Clara had isolated herself in her room, refusing to speak to anyone about anything pertaining to the upcoming nuptials. Yes, it was childish, but Clara was sick and tired of being manipulated into doing things she didn't want to do. This farce of a wedding was the pinnacle of her mother's long campaign to marry her to a titled gentleman. Hedra could not be reasoned with. Clara's tears and pleading went ignored. After one particularly heartfelt talk, her mother had simply smiled and said, "But he loves you. Do you not have a care for him at all?"

Of course, no one could understand the depth, the burning pain of his betrayal. And yes, her pride had been stung and she was fully aware that pride goeth before a fall. It was the one part of the Bible she refused to acknowledge. Every time she recalled her diatribes about class and status, she felt ill. He'd just listened and nodded—sometimes offering a tepid argument—and let her go on and on about how the aristocracy was an outdated concept and one that should be abolished.

Still, it was difficult to ignore his claims of love, made without hesitation and in front of her father. Her mother refused to listen to her when she wondered aloud how a man could claim to love a woman but lie and lie and lie to her.

"He had no choice," Hedra said, more than once.

Worse still was that she missed him. And hated herself for missing him. And she loved him and hated herself for that too. Since he'd gone to London, she had not seen him alone. The entire family, including Lord Berkley and her sister, had eaten together during one uncomfortable dinner. Nathaniel had sat across from her and stared at her throughout the evening, his eyes assessing and, well, cold. Which made Clara wonder if he loved her at all or if he were simply "paying back" her family for taking the diamond from them.

Gone were the easy smiles, the charming, self-effacing man she'd fallen in love with. In his place was this…this…*baron*. Ugh. She longed for the Nathaniel she'd fallen in love with, that tanned man with the too-long hair and the work-worn hat. In his place was a man who clearly had a valet, whose hair was carefully cut and neatly combed, whose clothes were impeccable and finely tailored. When he smiled, it never reached his eyes, and when he looked at her, there was none of that burning intensity she used to see. Or perhaps she'd imagined it. Perhaps she'd gotten so caught up in the secrecy of their relationship, the inappropriateness of it, she'd thought she'd seen something she had not.

Now, this very morning, she was about to walk down the aisle and marry a complete stranger. Perhaps not a *complete* stranger. But she did not know Baron Alford and she was afraid she might not love him as much as she'd loved her gardener.

Clara walked to the window and looked down at their little plot of land, at the roses that were just starting to bloom, at the carefully planned walkway and, in the distance, the hothouse that would give them flowers all next winter. She loved her garden. Laying her hand upon the cool window pane, she swallowed a knot in her throat, wishing she were still that naïve girl who couldn't wait to walk along those paths and imagine what more they could do to make their garden beautiful. Mr. Smee, she couldn't help to think, would have been so disappointed in Nathaniel, to know it had all been pretense. All those holes, all that tilling, and none it of it had anything to do with creating beauty or the love of gardening. Another wave of humiliation washed over her. Nathaniel claimed to love her, but how could he? It was far easier to imagine he held her in contempt, a silly country girl with simple pedestrian dreams.

Following the ceremony, they were leaving immediately for London, and then on to Cumbria, with its lakes and deep forests that were so unlike St. Ives. His estate was called Lion's Gate, and a more pretentious name for an estate she had never heard. Despite his claims of poverty, Clara couldn't help but think he was exaggerating. Perhaps what constituted poverty for a peer was different from what constituted poverty for ordinary folk.

She would be in charge of a staff, something her finishing school had well prepared her for. Her mother, for all her flaws, had done an admirable job of hiring and supervising the staff, despite her lack of experience. Mrs. Pittsfield had been a large help in that area.

Outside, she heard Harriet's laughter and felt a sharp twinge. Not only would she miss her sister, but it somehow didn't seem fair that Harriet would stay in St. Ives while she would be banished to the cold north, just a few hundred miles from Scotland.

"Now, what's the sad face for, miss?" Jeanine chastised happily. "All brides have the jitters. I expect even I will."

Now that, Clara didn't believe for a second. "I'm sure I'll be fine once the ceremony is over." *And I'm alone with him. In a train compartment. And then later in a hotel room in London. Oh Lord.*

Her mother had come to her room the previous night, clearly nervous, and blurted out, "You know what to expect on your wedding night?"

"In a manner of speaking," Clara said, even though she wasn't quite sure.

"Good then." And Hedra had left so quickly, a bit of dust was kicked up from the floor.

The physical part of her marriage was the least of her worries. She had a feeling Nathaniel would put her at ease and be considerate of her. If he could nearly make her swoon from his kisses, she imagined the act of union would be tolerable. It was the rest of her marriage that she worried about.

Before she knew it, Clara was in their carriage on the way to St. Ives Church, horrified that a throng of well-wishers were lining the street. Harriet had been married in Lord Berkley's tiny chapel with only family and a few friends present—including Harriet's small group of chums. Clara wasn't certain how her mother had managed it, but the church was packed with people, including her grandparents, who looked more than a little put out to have been summoned on such short notice to attend their granddaughter's wedding.

When the wedding party entered the church, her grandmother looked back and immediately stood to make her way to the back, where Clara stood with her sister and matron of honor. Clara watched her progress, struck by how quickly she walked and how tiny she'd become. Her grandmother, like so many older women she knew, was shrinking. She wore black, for the son who had died ten years earlier, but Clara suspected her *damawyn* secretly believed she looked good in the color.

"A bit fancy," she said crossly, looking Clara up and down in her wedding finery, then glancing around the copiously decorated church. Truly, her mother was a miracle worker.

"I couldn't get married in a pasture, could I, Damawyn? Not to a baron."

"Your mama says he loves you and that's all well and good. Answer me up, now, do you love him?"

Clara leaned down to her grandmother's ear and whispered, "I do, but don't tell him. I'm still quite cross with him for turning out to be a baron."

Her grandmother cackled. "He's an 'ansome enough devil, he is. Back along when I was a girl, he would have turned my 'ead."

"Damawyn, really," Clara said in mock horror. "You're a married woman."

"And an old one." She gave Clara a wink "But I'm not bleddy dead yet." Then her dear grandmother grew serious. "'Tisn't the worst thing in the world, marrying up like this. Look at 'arriet. She seems happy enough."

"I'm ecstatic," said Harriet at her cheeky best.

"I know, Damawyn. It's just not what I had in mind. But it will all work out in the end."

Her grandmother gave her a keen look. "Only if you want it to."

With that cryptic response, she headed back to her seat, where her husband had already nodded off, his head bobbing slightly as he snored.

Nathaniel had always considered himself to be a patient fellow, but it had been three weeks since his proposal—perhaps not the most romantic declaration, but he had proposed in a manner of speaking—and she'd hardly looked his way. She was not going to forgive him and he couldn't help but think she was being a bit stubborn about it all. What if this was a terrible mistake? What if she wasn't merely angry but had turned the corner to dislike?

What if she truly didn't love him?

Her mother, her father, even Harriet had assured him she did, and if she didn't now, she eventually would, but it was still maddening to wonder.

Nathaniel looked at his reflection with an assessing eye. He was dressed impeccably, with a rich blue cummerbund around his waist, a perfectly tied cravat around his neck. He'd borrowed Lord Berkley's valet for the day, having sent Mr. Standard on ahead to Lion's Gate to attempt to get the house in some sort of order and hire a skeleton staff before he presented his new bride. Mr. Standard had been trained as a valet, and for at least a while, he would serve in both that capacity and as butler until all Nathaniel's finances were in order. Thanks to the diamond, that would soon be resolved. Just three days prior, he'd gotten notification that the diamond had been exquisitely cut and was valued at a fortune. *The Times* ran a story on it and interest in the stone was reportedly high. Proceeds from the sale would most certainly be enough to pay his debts, get his tenants' properties in order, and begin repairs to Lion's Gate. Once the steelworks was up and running, he would have a regular income and could then continue making improvements all around. It was as if an unbearable weight had been lifted from his shoulders. So much so, he hadn't truly understood the extent of how heavy a load it had been before now. Even as a student, he had been aware of the debt his father was accumulating, of how it would someday be up to him to either rescue his inheritance or let it fall to complete ruin. Restoring not only his family's name but also its riches had seemed a lost cause, but one that was now within his grasp.

"Shall I trim your hair, my lord?" the valet, Mr. Jamison, asked.

Nathaniel turned his head this way and that, and finally rejected the offer, remembering how Clara had seemed to like running her fingers through his thick, wavy locks. He smiled grimly, wondering if he would ever feel such passion from her again. Surely, he could convince her he loved her and was worthy of her love.

"Nervous, sir?" Mr. Jamison asked.

"I am a bit, to be honest. I suppose when I see my bride walking down the aisle I shall be greatly relieved."

The valet chuckled and gave his shoulders a final brush before stepping back. "Do you need anything else, my lord?"

"No, Mr. Jamison. And please do again extend my thanks to Lord Berkley for your services."

Once Mr. Jamison had left, Nathaniel took a deep breath, a bit shocked at how it shook when he released it. He hadn't been lying about being nervous; he was damned uneasy. Clara hadn't spared even a smile in his direction since she'd agreed to marry him. It had become rather worrisome. He understood her anger, her hurt. Hell, he was angry at himself for allowing this entire situation to blow up as it had. Telling her he understood, telling her he loved her, seemed to do nothing but remind her of his perfidy. He could think of nothing that would make her understand that he *knew* he was a cad and unworthy of her. But this particular unworthy cad wanted her anyway.

He was the same fellow she'd kissed behind the shed, the same one who'd touched her, made her come, her body pulsing beneath his hand. She was the same girl who'd seemed to relish his touch, who whimpered when he sucked on her nipples. God, he had to stop thinking such thoughts or he'd been in a rare state when she did walk down the aisle. Yes, he was the same fellow he'd thought had managed to make her fall in love him with; only his clothing had changed.

She had fallen in love with a gardener, but the man she'd become angry with was the lying, manipulative baron. And there was nothing he could do about it.

St. Ives Parish Church had stood overlooking St. Ives Bay for centuries, its tall, square bell tower dominating the village. It had seen births and deaths, baptisms, countless Christmases, and on this day, it was about to see a local girl reluctantly marry a man nearly every girl of marriageable age would have given her eye tooth to marry. That was what Hedra had told her in any case.

Clara looked down the long aisle, bordered by white-painted arches that marched toward the altar awash with a rainbow of colors from the stained glass, a statue of Christ on the cross standing on a thick wooden beam that stretched across the aisle. She would have to walk beneath that statue of suffering, which made her own "suffering" seem rather paltry. The church's pews were filled to capacity, evidence that her mother likely had had invitations at the ready—or at least a list. Other than for Harriet's wedding, Clara had never seen her mother so happy. But try as she might, Clara simply could not call up the same enthusiasm.

It wasn't as if she were marrying an ogre; she'd told herself this countless times in the past three weeks. She was marrying a man she loved—or at least a man she *had* loved. Did she still love him even though she'd fallen in love with who he was pretending to be? Was he the same man?

Dash it all, why couldn't he have remained a gardener?

The organist, who had been playing soft hymns, suddenly stopped and Clara's heart nearly flew out of her body. Oh, goodness, this was it.

Harriet gave her a quick hug and whispered, "He loves you, he does," before beginning her walk down the aisle, her dramatic bouncing locks marking each step. Clara stifled a sigh.

"You'll be fine, Clarabelle," her father said, using the name he'd called her as a child. "I think it's our turn."

She gave him a tremulous smile and tucked her hand into the crook of his elbow. The aisle was long and shadowed between the entry and the stained glass window behind the altar, and with her veil obscuring her vision, she could hardly make out the reverend or Nathaniel, whom she presumed was standing at the end. As she walked, she looked at those who had gathered to see her married, old friends and families she'd known all her life, unable to bring herself to look up. Truthfully, she feared she might see that cold baron and not Nathaniel at all.

Please let him smile at me.

At the end, she turned and her father lifted the veil and beamed a smile at her, silently giving her courage. After kissing her father's cheek, she turned toward the reverend, aware that she hadn't spared Nathaniel a single glace. The reverend looked…odd.

Rev. Baker had been officiating masses at St. Ives Parish Church for as long as Clara could remember and she'd never seen that particular expression on his face before. He darted a quick look toward Nathaniel, then back to her.

Whatever…

Clara turned toward Nathaniel and froze. Her lips trembled and her eyes glazed over with tears. For standing there with her at the altar was not Baron Alford, but her own Mr. Emory, complete with dirty gloves, worn boots, and sweat-stained hat. "Oh."

Rev. Baker leaned forward. "This *is* Baron Alford, is it not?" he asked, giving Nathaniel another curious look.

"No, Reverend. This is Mr. Nathaniel Emory, our gardener and the man I fell in love with," she said, her throat closing on the last word.

And then, Nathaniel did something that made it even more difficult to remain angry. He started to cry. Oh, not copious, unmanly tears, but two tears, one from each eye, furtively escaped down his cheeks. "Shall we?" he asked. He sounded like a baron, yes, but he looked like her dear gardener.

"Yes. We shall."

Though Nathaniel had warned her that Lion's Gate was in disrepair and the village neglected for nearly a generation, Clara was still shocked by what they found when the hired carriage pulled up in front of the massive home. It looked completely uninhabitable, with broken windows, moss-covered stones, and a tangle of vines covering the façade. The drive was riddled with weeds, just coming to life after a long, cold winter, and the garden—if one could call it that—was completely unkempt, a hodge-podge of weeds and overgrown plantings that cried for attention.

It was beautiful.

Clara smiled but quickly hid her excitement from her husband. Despite her happiness at seeing him in his gardener's garb on their wedding day, Clara realized she had not yet forgiven him for lying to her all those months. She did try. Her head was constantly filled with silent urgings to get over it. She couldn't count how many times she told herself to stop being so stubborn, but every time she looked across and saw Baron Alford instead of Mr. Emory, all the anger came rushing back.

The journey from St. Ives to Cumbria was long and tiring and fraught with tension, as Clara wondered when—or if—Nathaniel would demand his husbandly rights. He had tried, that first night in London, but Clara had tensed and he had stepped back, his expression unreadable.

"We'll wait 'til we get home to Lion's Gate, shall we?" he'd asked, giving her a brief and entirely unconvincing smile. And when she'd quickly agreed, she couldn't help but notice he seemed disappointed. She was a bit disappointed, too, but couldn't find a way to bridge the gap that had sprung up between them the day she'd discovered his true identity.

Since then, he'd been a polite acquaintance, as if he didn't know what to do with her now that he had her. They were strangers. The one thing that had brought them together—her garden—was now gone. What did they have to talk about if not their plans?

Seeing the terrible state of Lion's Gate's grounds gave Clara a bit of hope. Perhaps their conversations could begin with the garden and then move on to other topics. She knew little about her husband other than that he was quite good at lying and was a baron. Just that thought brought back all those ugly feelings she'd been fighting each day since he'd asked for her hand.

"I know what you are thinking," he said, gazing out the carriage window with a frown. "But now perhaps you will understand my desperation."

Perhaps she would. Nathaniel had apologized for his behavior, more than once, and she was beginning to feel like a shrew.

"I understand everything," she said, then paused. "The garden needs work, does it not?"

He nodded solemnly. "It does. Everything needs work. I knew it was in disrepair, but it somehow seems worse now that it's spring. I cannot afford a gardener, and repairs to the house will have to wait until other, more pressing, matters are taken care of. The corn mill, the steelworks." He let out a sound of frustration. "Shall we go in? Perhaps Mr. Standard has performed a miracle."

Mr. Standard had not performed a miracle. He met them at the door, a panicked looked on his face, and it almost seemed to Nathaniel that he meant to stop them from entering. Instead, the butler forced the door open more fully, then stepped back and said, "Welcome home, my lord, my lady."

The door had not been repaired, obviously, and the two had to enter the house by stepping sideways. At least the leaves had been swept from the entryway and the long strands of cobwebs had been removed from the ceiling and light fixtures. Inside, the house was cold and dark and he could detect a lingering smell from the fire. Nathaniel wondered if it would be better for his new bride if they simply stayed at a local inn rather than the house.

For her part, Clara entered the foyer with caution and looked about, a bewildered expression on her face.

"Has no one lived here?"

"My grandfather did until he died, but he occupied only one room on the second floor. Most other rooms have gone unused for decades."

"We did our best, sir, but it took some time to find any locals willing to come all this way and back each day. The servants' quarters are uninhabitable, you see. A family of red squirrels seems to have taken up residence, and at some point there were bats. And the guano that accompanies such creatures."

Nathaniel tightened his jaw, embarrassed to have brought Clara to this home when she'd come from one far better. "We shall depart immediately for the village," he said. "You have done your best, Mr. Standard, but I fear I didn't realize the extent of disrepair."

He began to leave, but Clara placed a hand on his arm. He wasn't certain why that simple touch affected him so; perhaps it was because it was the first time she'd touched him since their marriage other than to be assisted up and down carriage steps. "I'm not afraid of squirrels."

He looked down into her face and tried to read her lovely blue eyes, those eyes he'd found so fascinating since that first day in the garden. "What about guano?"

"I have managed to clean your rooms, sir," Mr. Standard said hastily. "New linens, a fire in the grate. The maids have done an admirable job, sir. As it's Sunday, they are home, but you can meet them tomorrow and see for yourself how hardworking they are."

"I've no doubt, Mr. Standard. Very well, show me the rooms. We'll make the best, shall we? After all, I managed to do quite well living in the back of a shed." He turned to see if his comment had elicited a smile from his wife, but found that she was frowning, as she was wont to do whenever he referred to the past, no matter how obliquely.

After some consideration, Nathaniel had opted not to use his grandfather's rooms until they were renovated. When he moved into them eventually, he did not want to have any sad reminders of the only relative in his memory who had ever cared for him. Instead, he'd moved into his old rooms, on the opposite side from his grandfather's suite of rooms, and Clara had been placed in the adjoining suite. He prayed Mr. Standard was being truthful when he'd said the rooms were well prepared.

Clara preceded him up the stairs, and he laid a hand at the small of her back, more because he could hardly resist touching her than to assist her. He'd felt a bit crazed when he'd suggested they wait to consummate their marriage and she'd readily agreed. She'd agreed so quickly, in fact, that he'd been left reeling. Did she not welcome his touch anymore?

"Please show the countess her rooms first, Mr. Standard."

The butler nodded, proceeded down the hall, then opened the door with a flourish, revealing a brightly lit room that was, Nathaniel had to admit, breathtaking. Mr. Standard had, indeed, created a miracle.

Clara let out a delighted gasp and walked to the middle of the sitting room, decorated in soft pinks and yellows and immaculately clean. The curtains had been pulled back to reveal what was an impressive view of the gardens, which would give her delight when they were properly cared for. Of course, she went directly to the window and looked out for a long moment. So long, in fact, that Nathaniel began to wonder if she disliked what she saw.

But when she turned about, her eyes were alight and she was smiling in a way he hadn't seen in far too long. "Mr. Standard, it's lovely. When the maids return tomorrow, please do bring them up so that I may thank them personally." With that, she walked quickly to her bedroom, and Nathaniel followed, relief that she was pleased making his steps a bit lighter.

When he entered, he found Clara sitting on the bed, bouncing up and down a bit, and caressing the thick coverlet that covered the large four-poster. Nathaniel turned to Mr. Standard so quickly, he nearly struck the man by mistake. "That is all for now, Mr. Standard. I'll view my room later."

The young butler's eyes widened imperceptibly and Nathaniel had to give the man credit for simply nodding and leaving the room.

He was only a man, and his wife, his beautiful and still virginal wife was sitting on a bed. What else was he to do?

Shutting the door, he ignored a small sound from Clara, a sound that might be either excitement or outrage. Or fear.

Nathaniel turned and leaned against the door, his hands on either side, pressing against the wood as if Mr. Standard might barge back in. Clara's eyes widened and she sat still, her gaze unwavering.

"What are you doing?" she whispered.

A fair enough question. What the bloody hell *was* he doing? He didn't know. He only knew that she had to stop looking at him as if he were a villain. She had to love him again. She *had* to. Without knowing what he planned to do, he walked toward her, his eyes never leaving hers, and when he reached her, he dropped to his knees and laid his head in her lap, his hands clutching her skirts on either side.

"You must forgive me." The words felt wrenched from his throat and he swallowed convulsively. For a long, terrible moment, he stayed like that, hands buried in the soft muslin of her skirts, head pressed against her thighs, while she remained stiff and still.

And then, he felt her hand atop his head, a soft caress, and he squeezed his eyes shut, silently thanking God that she hadn't shoved him off.

"I forgive you." He looked up at her, studied her face, and saw tears in her eyes. "I love you," she choked out. "Even though you are a horrid, horrid man who did the most despicable thing and don't deserve my love."

He smiled. "I thought you said you forgive me."

Clara let out a watery laugh, then placed her hands on either side of his face and gave him a little shake. "I do forgive you but I'm still so angry. Each time I think about it, picture you there in the garden, I just want to throttle you."

"If I let you throttle me, will you feel better?"

She tilted her head. "I do believe I would feel better. How does one go about throttling another?"

"Like this," he said, quickly jumping to his feet and kissing his wife the way he'd wanted to since the day she'd stood there, fiercely angry, having just thrown a diamond worth a fortune at his head. God, she tasted good, felt good. Clara placed her hands against his chest and he thought she might push him back, but instead, she clutched at his lapels and let out a sound—half anger, half desire. And then, she loosened her death grip on his jacket and flung her arms around his neck and Nathaniel knew he'd just gotten his girl back.

"I'm still angry," she said breathlessly as he made a trail of kisses from her mouth to her jaw and then to her smooth, sensitive neck.

"I know. You kiss rather well when you're angry," he said, chuckling when she let out a growling sound. It was an adorable, womanly growl that he found rather delightful. "Shall we get undressed so I may ravish you properly?"

She gave him a wide-eyed look of innocence. "But I have no maid." Jeanine, soon to marry, had remained behind.

He waggled his brows at her. "I do believe I can act the lady's maid for this one day." He placed a kiss just where a small bit of cleavage showed above her modest gown. "I did rather well before, as I recall." He pulled away reluctantly and held out his hand for her to take, which she did without the slightest bit of hesitation. This day was getting better by the second, he thought.

"Turn around, my lady—" He was struck by the sudden realization that facing him was a daunting task of unbuttoning tiny seed pearls that ran from her neck to her waist. He began fumbling with them, his hands shaking a bit in his haste. "How much do you like this dress?" he asked casually.

She turned her head slightly, but he could see a small smile on her beautiful mouth. "Not all that much."

The final "ch" sound had not yet been uttered when he rent the dress in two with a satisfying rip that exposed her lovely back, now covered only with a chemise, corset, and corset cover and God and her maid only knew what else. "I give up," he said, then spun her around and gently pulled the dress down, relishing in her curves and the sound of her quick breaths. While he was busy with that, Clara tackled the ties and laces that held the rest of her clothing together, and before he knew it, she was standing there only in her shoes, stockings, and bloomers. Without warning, he lifted her and tossed her onto the bed, her breasts bouncing enticingly, and made quick work of the shoes and bloomers, but taking a bit more time with her stockings. They were the finest silk and looked rather lovely on her divine long limbs.

And then she was naked, lying in the middle of the bed, the soft curls at the apex of her thighs, slightly darker than the ones on her head, exposed to his hungry gaze. "You are the loveliest vision I have ever seen in my life," he said, hardly recognizing his own voice. Her skin was white and smooth, like a rose petal dipped in sweet cream.

When Nathaniel had been a boy, he and his friends would run to the nearest pond on a hot summer day and undress, leaving behind a trail of clothing until they were completely naked when they reached the edge of the lake. He'd always been good about stripping down quickly, but never in his life had he discarded his clothing as quickly as he did that day. By the time his smalls were off, Clara was laughing—a laugh that quickly ended when he stood up.

"Oh," she breathed, but Nathaniel wasn't sure what that single syllable meant. He hoped it meant she liked what she saw, but as a virgin, he realized she might not have any comparison to make. Of course, his member was erect, and that might be an unsettling sight to a girl who had so little experience.

"Here I am," he said, glancing down at his cock, which he had to admit looked a bit red and angry at the moment. And large. He was a large man, overall, and this part of him was no exception.

Clara darted a quick look at his male appendage. "There you are. Goodness." His low chuckle drew her gaze to his face and she couldn't help but smile. "We are both quite naked, it seems. In broad daylight, no less. I've heard that is not the done thing."

"I am the lord of this house and I say it is precisely the done thing. Besides, I could hardly wait until darkness falls. I'm about to die from wanting you."

Clara pressed her lips together in a failed attempt not to smile. "I shouldn't want you to die. I'm feeling a bit faint myself."

He laughed aloud at that, then, without warning, threw himself on the bed beside her and propped his head up with one fist while the other he laid gently on her stomach, just above her navel. Yes, they were naked, and yes, they were about to make love for the first time, but that hand on her tummy, gentle and light, for some reason put Clara at ease. It felt right, having his large hand splayed across her midriff.

"Do you remember when I had to leave St. Ives for an emergency? How I touched you?"

"I do. What was the emergency, if I might ask?" She felt him tense and suspected it had something to do with his being a baron, so put on a scowl, one he immediately erased with a searing kiss.

"Did you smell smoke when we arrived? That night, I received a telegram stating there had been a fire. Fortunately, damage was minimal." He kissed her again as if unable to stop himself. "Enough of that, my wife. Do you remember how you felt?"

She nodded, awash with the memories of all the delightful sensations he was able to produce.

"I shall endeavor to make you feel that way again, and then, my love, I shall endeavor to make myself feel that way." He paused and kissed her cheek and then laid a gentle kiss on one breast; he moved down further and drew her already hardened nipple into his mouth. Yes, she remembered this feeling, this unbelievable sensation that centered between her legs. Already, she could feel herself going languid in preparation for what was to come.

"Yes," she whispered, as he teased her other nipple with his fingers. He had only touched her this way once, but it seemed so natural, so familiar. So right. She laid a hand on his shoulder, felt his strength, his raw masculinity, and closed her eyes, losing herself in the sensations of lying with a man, hearing his harsh breath, inhaling his scent. His hand drifted down, tickling her, and Clara couldn't help but tense and giggle.

She felt rather than heard his chuckle, a deep vibration in his chest, and then he placed his hand against the apex of her thighs, applying subtle pressure. "You are wet for me," he said, bringing his head up to gaze down at her.

"I am." It was slightly embarrassing, this thing her body did whenever she was around him. Even when he was not kissing her, touching her, just being with him made her body react and ready itself for him.

He moved his hand slightly, one finger searching, and he let out a sound of male satisfaction when he found her sensitive spot, that wondrous bud where everything seemed to center in warm delicious sensation. "Someday, I am going to kiss you there," he said, his voice sounding oddly strained. "Someday, I am going to kiss every inch of your luscious body. But today, my love, today I don't think I will last past touching you." He pressed his manhood against her thigh and began rhythmic movements until he stopped, his body tense and trembling beside her. "You're too damned beautiful."

In an almost desperate way, he suckled her nipples, first one, then the other, while at the same time working his hand between her legs, and Clara knew her release was coming, fast and powerful, until all she could do was lose herself, push her hips up and against his hand. It came then, that powerful moment when everything disappeared but the pleasure that pulsed through her entire body. She was still pulsing, still reveling in what he'd done, when he moved between her legs.

Nathaniel braced himself over her, his body bathed in sweat, his eyes intense on hers. With one hand, he guided himself to her entrance. "I am sorry if this hurts, but God, Clara, I cannot wait." He pushed his member inside her, slowly, and stopped, letting out harsh breaths as he encountered her barrier. He kissed her, almost harshly, then pushed all the way, sliding in and filling her. Clara tensed, waiting for the pain that was supposed to come, but nearly laughed aloud when all she felt was a mild twinge, far less pain than even her monthlies.

"It only hurt a bit," she said, lifting up her head and kissing him.

He let out a low moan and starting moving, creating a rhythm that started off slowly at first, but soon became almost frantic, and Clara knew he was near to finding his own release. Without thinking, she lifted her hips and wrapped her thighs around him, drawing him in, losing herself to the rhythm he was creating. When she did that, his hips quickened, and then he arched his back, his neck muscles strained, his handsome face ravaged with pleasure as he found heaven too.

When Nathaniel's breathing became more normal, he started laughing and Clara joined in. "That was lovely," he said. He eased off her and lay back, his chest still heaving from their love-making. "And it will only be better next time," he said, a bit of wonder in his tone. "You are miraculous."

Clara giggled and tucked her head beneath his arm.

"You are well? I'm afraid I wasn't as gentle as I'd planned to be."

"I am perfectly well. A small twinge." She kissed his shoulder. "Do you know what I would like to do now?" Positioning herself half on his chest, she tucked her arms beneath her chin and gazed at him.

"I have an idea." He laughed. "The garden."

"Oh, could we? It's only that it's still quite early and the sun won't set for hours yet. I have such plans, Nathaniel."

After they'd freshened up and Clara assured Nathaniel at least a half dozen times that she was perfectly capable of walking—even after their vigorous "exercise" (he'd chuckled at that)—they went through the house and out the back entrance to what could only be described as the saddest bit of garden Clara had ever seen.

"It needs me," she said as they walked toward the overgrown, weed-filled shrubbery. Then she stopped still, her eyes going up to a wrought-iron arch positioned over a break in the rock wall that separated the lawn from what would one day be her garden. There, with vines already twining around it, in lovely scrolling letters, were the words, "Clara's Garden." It was not a new addition; the vines were proof of that.

When she turned to him, he gave her a sheepish grin. "I was perhaps overly confident of my abilities to make you forgive me."

In that moment, any lingering anger was swept away. That time in the garden, it had been real, it hadn't just been all a ruse. This small gesture showed he understood how important that garden was, how important her gardener was to her.

"Do barons work in their gardens?"

He smiled. "They do. Alongside their beautiful wives."

"Mr. Smee will help us," Clara said, feeling a bit choked up thinking about their mentor whom they would never meet.

"He already has," Nathaniel said, and he pushed ahead, stepping over twigs and overgrown grass that pushed through the long-neglected brick path. "Look here."

There, tucked behind the stone wall, was a long line of plants, a huge variety, all still in their burlap, waiting to be planted in the garden.

Clara gasped and ran to the plants, thrilled by what she was seeing. "All from Mr. Smee's garden?"

"A wedding present from his son."

It was silly, really, how seeing these plants made her heart sing, made her eyes tear. Or perhaps not so silly. Her husband, a baron, an aristocrat, understood how very important it was that she marry her simple gardener, her Mr. Emory. It seemed she had, after all.

About the Author

Jane Goodger lives in Rhode Island with her husband and three children. Jane, a former journalist, has written and published numerous historical romances. When she isn't writing, she's reading, walking, playing with her kids, or anything else completely unrelated to cleaning a house. You can visit her website at www.janegoodger.com.

JANE GOODGER

Behind a
Lady's Smile

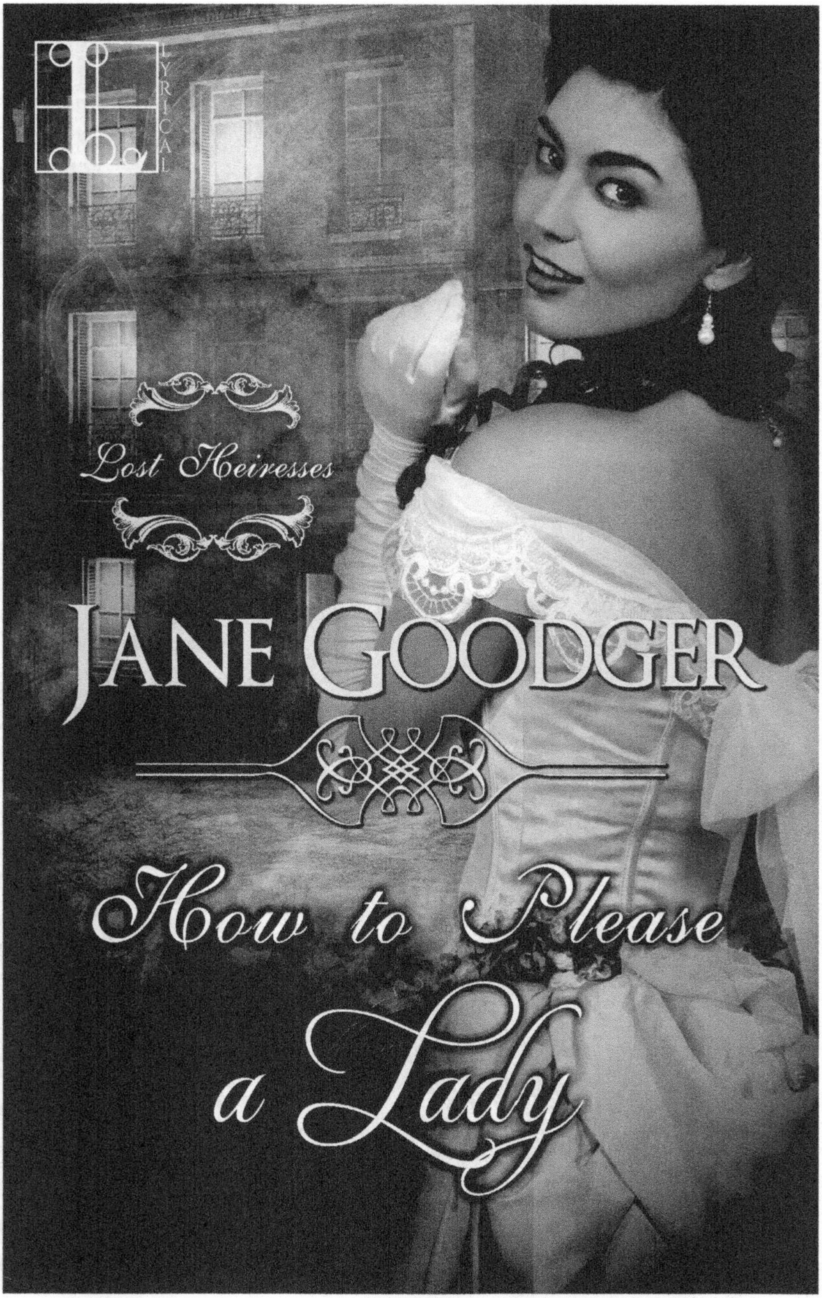
LYRICAL
Lost Heiresses
JANE GOODGER
How to Please
a Lady

Lost Heiresses

JANE GOODGER

Lady Lost

The Brides of St. Ives

The Bad Luck Bride

JANE GOODGER

The Brides of St. Ives

"An unforgettable read."
–RT Book Reviews, 4 Stars

The Earl
Most Likely

JANE GOODGER

Made in the USA
Las Vegas, NV
31 July 2022

52474765R10121